My Sweet Untraceable You

My Sweet Untraceable You

Sandra Scoppettone

LITTLE, BROWN AND COMPANY
BOSTON   NEW YORK   TORONTO   LONDON

First Edition

This novel is a work of fiction. Names, characters, places, and incidents are
either the product of the author's imagination or, if real, are used
fictitiously, for example, Cybill Shepherd, Colin Powell, Zsa Zsa Gabor, and
Sam Nunn.

Library of Congress Cataloging-in-Publication Data

Scoppettone, Sandra.
    My sweet untraceable you / Sandra Scoppettone.—1st ed.
      p.   cm.
    ISBN 0-316-77648-3
    1. Private investigators—New York (N.Y.)—Fiction.   2. Women
detectives—New York (N.Y.)—Fiction.   I. Title.
PS3569.C586M9   1994
813'.54—dc20   .   93-47426

10 9 8 7 6 5 4 3 2 1

MV-NY

*Published simultaneously in Canada
by Little, Brown & Company (Canada) Limited*

Printed in the United States of America

For Linda, always

Joy fixes us to eternity and pain fixes us to time. But desire and fear hold us in bondage to time, and detachment breaks the bond.

—*Simone Weil*

My Sweet Untraceable You

Chapter

One

BRUTAL.

Summer in New York City.

I am having breakfast in the air-conditioned Waverly
Place Luncheonette with my friend Lieutenant Peter Cecchi. He's my age, forty-five, handsome in a craggy way,
with brown eyes that have the flat, cool look of a man
who's seen more than any one human should.

We eat here a lot because it's a cop hangout, cheap by
New York standards, and the service is fast. The decor is
the same as in any other luncheonette — a square room
with booths, small tables, a counter and stools.

Cecchi is married to Annette and I'm married to Kip.
We're discussing them when Ruby Packard, the waitress,
comes over to the table without being called. She has Ann
Miller hair so sprayed into place it looks like a wig, and a
square thick body with sturdy legs. Ruby loves Cecchi.
She loves all cops, but Cecchi especially, because he's extra nice to her. When he and I are together, even if I ask
her something, she answers *him*.

"Cecchi, phone," she tells him.

Ruby's a woman of few words.

He thanks her and goes to take the call.

I pull some money from one of the innumerable

pockets in my lightweight khaki slacks and retuck my navy blue Gap T-shirt that doesn't match my eyes, as they are brown, similar to my hair, if you don't count the gray, which I don't.

When Cecchi comes back he says, "We got a stiff on Eighth Avenue and Twelfth in a Dumpster."

I wipe my mouth and stand up to go with him.

"I don't know," he says.

"Yes you do."

"Okay, Lauren, but stay out of the way."

Outside the air is thick and hot and the sun hangs in the sky as if it's loitering. A blue-and-white waits for Cecchi. He gets in front and I sit in back. The driver takes off fast, throws his siren. When we get to Eighth, we turn downtown on this one-way uptown avenue and pull next to a green Dumpster with the name Mazzafero on the side in big yellow letters.

It hits us right away when we get out of the cruiser. Hiding a body in New York City, especially in mid-July, isn't easy. Decomposition starts fast and the smell of death is like no other.

Cecchi pushes past some uniformed cops to the back of the Dumpster, where he hikes himself up on a ledge and looks over the side.

"Jesus," he says.

I move closer and that's when I start to gag. I swallow hard, then get myself under control. Like some of the others standing around, I take out my handkerchief and hold it against my mouth and nose.

Cecchi jumps down, his face the color of flour. He wipes some sweat from his forehead, pushes back the salt-and-pepper hair, and shakes his head. "Jesus," he says again.

I know it must be bad to get Cecchi that way and a big part of me doesn't want to look. But that other part of me, the part that needs to know no matter what, takes over.

Keeping the handkerchief over my mouth and nose, I

use my right hand to pull myself up. The leather soles of my sandals slip and I have to give it a second try. This time I make it and as my eyes come level with the top of the Dumpster I feel my heart whump like a fanfare for death.

She is lying faceup except there isn't any face. The flies have laid their eggs and the maggots are doing what they do best. Her brown hair is fanned out and laced with bits of garbage like ersatz ribbons. Her legs are spread-eagle, arms across her breasts, and her cotton dress has small blue horses on a field of white. I see enough and jump down.

As always, I wonder how and why a human being ends her life this way. Who was she? What did she do to achieve this inglorious end in a Dumpster?

"You know who she is?" I ask Cecchi.

He shakes his head no.

I could hang around and watch what happens next but I've been through this part before. It's a long process and I should get to my office. I ask Cecchi to keep me posted on the case, and head east on Twelfth Street.

For many of us there has always been a sense of danger in New York City but now, even in the daytime, I no longer feel safe walking the streets of Greenwich Village. I attribute this to the constant possibility of terrorists at work. I suppose it started with the explosion at the World Trade Center in February, and then the capture of the Fourth of July conspirators. I have the feeling that anything could happen at any time. This has always been true, of course, but this new threat hovers like pollution.

I have to keep going on; still, something of my love for this city has evaporated and a sense of sadness lives inside me in a way it never has before. I wonder how long I'll stay here, how long any of us can.

I walk the winding route and as I come abreast of a market on West Fourth Street I hear a man say to the owner:

"Give me all the change in your pocket."

I know this isn't a holdup because there's no weapon and what self-respecting outlaw would ask for change?

The owner, a small Korean man with large glasses, reaches into his pants pocket, pulls out his change, and gives it to the other man, who has a graying mustache to match his hair.

He arranges the money in a column, bends his arm, fingers on his shoulder, and places the change near the tip of his elbow, where it wobbles precariously. Then he flips it into the air and catches it in his hand. With a dispirited smile, he says, "I used to be able to do more but I'm too slow now."

From the sound of his voice and the look in his eyes, I recognize that this is his measure of aging and I empathize. We all have one or two.

"That's terrific," I say.

"Ya shoulda seen me in my yout' . . . sometimes a pile tree inches high."

I find this hard to believe but say, "That looked good to me."

His eyes take on a new luster. "Ya tink so?"

"*I* couldn't do it."

"Why should ya?"

"Excuse me?"

"That suppose to be some kinda compliment or somethin' ? Why the hell *should* ya be able to do it, huh? I mean, yer a girl."

A girl.

"A girl? Is that supposed to be some kind of compliment or something?"

"Huh?"

I wave a hand at him in dismissal and walk on. The hell with him. Let him mourn his youth alone.

By the time I reach my building I'm drenched in sweat. Each year the weather gets worse. But because Kip's work as a psychotherapist and my sporadic work as a private eye keep us here until August, we suffer through the weather, not gladly, but better than we suffer fools.

True, private eyes don't generally take August as vacation time (the way therapists do), and as I like taking my vacation with my lover, even after thirteen years, this is what we do. But June and July in the city are nightmares. Sometimes even May. This particular July is the July from hell.

My office, on West Fourth overlooking Seventh Avenue, is not air-conditioned. I have a fan, one of those big jobs, and it helps but doesn't do the entire trick. I would happily buy an air conditioner if the wiring in this building were up to it. I could report this violation but then my rent would go up, so I take the heat like a woman.

On my office door is "Lauren Laurano, Private Investigator." When I open it I feel like I've entered a pizza oven. Immediately, I turn on the fan, which whirs like a cement mixer. Hey, it blocks the street noises.

I sit at my desk, where there are what I consider the essential tools of my trade: phone, Toshiba color notebook computer, modem, mouse, and mouse pad.

I already regret that I didn't stop for an iced coffee and chocolate doughnut. Breakfast seems so long ago. I hang my purse over my chair. Inside is a .38 Smith & Wesson. Strapped on my ankle is a .25 and in my desk drawer a .44 Magnum.

I feel: secure, happy, and hot.

I power up my computer. It spins into action, doing its things, then takes me right to Windows (I've set it up this way), where I double-click my mouse pointer at the icon for Unicom, the telecommunications software I use with my modem, and wait for the program to come on the screen.

I never cease to be amazed that I know how to do this. Only a few years ago I was completely computer illiterate, but I had to learn to use one and a modem to help solve a case. To say that I became obsessed with the technology wouldn't be extreme.

Kip would probably say that for a while I became a bulletin board freak. These are on-line boards run by ordinary people where you can write and read mail, join conferences, better known as Sigs (special interest groups), and get files (shareware software), among tons of other activities.

With the passage of time, I've become more normal about the whole thing and now I basically use one BBS called the Invention Factory, where I log in every day, check the new files, and get my mail from various Sigs and my E-mail friend, David.

As I'm about to instruct my modem to dial I.F., there's a knock on my door. The glass is smoked and I can see only the outline of a short person (probably five one or two, around my height) and guess that it's a woman. I abandon my dial and tell the intruder to come in. I can't help it, I wanted to read David's letter to me, and even though this may be a client, I see him/her as an interloper. David will have to wait until later.

The door opens and a man enters. He is, unfortunately, in this world we inhabit, extremely short for a man.

"Miss Laurano?"

I think about correcting the Miss to Ms. but don't out of sheer lethargy, and simply nod. "Come in, sit down." There's a green armchair on the other side of my desk.

The man wears New York black. In this case it's a T-shirt, jeans, and boots. I wonder how he stands the boots on such a hot day, but I've noticed certain boot wearers tend to don them year-round. This man is muscled as though he works out: prominent pecs and whatever the hell the rest of the bulges are called.

He clicks his way across my wooden floor, indicating he has taps on his soles and heels, and before he sits, stretches out a manicured hand to me.

"I'm Boston Blackie," he says.

Oh, please. Digging in my tattered memory, I recall my parents talking about a radio show of the same name. And I think there were a few Boston Blackie movies. Was he a P.I.?

I take his hand. "Would that be *Mr.* Blackie?"

"Just Blackie," he says seriously.

"What's the Boston part?"

He looks at me as if I'm an imbecile. "That's where I'm from."

"I see." Perhaps I should feel stupid but I don't. "This is to distinguish you from Miami Blackie, Detroit Blackie, and Kansas City Blackie?"

"Ya know 'em?" he asks, eyes forming accusing blue slits.

"Not personally," I assure him and am astonished by my joke that turns out to be real.

He relaxes some, although the lips are stern and straight.

"What can I do for you, Blackie?"

"Ask not what ya can do fer Blackie, but what Blackie can do fer ya."

I'm speechless.

"Mind if I smoke?"

"Actually, I do. I'm allergic," I tell him, which is untrue but is the only thing smokers accept. "So, Blackie, what can you do for me?"

"I can hire ya," he says, as though this is a reasonable answer to my question and his lofty pronouncement.

I decide to let the whole thing pass. "Hire me to do what?"

"Yer a P.I., ain't ya?"

I allow that I am.

"So, I can hire ya to do a case."

"I don't *do* cases, Blackie. I *crack* them," I say facetiously.

"Whatever." He's more sullen than before, if this is possible. "I want ya to find my mother."

"She's missing?"

"Yeah. Has been fer years."

"How many years?"

"Thirty-eight," he says without hesitation.

"Since you were born," I intuit.

"Yeah, right. Hey, yer good."

"Thanks."

"Yeah, Goldie said ya was but I dint wanna believe him, yer bein' a girl."

This one I can't let go by. "Woman."

"Whatever."

"Who's Goldie?"

"A pal," he answers suspiciously.

I don't know any Goldie. "Is this Grand Canyon Goldie?"

"I thought ya said ya dint know him."

"You're not serious, are you?"

"About what?"

"His name is *really* Grand Canyon Goldie?"

"Look, ya know him or what?"

"It was a guess. I don't know him. How does he know me?"

"Guy inside told him about ya. Joe Carter."

Joe Carter. A murderer I'd caught a few years ago. It was funny to think of Carter recommending me. But I *had* helped to put him away, after all. On the other hand, it gave me the creeps to think of Carter talking about me.

"So," Blackie says, "is it a go?"

"Is what a go?"

"You and me. The case. Ya gonna *crack* it?"

"I don't even know what the case is."

"It's the case of the missing mother," he says, straight.

"If she's been missing for thirty-eight years it's not going to be easy. Trails grow cold. I'll need a lot of information. You have something for me to go on?"

He reaches into the pocket of his T-shirt, pulls out a photograph, hands it over. It's a black-and-white picture, the edges yellow and curling. A woman stands against a car, circa early fifties, wearing a skirt and sweater, loafers and socks, and a strand of pearls. She's quite beautiful but she appears to be unhappy. I wonder why there are so many photos of people standing against cars and if subjects still pose this way.

"This is your mother?" I ask.

"Yeah." Blackie's voice catches, as if he's moved.

I turn the photo over. In pen someone has written:

Susie Mcmann, Stone Ridge, N.Y., 1953

I know that Stone Ridge is in Ulster County, upstate. "Were you born there?"

"New Paltz. Grew up there, too."

"Is your name Mcmann?"

"No. That was *her* name. I got my father's. Black."

"Ahh," I say, as if now I understand everything instead of simply the origin of his moniker. "Wait a minute. I thought you said you were from Boston."

"Later, when I was sixteen, we moved there. But she didn't. I mean, she died in an accident right after I was born."

"Accident?"

"That's what they tole me."

"Who?"

"Father, grandma, everybody."

Suddenly I feel a sadness for this man who was left without his mother.

"They said she died in an accident but you don't believe it and now you want to find her? This can be risky, you know." There's no good way of saying what I have to tell him. "She might not want to be found."

"Ya think she dumped me, huh?"

I don't know what to answer.

"Guess I didn't put it right. I want ya to find her body. She's dead all right."

"She's dead but not from an accident?"

"Yeah, that's right. That's what they *tole* me but I know better."

"Why would they lie to you?"

"Because my father killed her."

Chapter

Two

━━━━━━━━━━━━━━━━━━━━

"ARE YOU SERIOUS?" I ask him.

"Ya think this is a joke?"

I almost do but I don't say that to him. "How do you know your father killed your mother?"

"Listen. Ya live in a small town, ya hear all kinds of stuff. Ya gotta know what to believe, what not to believe, know what I'm gettin' at?"

"Explain."

"It's complicated," Blackie says.

"It usually is."

"It's hard to describe."

"Try." I'm beginning to suspect the man has nothing substantial to go on.

"I don't think my mother died a natural death. There's no gravestone or nothin'. And I don't believe there was an accident. They tole me she was burned up and wanted her ashes strewn in the woods."

"You mean cremated?"

"Burned up."

"Okay, burned up. I have to tell you that not having a stone isn't proof of murder."

He jumps to his feet. "Look, if I had proof I woulda turned him in a long time ago. I don't got proof. What I got are . . . are . . ."

"Feelings," I supply.

This embarrasses him. "Well, yeah, I guess ya could say that."

I do and I hate it. Feelings aren't facts. And facts are what you need in a murder case of any kind. "Why don't you tell me some of the things you've heard over the years?"

"I heard she run away. I heard she died in this auto accident, which is what the old man and his mother say."

"That's what you meant by burned up?"

"Yeah," he says as though perhaps I'm not smart enough to hire.

"There must be some record of the accident."

"Records can be made up, know what I mean?"

What I know is that Blackie believes what he wants to believe. "What else?"

"I heard I wasn't really my father's son, that my mother wasn't really who she was, that I was the grandson of a powerful and rich man."

Where have I heard this before? Maybe it was in a Boston Blackie movie. It certainly could've been in a Ross MacDonald novel. "What makes you think your father killed your mother?"

"It's just one of those things."

"A feeling?"

"Yeah."

Great. "So why now? Why haven't you pursued this before?"

He looks down at his boots as though they'll provide an answer, but all he says is, "This and that."

"Look, Blackie, we have to get something straight. If you want me to do my job, you have to tell me everything you know and make sure it's the truth."

"Slammer," he mumbles.

Ah. "You've been in jail?"

He nods. I don't have to know why unless it has some bearing on the case, which is what I ask him.

"Nah. Drugs. I've been clean fer about a year. I been on the program and they tell ya not to make any major decisions the first year so I waited. Now I got my act together, I'm ready to go after the bastard."

"I see. Can you pay me?" I hate talking money but I have to.

"Oh, don't worry about that. I'm loaded. It's clean. I got some great stock tips from Goldie."

This is getting ridiculous. A recovered drug addict plays the stock market using tips from a con? On the other hand, why not? But I need to be sure.

"You swear this is legitimate money?"

"I swear. What's your fee?"

I tell him and he gives me a week's retainer, shakes my hand, says he'll call me, and leaves.

I never had the chance to say I'd take the case but, hell, money and I have a way of not getting together and a case is a case. I enter all the information I've gotten from him into my database. It takes time but it will be worth it later on. I don't have a lot of hope for solving this one, because it all seems vague. Still, I'll do my best. No matter what Blackie's past has been he seems like a decent guy.

When I finish with my work I dial the Invention Factory, log on, and go directly to my mail. David and I upload our letters to the Main Board because we both live in Manhattan, although we've never met. This would spoil everything. We mark our letters "Private" so that no one else can read them. Of course the Sysop, systems operator, could if he wanted to but I trust that he doesn't.

I download the mail. It takes about six minutes because I read other conferences as well. Lately I've been reading *Gay Issues, JFK Conspiracy, Strange,* and *Word.* That's the software program I use. *Strange* deals with paranormal experiences, UFO sightings, et cetera. There are hundreds of conferences to choose from but one only has so much time.

When the download is over I log off, then open the mail packet in my Winqwk program, which is how you read and respond to mail. I'm only prepared to read David's letter now.

Dear Lauren,

I don't have a whole lot of time today because I'm helping Mario hang his new show. I think it's great that he's exhibiting again and I hope it won't be his last . . . you know what I mean? Don't despair, my friend, you'll get a new case soon and then you'll be griping about having to work, if I know you. I'm sure Kip doesn't mind picking up the slack when you go caseless, so to speak. Anyway, after I help Mario I'm going to get my hair cut, meet Destiny for lunch, and then I have a rehearsal for the new play. So it's one of those days. I predict that a case is going to walk through your door today. Love you lots and lots.

David

Mario Trinchieri, a painter, has AIDS and hasn't had a show in almost three years. Destiny is a transsexual and the play David's directing is one of his own that will be performed by his company: the Nonsensical Nomads. I've never seen one of David's shows and we're not sure if I will this time or not. It's all about preserving our physical anonymity to each other, even though we probably know more about the other than almost anyone else. Kip, of course, thinks we're crazy. She doesn't understand why we don't want to meet if we like one another so much. I can't explain.

David is *almost* right about Kip and paying the bills when I don't have anything to contribute, but sometimes Kip and I have money problems. She can go on for a long time not saying a word, then some little thing will tick

her off and she throws the inequity of our earnings in my
face. It's not a pretty sight.

Kip has loads of money, we consider ourselves married, and some time ago put our finances together. So I
don't think it's actually about money when this comes up.
She knows I'm insecure in this area and hey, don't lovers
always look for the most vulnerable spot to attack? Why
is this? I don't know the answer but I know it's true of all
my friends who are couples.

I quickly type out a letter to David telling him I got a
case, thanking him for his good wishes, and saying that
I'll write in more detail later. Then I log on to I.F. again,
upload my reply, which takes a second or two, log off,
and power down my machine.

It's eleven fifty-eight and I'm going home for lunch
with Kip. We can't always do this but occasionally our
schedules mesh and we like to take advantage of it when
possible. And now that I finally have a case, after weeks
and weeks of stagnating, who knows when this opportunity will arise again.

I cross Seventh Avenue, nearly get knocked down by a
cab, almost get creamed by a biker wearing a Walkman,
and finally get to the other side. Near the corner is a new
Japanese restaurant which has replaced a health food
joint that had succeeded an Italian restaurant which had
followed a coffeehouse which had been taken over by a
Greek fast-food spot which had become a seafood place
which had supplanted a Japanese restaurant all in the
last eighteen months. I mentally wish the new place good
luck but don't hold much hope for it. Some spots seem to
be jinxed.

When I reach the corner of Perry Street I can't believe
what I see.How could I have forgotten? It's the ubiquitous dread film crew with all their paraphernalia. But
this time I can't complain because this is a movie written
by Rick, my upstairs neighbor and good friend, and

Susan, another good friend. And it's no accident that they're shooting here. Rick and Susan's screenplay is about a P.I. who lives on Perry Street named Lauren Laurano. Cybill Shepherd plays the P.I. This casting is certainly not art imitating life! I wish.

As I start down my block a man in jeans and a T-shirt that says SADDAM SUCKS stops me.

" 'Scuse me, lady, but would you mind going around the block 'cause we're shooting here."

"Shooting whom?" I ask, playing dumb.

He smiles condescendingly. "Nah, not like that. We're shooting a movie. You'll want to see it when it comes out, and if you go around the block you'll make it easier for us to do our job and then you'll be part of the making of this movie."

This might be one of the worst reasons ever given for a person to not interfere with a shoot.

"I don't want to be part of this movie," I say.

He's not amused. "Well, then, could you just go around the block anyways?"

"No. I live on this block."

He narrows his already scrawny eyes. "You got identification?"

"You're kidding."

"Nope."

This is a dilemma. I can make a scene, show my P.I. license, or I can simply explain. The problem is that in New York there's no such thing as "simply explain." It's a concept that has not arrived here yet. Still, I try.

"What's your name?" I ask.

"Why?"

"Because I want to address you by name when I explain who I am."

"Who *you* are?" he says disdainfully.

I'd like to tweak his ruddy nose. This is already ridiculous and it's only taken about one minute of my time. "Okay, so you don't want to give me your name. Fine. My name is Lauren Laurano, I'm a private eye, I live in the building where you're shooting the exterior, and, in a way, this movie is about me." I immediately regret that I've said the last part of my sentence.

And I'm right to do so because this twerp looks at me as if I'm an escapee from a Star Trek convention. Next, he laughs. Loud and long.

It's then that I'm rescued.

"What's going on?" Rick says, running up to us. He's fat again and has huge circles under his eyes. I wonder if the gain in weight has to do with this film, or William, his lover.

The guy explains to Rick that he's trying to keep this annoying and absurd person off the set.

Rick rolls his eyes at me. "Dwayne, this is Lauren Laurano. She lives here. In fact, this movie is sort of about her."

I should've guessed his name would be Dwayne.

Dwayne looks at me, then back to Rick. "Cybill's playing *her?*" he asks incredulously.

"Central casting," Rick says, and takes me by the arm as he leads me down the block. "Don't blame Dwayne, he's just trying to do his job."

"I blame his mother for naming him Dwayne. He never had a chance."

"Too true. We're going to start shooting in about five minutes. You want to watch or go inside?"

"I think I'll go inside." I know that five minutes probably means an hour or so.

Susan walks toward me. "Lobes," she says and opens her arms for a hug.

"Tone," I say. We often play at being mobsters of the Italian type because: 1. It's easy. 2. It's fun. 3. It started as a way to rag me because I get so fed up with books and movies that portray Italians *only* as criminals. 4. Tone is short for Tony, a stereotypical mob name; Lobes is the diminutive of earlobes, of which neither of us can remember the origin. But we like the way it sounds.

Susan is married to a nice guy named Stan who's a film editor. We often spend evenings with them and sometimes go for weekends to their house on Sunrise Lake in Pennsylvania. Kip and Stan like to do unbelievable things like taking walks, biking, swimming, or sailing. Susan and I like to stay inside and watch movies. We're a very compatible foursome.

"So, congrats on your first day of shooting, Tony," I say.

"Thanks. I can hardly believe it's finally happening."

"You should've used me as a model a long time ago."

Susan says, "It's only happening because YOU are somehow involved, right, Lobes?"

"Only reason."

Susan has a pretty face, smooth skin, and lovely brown eyes. She's in her forties and dyes her hair (as does Rick) because in the movie business THEY only want youth. So her hair has a reddish cast to it. Basically, Susan wears one outfit for winter and one for summer, although there are many variations on each. Today she wears a green shirt with a V neck, jeans, and Reeboks. In the winter the shirt is a turtleneck. This has nothing to do with money. She likes the way the shirts fit and feel and sees no reason to wear anything else. Unless she has to *take* a meeting here or in Hollywood. Then out come the heels and hose, et cetera.

"So you going to watch, Lobes?"

"Nope. I'm going to eat lunch with *the little woman.*"

"Don't blame you."

"See you both later," I say, starting toward my door. But I stop when I hear a young actor addressing Rick.

"Rick, I can't say this line. I can't find any motivation for it. I mean, why would my character say this? There's absolutely nothing anywhere in the script that gives me an inner life to say this line."

Rick looks down at the script where the actor is pointing his finger.

"There's no subtext for this," he whines on.

Susan looks over Rick's shoulder at the script. Then she and Rick look at each other. Finally, Rick says:

"'Take this tray.' The line is 'Take this tray,' Gary. What's wrong with it?"

"I don't know anything about this tray."

"What's to know?" Rick asks.

"Jesus," Gary says. "I don't want to bother the director with this. I thought you could help me. I mean, where does this tray come from? Whom does it belong to? What provenance does it have? Is that too much for a poor actor to know?"

Rick puts an avuncular arm around Gary's shoulder and begins talking to him sotto voce. As I turn away to go inside, I wonder how Rick, Susan, and the poor director stand it.

I open the door to our brownstone. Kip bought it some years ago, and we live on the first two floors while Rick and William live on the third. The fourth is occupied by two leftover people from the sixties who continue to smoke pot, which drifts into the halls at times. We refer to them as the PITAS (Pains In The Ass). We've been trying to evict them for years but so far it's been impossible.

There are two entrances to our duplex and I take the one directly into the kitchen to wait for Kip. We've been trying to cut down on our cholesterol — well, Kip has been trying to cut down on *my* cholesterol — so I know that lunch will be some sort of salad. Eeeeew. Still, it's worth it to have lunch with her.

I open the fridge and there the horror sits in a big bowl secured with aluminum foil. When I put it on our round table I remove the covering, look inside. Just as awful as I knew it would be. But I have to hand it to her; it contains about sixteen different vegetables. I didn't know there were so many. My mind drifts to thoughts of mud cake.

As I set the table I hear the door open and when I turn around my lover's heart hosts a hurricane. This doesn't happen all the time, of course, not after all these years. Still, once in a while, it's as if I've never seen Kip before, or perhaps it's because I *have,* and know what possibilities exist.

She is tall and thin . . . well, tall to me as almost everyone is, about five six . . . has dark hair, and eyes that, when sad, could break your heart. I'm not alone in thinking she's stunning. And the way the woman dresses! Today, she wears a lime-green silk blouse, gray slacks of some lightweight material with a thin gray belt, and matching shoes. Around her neck, on a cord, are her glasses.

"Hello, my pet," she says facetiously, kisses me sweetly.

"Mmmm," I say.

We look into each other's eyes.

"God, I love you," she says.

"That's good."

"*That's good?* This is what you say when I tell you I love you? Excuse me, sister."

"You'd prefer 'That's bad'?"

"So amusing. I see you found our scrumptious lunch."

I smile weakly.

"Lauren, it's for your own good."

"I hate things that are for my own good."

"Yes, I know. And speaking of your own good, I was cleaning out a cupboard this morning and found all these crumpled wrappers from Tootsie Roll Lollipops."

"You did?" I can't believe I forgot to throw them away. "Must be Rick's."

"That was my take on it, too. It's not funny, you know."

"There's no fat in them."

"What about your teeth? They're going to fall out of your head, and when they do, dumpling, I'm not going to be there to catch them."

"Where will you be?"

"Oh, I'll be reading or something. I'm just not going to catch your teeth."

"That's a relief."

We sit down and Kip serves us. "Did you read the paper this morning?" she asks.

Oh, no. The press has been giving President Clinton a very hard time, and the raves and rants of Kip Adams are in full swing.

"The honeymoon is over, they say. Honeymoon? It's been more like date rape."

"Why are you continuously shocked by this, as if it's something you've just discovered about the press?"

"Because it gets worse with every passing day. The man can't do anything right, as far as they're concerned. And the public's no better. Do you know that when we bombed Baghdad he went up eleven percent in the polls?"

"You've mentioned that," I say, trying to sound even.

"They want to reduce the deficit but nobody wants to sacrifice. What do they think the man is, Merlin the Magician? And Hillary. God. A caller on the Bob Grant show said that her haircut was to 'make her look like June Cleaver and not the lesbian she is.' Can you believe that?"

"That she's a lesbian?"

"Lauren, please."

"What?"

"You're missing the point."

"The point is that you must be crazy to listen to the Bob Grant show."

"No, that's not the point. The point is that people say she's a lesbian because she's strong. They use the word as an epithet."

I slap my hands across my breast in mock horror. "No! That can't be possible. Who would do such a thing?"

A smile flashes across her face, then vanishes, leaving no trace. "Okay, okay. I know we're the targets now that the abortion issue is dead, but I can't bear this constant attacking of the Clintons."

"What would happen if you didn't read the paper or listen to right-wing radio programs or watch the news?"

She looks at me, astonished. "Are you nuts?"

"Seriously. Think how relaxed you'd be if you weren't on constant asshole alert."

"Relaxed? I'd be a basket case not knowing what was going on."

"You're a basket case *knowing*."

She reels back in her chair, blinks at me as though I've suggested she's a Rush Limbaugh fan. "What in hell does that mean?"

"Frothing and fuming all the time. Shrieking about Nunn this, Powell that."

"Lauren, I *never* shriek."

"You do." I pop some salad.

"How can you say that?"

"Kip, face it, you're hysterical when it comes to politics."

"I'm not hysterical. I'm concerned."

I laugh.

"And frankly," she continues, "I think you should be *more* concerned."

"I am in my own way. My own *quiet* way."

"How? By calling bulletin boards and downloading the *Politics* conference?"

"How'd you know there's a *Politics* conference?"

A smile sneaks across her mouth. "I have my ways."

I suspect her way is a good guess. "I don't download that one. I hear quite enough at home, thank you."

"Lauren, aren't you interested in the news?"

"Of course I am. It's just that you get so crazy."

"Crazy, hysterical, and shrieking. Very nice."

"Anyway, I have my own news."

"What?"

"I got a case today."

"Oh, that's great, sweetheart. Tell."

"Only if we can put Nunn and Powell on the back burner for now."

"Hey," she says, "they're back there, babe. Can't you smell them?"

I can't top that one so I begin to tell her about Boston Blackie.

Chapter

Three

════════════════════

"DID YOU TRY to talk him out of it?" Kip asks.

"I never got the chance. The man is determined, and it was clear that if I turned him down he'd hire someone else. I said that I didn't have much to go on and indicated it would be a tough case. I think that's being ethical," I say.

Kip smiles at me, the kind that conveys cockeyed devotion; the good kind! "Of course it is. Is Mr. Noir's father still alive?"

Kip and I give our clients code names and I'd named Blackie "Noir." Not terribly original, I admit.

"He's alive and back in Stone Ridge with his ancient mother."

"Is he an only child?"

"As far as I know. He never mentioned anything about his father remarrying."

"That's odd in itself," Kip says.

"Why?"

"Widowers usually remarry in the first two years."

"Maybe he's the classic mama's boy."

"Has Big Daddy lived with her all this time?"

"Seems he has."

"Maybe Grandma didn't like her daughter-in-law."

"Always a possibility."

"So Grandma might have done the deed?"

"I suppose so," I say, reluctantly. Kip knows why.

"Lauren, you have to get over this. It's a real blind spot with you and I'm sure it affects your work."

"You're right," I say. But I can't help it. I find it difficult, even though I know they do it, to see women as murderers.

"Want me to start naming them for you?" She's referring to known female killers.

"No thanks." I've heard the list before. Compared to men it's a rather short one, but I don't bother mentioning this again. "Mr. Noir didn't have any suspicions about Grandma. He was very definite about the perp being his father."

"So? That's natural. Maybe he had a rough time growing up with his father. Grandma was probably the nurturing one."

"Nurturing but a killer?" I say.

"It happens. If there can be 'nice quiet boys' there can be 'nice quiet grandmas.' "

"You have a sick mind," I say.

"You would too if you saw the people I see every day."

"I see worse. At least yours are in treatment."

"Yeah, like W.W." This refers to Willie Whore, who can only do it with prostitutes. "Any minute I think I'm going to pick up the paper and see that I've been treating another Joel Rifkin."

"Wouldn't you know? Wouldn't he have told you?"

"Probably not. Of course, W.W. *is* in therapy. Something I don't think Rifkin or Dahmer ever did."

"Or any of them, as far as I know. What would you do if W.W. turned out to be a serial killer?" I ask.

"What *could* I do? I'd faint."

"You're so butch."

She laughs.

"So, who do you have today?"

"Two regular neurotics and Yellow Ribbon."

"Eeeew."

"I know."

Yellow Ribbon likes to be peed on. "What do you say to him?"

"About . . . *it?*"

I nod.

"Well, I don't say 'Eeeew.' "

"You don't?" I reply with mock surprise.

"Maybe I should. Maybe today I should give in to all my real responses. I wonder what they'd do?"

"Are you telling me that you fake what you feel, Kip?"

"Of course not. It's just, sometimes I don't show, well, distaste. I'm not there to make judgments, but occasionally I can't help feeling negative. In case you haven't noticed, I *am* human."

"Actually, I have noticed that," I say, smiling salaciously.

She gives me a look. This is the one that hits me right in the solar plexus, then works its way downward.

"So what's your next move?" she says.

I look at my watch. "Do you have time?"

"I didn't mean *that,* although I wish we could."

This is one of those times I envy hets and gay men. They can do it in minutes. Even when we don't want to make it a production number, it's a production number. We've gotten it down to twenty minutes when we've had to, but never less.

"I meant," Kip says, "your next move on your case."

"Oh, that."

"Yes, love, *that.*"

I sigh and return my thoughts to business. "How would you like to take a drive upstate this weekend?"

"To Stone Ridge?"

"The very same."

"Will you take me out to dinner at an idyllic place?" Kip asks.

"Yup."

"Will we stay overnight at some sylvan inn or B and B?"

"Some what?"

"Bed and breakfast," she says.

"Kip, I know what a B and B is. What's a *sylvan* one?"

"How can I be married to such an illiterate?"

"Just lucky, I guess."

"It means wooded, foresty."

"*Foresty?* Oh, that's very literate."

"Never mind. Where was I?"

"In a sylvan."

"Right. And once we're in this place will you make mad and passionate love to me?"

"Absolutely."

Slowly, she smiles and the look comes back. Then she says, "No, don't think so. I'm pretty busy."

"My little romantic."

When I come out of my apartment I find that I can't open the front door. No matter how I twist and tug, the damn thing won't budge. I get a chair from the hallway, put it in front of the door, and stand on it so I can look through the small panes at the top. The moment my face comes level with the windows I hear something that sounds like a wounded elephant.

It turns out to be a collective groan from the film crew and cleverly, because I'm a detective, I figure out that I've ruined a shot.

"CUT. Who the hell is that?" says a man's voice. I assume it's the director, Barry Berry.

My front door opens and reveals me standing on the chair. Do I feel like an idiot? Nahh!

"What in the bloody hell do you think you're doing?" Barry Berry is a medium-sized man with thick eyebrows like two small gray hedges above penetrating puce-colored eyes and a commanding nose. He wears a red tank top, safari pants, sandals, and a tan hat, the brim turned down all around. Stuck in the corner of his mouth is a thin brown cigarette, the smoke pluming around his head like a halo.

It's difficult to know how to answer this question but I try. "I think I'm standing on a chair in my doorway."

"Oh, you do, do you?" When he speaks to me he doesn't remove the cigarette. "We're trying to make a film here."

I hate it that he says *film* instead of *movie*. "Yes, I know."

"You know," he repeats, exasperated. "Well, if you know, why are you standing on that bloody stupid chair?"

Rick and Susan to the rescue again.

"Barry, she lives there."

"I don't give a damn where she lives, she's ruined the bloody shot. Why can't these people be controlled?"

I climb down from the chair, return it to its place, and venture out the door.

"Miss," Barry Berry yells.

"*Moi?*" I say.

"*Vous*," he says, completely missing the irony. "Dear girl, I know that you live here but we're trying to make a film." He loops his arm through mine and begins walking with me as if I'm his charge. "The thing is, pet, it costs bundles of money to make these bloody things and every time a shot is called off, that's more money and more time. You do see, don't you, love?"

What I see is an impersonation of a motion picture director. It's as if this man learned his lines from one of the innumerable movies made about the movies. Which is disconcerting because I'm not sure of my role, therefore my lines. Still, I do my best.

"How would you like me to enter and leave my home?" I ask.

He gives me a cultivated chuckle. I'm not charmed. "If you would simply wait, dear girl. That's all I ask. Wait," he says, dramatically hitting the *t* with emphasis.

"For what?"

"For the shot to be over." Berry looks at me as if I'm definitely not Mensa material.

"But," I say slowly to further his impression, "how will I know when the shot is over if I'm inside?"

He stares at me. And stares at me. Because he doesn't have an answer.

"Exactly," I say, move out of his grasp and down the street.

Behind me I hear him yelling to his crew: "The bloody people must be controlled."

As I come abreast of one of the trailers the door opens and Cybill Shepherd comes out. I can't help myself. I stop and stare.

"Hi," she says to me, and smiles.

"Hi," I say.

She's much taller than I thought she was and not as thin, although not fat or even plump by any stretch of the imagination. She really is quite lovely-looking. Suddenly it hits me in a way it hasn't before that she's portraying *me*. Sort of. Rick and Susan have *based* their character on me. It's heady stuff.

Suddenly Susan is by my side. "Cybill," she says. "This is Lauren Laurano, you know, the P.I. who's the prototype for your character."

"Oh, wow," Cybill says, stretching out a hand to me. "I can't believe I'm really meeting you."

This has got to be a joke, I think, as I shake her hand. Immediately I notice that it's a good handshake, so rare to find these days.

"You must lead a very exciting life," she says.

This is absurd but I can tell that what she's saying is absolutely genuine. Here is a woman without artifice. I almost can't stand it.

"Well, not as exciting as yours," I say like some bumbling fan.

She laughs. It's the Cybill/Maddie laugh and I feel I

know her, but it's only because I'd loved *Moonlighting* and watched it religiously, until they gave away the show to Mr. One-Note, Bruce Willis.

"Honey," Cybill says, "this old life of making movies is about as dull as it gets. When you have some time I'd really like to talk to you."

"You would?" I say, shocked and sounding silly.

Fortunately, Cybill doesn't seem to notice how gauche I am. "Crime fascinates me and you must have so many stories."

"A few." I try for nonchalance but don't think I'm making it.

From a distance we all hear: "Where's that bloody woman?"

"That's me," Cybill says. "I have to go now. Hope we'll talk soon."

"Soon," I agree. Gape-jawed, I watch her go down the street.

Susan says, "Terrific, isn't she?"

I nod. I shouldn't be surprised by anything Shepherd does, because she was the only movie star who showed up at the gay march on Washington in April.

"Later, Lobes," Susan says, and follows Cybill.

Cybill.

Why have I never noticed what an exquisite name it is? Why have I been so uninterested in blondes? It's clear to me now that blondes are beautiful and I'm ready to dye my hair in a trice.

Okay, so I'm smitten. What of it? What full-blooded lesbian wouldn't be?

Kip's face looms large in my mind's eye.

Guilt.

What's to be guilty about? Am I never to find anyone else attractive? Let's face it, there are a lot of attractive women in the world and there'd be something wrong with me if I didn't respond to Cybill Shepherd. Right? Not that I think for one instant of doing anything about it even if Ms. Shepherd were of a mind, which she's not. I'm definitely not one of those people who think anyone who's nice to them is coming on. And I certainly don't believe that any straight woman can be had, a sentiment I deplore.

Anyway, finding Cybill attractive is nothing to be guilty about. If Kip did the same I'd completely understand. I would even discuss it with her. We're adults, after all.

I try to imagine our conversation.

I keep trying.

For some reason nothing comes to me. Well, hell. I realize that I've been standing and staring and that will get me nowhere on this case. I have to get back to my office and do a background check on my client, his father, and his grandmother.

Hey, it's easy.

Even children can get information if they know how to use a computer . . . according to *Sleepless in Seattle,* that is. At least for once it was a girl child.

Who says things aren't improving for women?

From a distance I hear, "Would you please get the bloody hell off my set?"

I laugh, wonder what poor fool the faux director is yelling at now. And then I feel the tap on my shoulder and I know, without being told, because I'm a P.I., it's me.

Chapter

Four

IT'S FRIDAY NIGHT and the cares of the week are behind us. This is a lie, but I wish it were true. Our friends Jenny and Jill have decided to take the weekend off and go to Stone Ridge with us. They own the wonderful Three Lives Bookstore in the Village and almost never get to go away except on Tuesdays and Wednesdays. But Hilary, their manager, agreed to switch with them.

The Js, as we call them, are our best female-couple friends. They've been together for sixteen years and introduced us. Last year Jenny finally turned forty (something we'd all been waiting for . . . all but Jenny).

Jill has deep red hair and green eyes and grows more attractive as she ages. Sometimes she speed talks and we have to make her slow down. She's smart, creative, and fun to be with.

Jenny is also all those things, but she's taken on the role of "the brat," even though this isn't who she really is, because it amuses us. She's shorter than Jill, about my height, has curly brown hair, wears glasses, and in a good light resembles Debra Winger.

And then there's Theo.

Theo is their dog, an adorable Welsh terrier. She's very well trained as she's been to school for six hundred years.

The Js made the mistake of never leaving Theo alone when she was a puppy so, when they tried, it was a disaster. Theo howled the entire time they were gone. Now they can go out without her for a few hours but *choose* to bring her along on this trip. We don't mind, although it means we have to stay at a motel, which is truly my preference because I don't like the bathroom situations at quaint country inns and B & Bs. I've assured Kip that I can be as romantic in a motel as I can in a cramped room in someone else's house.

Kip drives our red Range Rover. It's not that she doesn't like the way I drive; it's that she doesn't like the way I drive. I make her nervous. This is interesting because Kip is the one who's had two accidents while my sheet remains clean. The accidents were not her fault. Still. But these are the compromises one makes in a long-term relationship. After all, does it matter that I get less and less confident about my driving skills?

Another reason we've asked the Js to join us is that I'll be off doing detective things, which would leave Kip alone. This way she'll have company. In the morning we'll pick up a car we've reserved for the three of them. And Theo.

A tape of Bobby Short plays softly and we're all in good moods. Even Theo, who's asleep, head in Jill's lap. I wish this were going to be a holiday for me but during the day it'll be work. At night I can join the others . . . I hope. Sometimes night calls are the only ones you can make. I remind myself that this is a weekend and perhaps that will make the difference in finding people at home.

"Are we there yet?" Jenny asks, exercising her brat role to be funny.

"Only two more hours," says Kip.

The best thing about this drive is that there isn't much traffic. If we were going to the Hamptons on a warm July night it would take forever.

"So who are you after this time?" Jill asks.

I can't actually divulge this information but I can tell them in a vague way. "A mother, missing for thirty-eight years."

"Mine's been missing for forty-one," Jenny says.

"Forty-three" from Kip.

"Forty-two," says Jill.

"Forty-five," I say.

Jenny says, "You always win, Lauren, because you're the oldest."

"Thanks, I needed that." The truth is that my mother is probably the most absent as she's an alcoholic in denial. Jenny is close to her mother, Pat, who is a playwright and lives in SoHo. Jill's mother's in Florida, but since Jill's father died, mother and daughter have become closer. And then, of course, there's Carolyn, Kip's mother. Carolyn has been on the case since day one. Hardly missing in any way. And since she remembered my last birthday by phone *and* card, as far as I'm concerned, she's perfect.

It's Kip who's given her mother the most support during Tom's illness, although her two other siblings have been helpful. Tom, Kip's youngest brother, has AIDS. He, and his lover Sam, live in San Francisco.

Tom was diagnosed three years ago and has had several outbreaks of the disease. About two years back, they came to New York for alternative treatments. There's no way to gauge what good they did, but maybe they've delayed the inevitable. The last time we spoke to Sam he told us he thought Tom was steadily going downhill. Aside from the pain of losing Tom, when I think about this, I always feel a little frightened because of what we've agreed to.

The world prognosis for AIDS is worse than ever, and what came out of the convention in Germany this year was essentially that no one knew anything; that the existing drugs probably don't work; and that there's no cure in sight. At least Clinton seems to care, a positive change from the last twelve years, and has appointed an AIDS czar. Still, whatever happens will be too late for Tom and that's the hardest part for Kip to assimilate.

"Are we there yet?"

Nobody answers.

My background checks on Harold Black, Blackie's father, and his mother turned up nothing. Black appears to be a solid citizen, not even a parking ticket to his name.

Jill says, "Have either of you ever been anywhere in Ulster County?"

"Only Woodstock," Kip answers.

"Yuck."

"It's like being on St. Mark's Place," Jenny says.

"No," I say. "It's like being in Woodstock in the sixties."

"Some of it's beautiful. The houses are great. It's just that it gets touristy in summer and the center of town caters to leftover hippies," Kip says.

"Good bookstore there," I say, speaking of the Golden Notebook.

"Just what I can't wait to see," says Jenny.

"There's no rule that we have to go to Woodstock," Kip says. "I mean, the Woodstock police aren't going to come and drag us there."

"How about the lesbian police?" asks Jenny. "Aren't there lots and lots of dykes?"

"Yes," I say. "I think there's a big gay and lesbian community in Woodstock."

"I hate that," Jenny states.

"What?"

"Gay and lesbian *community*. Do we ever say there's a big *heterosexual* community anywhere?"

"We don't have to," Jill answers. "It's understood."

"Well, I don't understand it," Jenny says. "Are we there yet?"

"Shut up," we say in unison and all laugh.

At the ungodly hour of five-thirty, I'm awakened by the din of birds! This is almost worse than the sound of garbage trucks. It never occurred to me to bring my earplugs to the country. I stare at the back of Kip's head, hoping she'll wake too. It doesn't work.

We are in the New Eastern Motel. I would hate to see the Old Eastern Motel. Not that there's anything terrible about our room, it's just decorated in Early Monotony. The truth is that both Kip and I love staying in motels, no matter what they're like as long as they're clean.

Quietly, I get out of bed, walk to the bureau, where I find the local phone book, and bring it to the round Formica table, where I sit on an orange plastic chair. Why are they always orange?

Blackie gave me Harold's address so I don't need to look up that one. I turn to the Ms to see how many Mcmanns there are. There are lots. Tracking down relatives of Blackie's missing mother out of this mess of Mcmanns is going to be a challenge. I could tear out the page but I'm more conscientious than that, so I dutifully open my briefcase, take out my notebook, and begin copying the names and addresses. When I finish this I put away the notebook, withdraw my notes about the case from my briefcase, and take them back to bed to read.

Goddamn birds.

Kip stirs, opens one eye.

"Hi," I say cheerfully and quite loud.

"What time is it?" she mumbles.

"Ah, five-forty."

"Are you insane?"

"The birds woke me."

"This is grotesque. Go back to sleep."

"I can't."

"Try."

"I know I can't."

"Then read."

"I am."

She raises herself up to see what I'm reading. "Read the book you brought."

"Why do you care *what* I read?"

"I don't." She turns her back to me.

I put my stuff on the floor, then lean over and kiss Kip's neck.

"Stop," she says.

"I thought you wanted me to make romantic and passionate love to you."

"At the proper time," she says.

"When's that, when you have on your white gloves?"

It gets a grudging snicker.

I put the tip of my tongue in her ear and she screams and jumps, smacking her head into my mouth and teeth, and I scream.

"Oh, God, honey, did I hurt you?" she asks.

"Don't be silly, you know I love pain."

She sits up, puts her hands on either side of my face, turns me toward her. There are little stingy tears in my eyes from the collision.

"You're crying," she says, horrified.

"Not."

"What can I do?"

I look deeply into her eyes and give her my most lascivious look.

"I thought you were in pain?"

"I'll sacrifice myself," I say, smiling.

"What a gal!" she says and reaches for me.

Later in the morning we join the Js and stumble into a charming breakfast place that triggers deep discussion.

"Sometimes," Jill observes, "country women have that look."

Jenny says, "Please, get a grip. These are dykes."

"You know what you're saying, then, don't you?" Kip asks.

"What?"

"That you can tell a lesbian by looking at her."

"This is news?"

I tuck into my apple pancakes. "You're saying there's a stereotype."

"Well, there is," Jenny says obstinately. "And there isn't. But these nice women behind the counter are dykes."

The trouble is I agree with her. Sometimes you can just tell. "So we've discovered a lesbian restaurant first time out?"

"It's hard to believe one would be here in . . . where are we?"

"Hurley."

"I mean," Jenny says, "what are they doing here?"

"What are *you* doing here?"

"*They* live here. I'm visiting."

I glance around. The clientele is routine, so nothing's to be learned from them. There are two waitresses who look like two waitresses anywhere.

The place itself is one large room painted yellow and white, with pine tables and chairs, two display cases that house pastries and deli items, and a self-serve coffee island. Pastoral scenes adorn the walls and the menu's on a blackboard. Flowering plants hang from the ceiling.

"You know," Kip says, dreamy. "I can see it."

"See what?"

"Living here."

"Oh, no," I say. "Here she goes." Wherever we visit, Kip decides she wants to live there. Passing through the Adirondacks one time, we stopped for lunch, she found *Adirondack Magazine* and subscribed to it. Now they are stacked, unread, in a corner of our living room.

"Let's take our vacation here, Lauren."

"And do what?"

"You're so unreasonable."

"Excuse me?"

"No imagination," Kip says to the others.

"Kip, we don't know anything about this area. We might hate it."

"I love it already," she says absurdly.

"You haven't even spent *one* day here."

"But I can tell," she goes on. "The peace, the lack of noise, stress."

"Think of those noisy birds," I say.

"I couldn't stand it," Jenny says.

"What?"

"The peace, the lack of noise, stress."

Jill says, "The problem is, there isn't any water."

"I saw ponds," Kip puts in.

"Yuck. Ponds," Jenny says. "Creepy, crawly."

"You know where we should go?" I say. "The North Fork."

"Long Island?"

"Lots of water."

Jenny brightens. "We could have a boat there, Jill. Think about it. Theo would love it."

"Notice," Jill says, she doesn't say *I'd* love it."

Kip asks, "You mean, you'd live there all the time?"

"Of course not," Jenny says. "Days off."

"Isn't it awfully crowded there?"

"That's the South Fork," I say. "The Hamptons."

"Maybe I'll find the perfect house here," Kip offers.

"For what?"

"Our vacation."

"Please," I beg her, "don't do anything without me."

"Of course not, darling. You'd have to see it before I put any money down."

I feel the mention of money is code for *I'm paying so what have you got to say about it, anyway?*

"Kip, don't be impetuous, okay?"

"I just want to explore," she says.

Why is it I don't believe her? I give Jill a look and she imperceptibly nods, a sign that tells me she'll do her best to keep Kip from doing anything rash. I feel better.

"I have to get going." I stand up and my napkin falls to the floor as it always does.

"Lose something?" Kip asks.

"Your mind," I answer. "I guess I'll see you all back at the Hearst Castle later. Try to find a good place for dinner." I lean down and kiss Kip on the top of her head, say good-bye to the Js, and I'm off.

While Kip was showering I'd made a phone call, starting alphabetically, and come up with a winner first shot. The listing was an A. Mcmann, who turned out to be Susie's sister, Almay. Blackie never mentioned an aunt, but maybe his father and grandmother never let him know he had one. After getting directions from Almay I'd made an appointment to visit.

I put the key in the ignition and start up the car. At last, alone behind the wheel! The countryside *is* pretty. But like so many places in New York State (maybe elsewhere) the landscape, with its beautiful farms and stone houses, is ruined by the trailers that dot the scene like warts.

Almay Mcmann lives in one of these abominations and it's aqua. The front yard is littered with hubcaps, old tires, and unidentifiable pieces and parts. There is also a yellow dog that lies on the ground. I can't help thinking that this is like a scene from a documentary about the trailer crowd, I mean, yellow dog and all.

I have to admit, as I park the car in the dirt driveway, I'm slightly frightened to get out because the dog's tail is not wagging and he's looking at me ferociously. As I weigh the problem of what to do, the front door of the trailer opens and a woman steps out. I roll down my window.

"Ms. Mcmann?" I call.

"Yup."

"The dog won't bite, will he?"

This gets an inexplicable roar of laughter from Mcmann.

"You the de-tective called?" she asks in a deep froggy voice.

"Yes."

"C'mon out. You don't have nothin' to worry over."

I take Mcmann's word for it and ease myself out of the car. Before I can close the door the dog barks and runs toward me like he thinks I'm lunch.

Chapter

Five

THE DOG GROWLS and pulls back its lips and I see that Mcmann hasn't lied to me. No teeth. And *now* it wags its tail.

I exhale and only then realize I'd been holding my breath. Mcmann is doubled over with laughter, a sound like gears being stripped. Cautiously, I reach down and pat Yellow Dog's head. The tail goes crazy.

As I walk toward the woman, I suppress my annoyance at having been had. Up close I see, when Mcmann smiles at me, that she resembles the dog. No teeth. At least not in the front. She's large and lumpy as though she's stuffed with pillows.

Her face is odd. The eyes are concealed by dark glasses, which I find strange in itself. Why would this sort of woman be wearing sunglasses? But I recognize my reaction as a kind of elitism. This is stupid. They're not Ray-Bans, after all.

A broad nose spreads across her face like putty and her skin has a sallow look to it, as though she hasn't been outside in a very long time.

"Tole ya nothin' to worry over. Vicious ain't had a tooth in her head fer five years now."

"*Vicious?*"

"Well, we all got a past, ain't we?" And this collapses her into the same screeching laughter as before. I wait it out.

It's hard to tell how old Mcmann is, but I guess her to be in her late sixties. A greasy gray scarf is worn babushka style and a few strands of tangled white hair crisscross her forehead like latticework. I gauge her weight to be about two hundred pounds, although it's hard to tell with all the clothes she's wearing. There is layer after layer of what appear to be sacks. I decide they're exceptionally old dresses, one over the other, maybe up to seven or eight. Under the nest of dresses are green pants in shreds around the ankles. Her feet are shod with hoary black Keds, no laces. And she wears a pair of fire gloves, yellow and blue.

Six months later she stops laughing. "So yer the detective, huh?"

I nod.

"You might's well come inside."

I have no desire to do this. "We can talk here."

"Got somepin' on the burner," she says, turns, and makes her way up the two cement blocks and through the door.

Vicious and I are left alone. I have to go in. As I get to the top step I smell something like burning beach balls, and when I step across the threshold it's as dark as the inside of a whale. I'm temporarily blind.

"So whatcha want?" she asks me.

I stand still in the doorway and even though my eyes start their adjustment, I ask, "Do you think we could put on some light?"

"Don't have none. I'll open a shade."

I vaguely make out her outline as she waddles to a small window, snaps up a tattered blind. A thin finger of daylight enters the trailer and I'm able to see it in all its grandeur. There are broken chairs, a foam rubber couch, its insides erupting like deformed flowers, and a tortured table.

Almay toils at the hot plate. "So whatcha want?" she repeats, and comes toward me, a dripping wooden spoon in her hand.

"As I told you on the phone, I'd like to talk about Susie."

For a moment she looks at me as though she doesn't know who I mean. Then the dawn breaks across her face like a silent burp.

"My sister," she says gloomily.

"Yes."

She takes off the sunglasses and I see tears in her eyes. With the huge gloved hands she slaps at them as though they're flies, then quickly replaces the glasses.

"She was a good one." Almay goes back to the hot plate, where she stirs the concoction once more, turns it off, and places the spoon on a dish. Returning to me, she says, "Let's sit." She gestures to the couch and lowers herself into one of the broken chairs so that she's on an angle.

I take the sofa. The phrase "as comfortable as a rock pile" comes to mind. "Can you tell me something about her?"

"She sure was purty."

Purty. Oh, come on, I want to say, but don't, not wanting to break the flow, phony as it sounds.

"Us Mcmanns, we ain't a good-looking lot on the whole, but Susie, she were different. Not only a looker but smart as a whip. She didn't take after the Harris side, my mama's people, who wasn't yer beauties to look at neither. Lotsa times people kidded my mama, saying Susie couldn't be a Mcmann."

Blackie's words about various rumors as to the line of heritage of his mother come back to me.

"And your mother, what'd she say when people kidded about that?"

"Kidded them right back. Said Susie was a change-ling."

I have to force myself to accept this dialogue but it's hard. After all, we're only two hours from New York City, not in the heartland. But what do I know? Maybe this is how some people talk up here. No maybe about it: she does.

"Is it possible that your father *wasn't* Susie's father?"

"Oh, I'm sure he weren't," she answers, surprising me.

"Really? Then who was her father?"

Almay gives me the once-over as if I've only then appeared. "Why ya wanna know about this? What difference does it make now?"

"I've been hired to find out what happened to Susie."

"Hired? Who hired ya?"

"I can't tell you that."

She reaches into a pocket and pulls out something that looks like an old twig, places it between her lips, and lights it with a wooden match that she strikes against the underside of the table. "Don't matter. Must be the boy."

"The boy?"

"Susie's boy."

I say nothing.

"So who was Susie's father?"

"Ain't got no proof."

"That's okay," I assure her.

She huffs out a cloud of smoke, grimy and smelly. "Hearsay's what it'd be. And simple 'rithmetic, like puttin' two 'n' two together, know what I mean?"

I urge her on.

"Don't make no judgments, now. My mama weren't no tramp or nothin'. It was against her will, ya know what I mean? She worked fer these folks down in Kingston, in one a them big houses the rich folks used to own. Now it's all differnt. I was a growed girl when Mama got in the family way with Susie, and I hear them fightin' all the time, my papa and mama. Hear him say the baby weren't his. Couldn't be. Guess ya know what that means." Almay acts as if the thought of her parents *not* having sex is somehow more embarrassing than them having it.

"Well, she cries and yells while my papa beats the tar outta her but she keeps on sayin' the baby's his. He don't buy it and says it's the bastard of Nicholas Parrish, the man Mama works for. She cries some more but she don't never say he's right. I think he were."

"Why?"

Almay laughs again, shrill and grating. " 'Cause Susie looks just like Parrish. He was a handsome one and Susie, well, I tole ya, she was purty. Same eyes as Parrish, same nose. And then there's the chin." She runs a fore-finger straight down the middle of her own chin. "Cleft. They both had it."

I recall the photograph of Susie but not the cleft. Still, it was taken at a distance and perhaps didn't show.

"Why didn't anyone else make the connection, then?"

"Who says they dint? Whatcha think they was sayin' to Mama when they remarked like I tole ya?"

"You mean everyone knew but they wouldn't come out and say it?"

"That's it."

"What about Parrish? Did he know?"

"Beats me."

"Okay, let's say you're right and Susie was Parrish's child. What happened to her?"

"Ya mean when she growed up?"

"Yes."

"She married a sommabitch name of Harold Black and had the boy. Franklin."

"Franklin?"

"Yup. That's what she named the pup."

"The pup?" I can't help myself.

"Ya know, the tyke, the little guy, the peewee, the . . ."

"Never mind. I understand."

"So why's ya askin' like ya don't get my meanin'?"

I take a stab at it. "You speak in a rather colorful way."

"That good or bad?"

"Neither. It's unusual."

She stands up, paces back and forth with long strides. I'm afraid I've upset her. "Ms. Mcmann . . ."

"Miz? Sounds like a bee or somepin'."

I open my mouth to elucidate, then close it. There isn't time to explain the last twenty-five years to this woman. "*Miss,*" I say cravenly. "*Miss* Mcmann."

"Oh. Thought ya said *Miz* like one of them bra burners."

I'm speechless and ashamed.

"Call me Almay."

"Thank you." There's something about Almay . . . something I can't put my finger on, and I don't think it's just that she reminds me of Mammy Yokum. Anyway, I decide to drop the questioning of her speech and get back to what I want to know.

"So she had Boston . . . Franklin. Then what?"

"Then she was gone." She sits on the chair again.

I notice that this time she doesn't say *were* for *was.* But I'm not sure what it indicates. "What do you mean, gone?"

"Died. In a accident."

"My client doesn't think so."

"Client, huh?" She gives one sharp yap of laughter. "What's he think?"

I don't know whether to tell her or not but she interrupts my thoughts before I can decide.

"He prolly tole ya Harold killed her, huh?"

"My client suggested that, yes."

"Franklin was never no good, ya know. I heard he got sent up for a long time. Spent time in juvie prison, too. Used to break into summer places."

"Is there anyone else I can talk to who might tell me more about Susie?"

"Nothin' more to tell. Susie died in a accident on August fifth, 1954. Look it up if ya don't believe me."

"What about Parrish?"

"What about him?"

"He still alive?"

"He left the county a long time ago."

"And your parents?"

"They's all dead, all a 'em. It's over, that life. Don't go mixin' in to somethin's none a yer bidnezz and ain't a damn thing to do about it. Go home."

Almay squints at me, giving herself what she imagines to be a fierce look. I don't like it but it doesn't scare me.

"Look, ya come here to find out about Susie and ya found out. So why don't ya go home."

"Is there some reason you don't want me to stay in Ulster County?" I ask.

"Meanin' what?"

I take a shot at it. "Maybe you're not telling me everything. Maybe you're afraid I'll find out something you don't want me to know."

She cackles. "Yer like somethin' out of the movies."

Funny, but I was thinking the same about her.

"There ain't nothin' here fer ya, girlie. Ya go back to where ya come from and ya tell Franklin they's all dead and nobody kilt nobody." She turns her back to me, turns on the burner again, and stirs the awful-smelling stuff on the hot plate. It's clear to me that Almay has said her last so I smile at Vicious and leave. At least I have a new name: Nicholas Parrish.

The Stone Ridge Library is what one always imagines a small-town library looks like. It is white fieldstone with white wooden window frames. There's a good-sized parking lot and some lawn. In the back there's a red barn.

I park, get out, cross the gravel onto a paved path and

up a step to a small porch with an overhang and a locked box where you can drop your books if the library's closed.

I open the screen door and go in. It is exactly the way I thought it would look. The librarian's desk is to my right, the card catalog next to it.

I stop at the desk.

"May I help you?" she asks. She's an attractive young woman with long auburn hair and a cheery smile.

"I'd like to look up some information in the local paper for the year 1954. Do you have that?"

"You're in luck. We just had them all put on microfilm going back to the thirties. The machine's in the basement and the film is catalogued in big steel drawers. I don't recognize you so I assume you don't know your way."

"That's right."

She gives me directions. I thank her and go into another smaller room, which leads to still another room about the same size. I open the door that has a sign on it telling me where the microfilm is kept.

I switch on the light and go down some steep wooden stairs to a very cool, surprisingly unmoldy basement. Even Kip, with all her allergies, could come down here. Longingly I wonder what they're doing right now, if they're having fun, and self-pity races through me like the chocolate ribbon in vanilla fudge swirl.

I'm used to using microfilm to look up things and Almay has given the exact date, so it doesn't take me long to find the right reel.

I take the spool out of its box and thread it through the machine, then press the control and the pages blink by on the reader, a giddy glimmer of seasons, styles, and lives of thirty-nine years ago. Someday you'll be able to type in a date and keyword and the story you're looking for will appear in a millisecond. But that hasn't happened yet, and it takes me two years to get to the right issue and page.

Susan Mcmann Black, 19, Dies in Car Crash

While on her way to Kingston from her home in Kripplebush, the young Mrs. Black, who was driving a 1950 Chevrolet, was struck by a trailer truck at the intersection of Routes 209 and 213. It was thrown 50 feet before it landed and burst into flames. By the time the fire department arrived, there was little left of the car.

Edward Geiger, the driver of the truck, who remains in stable condition in Kingston Hospital, said that Mrs. Black made the turn from Route 213 without stopping to look and he didn't have time to put on his brakes.

Mrs. Black is survived by her husband, Harold, and her son, Franklin. There will be a private service.

So there it is in black and white. Who can question this? Why doesn't Franklin "Boston Blackie" Black believe this version of events? Why does he really think his father killed his mother? What was it he'd said? Something like "Records can be made up"? Still, I make a copy of the obit. I'll have to go over this with Blackie. Maybe when we're both looking at it in print he'll tell me why he doesn't believe the official explanation of the death of his mother.

Back at the desk I ask the librarian if the old chief of police is still alive.

"Sure is."

"Can you tell me how to find him?"

"You bet."

After she gives me directions to the home of ex-chief

Breese, I ask the woman if she knows what happened to Nicholas Parrish. Almay said he'd left the county but you have to check everything. The librarian doesn't know who I mean, so I request a local phone book.

He's not listed.

Maybe Harold Black can tell me what happened to Nicholas Parrish, the possible father of Black's dead wife.

Chapter

Six

IN CONTRAST TO ALMAY MCMANN, Harold Black and his mother live in luxury. Their village is Kripplebush, in the township of Rochester. The street is Cooper and the frame house is set back from the road with a blacktop driveway that sports a

**PRIVATE DRIVE
KEEP OUT**

sign on a sawhorse. However, there is room to park on the side of the road. I haven't bothered to call the Blacks and now I wonder if this is a mistake, considering the sign. At least it doesn't warn me to beware of a dog.

From the road, through windows near the top, I can see that some sort of vehicle is in the closed garage.

I walk up the footpath to wooden stairs, which lead to a deck. On the door, a Christmas wreath that's turned brown hangs in the middle. I knock.

I knock again.

"Mr. Black," I call. After a moment, I hear sounds and then the door is flung open. A stooped man, probably in his sixties, wearing a blue short-sleeved shirt and old gray trousers, worn, tan slippers on his feet, glowers at me.

"Yeah?"

"Mr. Harold Black?"

"Yeah?"

"My name is Lauren Laurano. I wonder if I could come in and talk to you."

"Jehovah's Witness, are you?"

"No." I hand him my card.

A week later he says, "Private investigator? What are you investigating?"

"I'd like to talk to you about your wife."

"Wife?"

"I realize that it was a long time ago but I'm referring to Susie Mcmann, who died in 1954."

"Susie," he repeats, no expression.

"Yes."

"Like you say, she died in 'fifty-four."

"You might be able to tell me something about what she was like that'll help me."

"Help you what?" He squints, puts a hand above his eyebrows as though the sun's in his eyes, appraises me, then looks back at my card, dwarfed in his large sun-tanned hand.

"Help me in my inquiry," I say, sounding like a detective on PBS.

"Your what?"

"Mr. Black, I've been hired to look into her death."

"Who wants to know about the bitch?"

"I can't tell you that."

He laughs. "Privileged information, huh?"

"Yes."

"I know where the sun sets," he says, pride swelling his sunken chest. "I pay attention."

"Good."

"Well, guess you can come in but I don't have anything much to say about that bitch."

I note that this is the second time he's called her *bitch*, a word that I've developed a theory about, although he hasn't used it in the precise way I mean.

He steps to one side and motions me in.

"Thanks."

We are immediately in the living room. The furniture is neither old nor new, and is characterless, like the type one might see on a fifties sitcom.

Black motions me to the beige sofa and sits in a beige chair across from me, his feet on a tan vinyl hassock.

"Is your mother home?" I ask, as though Black is a kid.

"What do you want with her?"

"I thought she might have something to say about Susie."

"Nothing good," he says, eyes sparking for the first time. "Yeah, she's home. But she's resting now."

"Maybe later," I say.

"How long you planning to stay?" He looks worried, as though I might be the woman who came to dinner.

"I meant if she's up when we're through," I reassure him.

He grunts, satisfied with my answer.

"When were you and Susie married?"

"How'd you know my mother lives here?"

"I'm a detective."

"He told you, didn't he?"

"Who?"

"Franklin."

It seems there's no mystery for anyone as to who my client is, and no one who calls him Blackie. I say nothing.

"More privileged info, I know. What difference does it make when I married the bitch?"

"It doesn't, I guess. When did she disappear?" I want to see what he'll say to this.

"Disappear? She didn't disappear, she died in an accident when she was . . . she died."

"When she was what?" I ask. "What were you going to say?"

"Nothing. He say she disappeared? What did Franklin tell you?"

"Mr. Black, I'm asking you."

"You got a warrant?"

"Of course not. If you want me to leave, I will."

He stares, twists his nose between thumb and forefinger. "This is old stuff, I don't know what more the boy wants. Susie died right after he was born. Automobile accident. She was on her way outta here when it happened. Bitch," he says venomously.

Now he's used it the new way. It's my theory that it's no longer acceptable for men to call women *cunts* so they've replaced it with *bitch,* a fairly common epithet, though not totally acceptable in some circles. Still, one can get away with it without actually being considered outrageous. Nevertheless, the word *bitch* now carries the same scorn and hatred of women that *cunt* used to.

Black says, "She never loved me. She was just biding her time to get the hell out of here. The whole time she was saving nickels and dimes from the house money, just so she could hightail it out of here when she had a big enough stash. Didn't give a good goddamn about the boy, me, nobody."

"How long had you been married when she left?"

"Eight months. I *had* to marry the bitch. Well, hell, it was the right thing to do."

"And you believe in doing the right thing?"

"Right. That's why I voted for Perot. There's a guy that knows what's right and what's wrong."

I don't engage and thank God Kip's not here.

"So the truth is, Mr. Black, you weren't in love with Susie Mcmann."

His face goes slowly red and he works his lips as if he doesn't have teeth. "I didn't say that," he sputters. "Never said that. Media people get everything wrong."

"I'm not in the media," I say, bewildered.

"That's just what I mean: did I say *you* were in the media? Did I?"

"No."

"Damn right. So don't misinterpret or I'm calling this interview to a close."

Interview. Media. What does he think this is? I decide against trying to understand this bizarre take on our conversation and press on.

"Then you're saying you *did* love her?"

"Why does it matter whether I loved a person all those years ago?"

I can't tell him that his son thinks he murdered her so this is not easy to explain. "I'm trying to form a picture."

"You think she left because I didn't love her, that it?"

"It could contribute," I say carefully.

"Well, it didn't. For your information I *did* love her back then. *She* didn't love me. Or the boy, like I told you. Imagine leaving a baby to fend for itself."

"Actually, she didn't. The baby had you."

"Still, it wasn't natural. Then Susie Mcmann was always a little bit unnatural, you know what I mean?"

"No, I don't."

"Big ideas. Thought she was better'n everybody round here. Being a wife and mother wasn't enough for Susie. She wanted to be a movie star."

Here's a new wrinkle. "A movie star?"

"Yeah, she wanted to go to Hollywood, be a star. Stupid woman."

"So you're saying that when she left your home, left you and the baby, and had the accident, she was on her way to Hollywood?"

"That's what I just said, didn't I?"

"And you knew that because she left a note?"

"Note? No. Nothing."

"Then how did you know she was leaving you?"

"Some things you just know." His angry words chip the air like splintering glass. "Anyway, she was always saying that was what she wanted to do and she took all her clothes."

"Did you identify the body?"

"Couldn't. Burned to death."

Suddenly it occurs to me that Susie Mcmann was never identified so maybe it wasn't Susie Mcmann in the accident. Maybe it was someone else and Susie *got* to Hollywood.

"You ever go to the movies?" I ask him.

"When there's somethin' good, like *Last Action Hero*. I don't go to those sex pictures, though. Jesus, I love that Schwarzenegger. I mean, there's a guy's got it all: money, macho, and a beautiful broad. What I like best is that those Kennedys must've taken a shit fit when she married that guy. Wish I could've been there."

I ignore this diatribe. "If you saw Susie in a movie would you recognize her?"

"How could I see a dead person in a picture?"

"Let's pretend she didn't die in the car accident and that she did get to Hollywood and she did get into the movies. Do you think you'd recognize her?"

"Probably not."

"How come?"

"Makeup and stuff, not to mention that she'd be fifty-eight now." He holds out a hand in front of him, gazes at the back of it. "Changes," he says ruefully, inspecting his skin.

I sympathize, having noticed that my own skin's not totally smooth the way it was even five years ago.

"But this is stupid. Susie's dead."

"Harooold?" a voice calls from the back of the house.

Black sits up straight as if he's heard the voice from hell. His mouth twitches. He stands up. "That's my mother."

I nod and smile understandingly, as if to let him know why the sound of one's mother could put fear in the heart of a man in his sixties. My own mother's voice doesn't frighten me, but when I hear it, it registers in a way no other does.

"Haaaarooold?"

"Maybe you better be on your way now," Black says.

"I'd like to meet your mother."

He gulps air like a drowning man. "You sure?"

I've never been surer. This is one woman I have to see.

"Okay," he says, conveying that he's not responsible for what might happen.

While Black is gone I take the opportunity to look in a few table drawers but there's nothing of any use in them. I'm struck once more by the dullness of the room, not a photograph or a knickknack anywhere.

When he returns, Black leads a small bent figure into the room. I stand as I always do when my elders enter. How long can it be until someone stands when I come into a room?

Black says, "Ma, this is a detective," as if I'm a new piece of furniture or an appliance she's never seen.

"How do you do?" I say.

"Not well at all," she answers in a wobbly voice. "Do you have a name?"

I tell her as Black helps her to a padded rocking chair.

There's only one explanation as to why a man of Black's size would be afraid of this shriveled woman. MOTHER. Mrs. Black looks like she's in her eighties and I begin to wonder about the longevity of the people from this part of the country. I'm sure it's not due to yogurt.

She wears a pair of old brown trousers and a gray sweatshirt. Her marshmallow-colored hair is worn short and straight, parted on the left. Her eyes are a glassy blue like two wet stones, and her nose is slightly hooked above a mean mouth. I doubt if she weighs a hundred pounds.

"So what're you detecting?"

Black gulps like a fish.

"Susie Mcmann."

"That slut," she says.

"You didn't like her?"

"Does it sound like I did?"

I deserve this.

She then tells me the same story that Black has told me. "I suppose," she goes on, "that ungrateful boy's telling tales again. Thinks his slut of a mother's alive."

It's tempting to say that Blackie believes she's dead and that Harold killed her, but I know I can't. Why didn't he believe the obituary? I'm anxious to get back to him and ask.

"We gave him everything a boy could want," the old woman says.

"What did you tell him about her?"

"Franklin? We told him the truth. That she was running away and had the accident. A child should know about his mother."

If he had been told that she was running away he certainly hadn't passed that on to me. Abandonment, whether it's for a career, a man, a life, is still abandonment and no kid is going to comprehend this. Could it be that Blackie chose not to believe what he did because it hurt less?

"He should let things lie, that boy. What's he trying to prove?"

I must pretend I don't even know him. "Have you lived here all your life, Mrs. Black?"

"Why?"

"Curious."

"We lived in Boston for a while."

"And you never let him know about his aunt, even when you returned here?"

The Blacks look at each other, then back to me.

Harold says, "I don't have a sister."

"No, I mean Susie's sister, Almay Mcmann."

"Almay?" Mrs. Black says. "What kind of name's that?"

"I don't know," I say, "I wanted to ask her but . . ."

"You spoke to this Almay?" Black asks.

"Yes. I saw her."

"Then you saw some fake."

"That's right," the old woman concurs. "Susie Mcmann was an only child."

Chapter

Seven

AS I CAREFULLY RETRACE MY ROUTE I try to figure out some kind of truth about Susie Mcmann. I have a woman named Almay who says she's Susie's sister but, according to the Blacks, can't be because Susie was an only child. This bogus sister, along with the husband and mother-in-law, says Susie was killed in an automobile accident. And my client, Boston (Franklin) Blackie, is convinced Susie was murdered by his father even though he's probably seen the obituary.

So who the hell *is* Almay? Why would she say she was Susie's sister? What would be in it for her?

I make the all-important turn at the old Kripplebush schoolhouse and take the road to Krumville. I find the bend into Almay's and take the dirt road that leads up to her trailer.

There is no yellow dog lying in the sun.

I get out of the car and call. "Vicious?"

Nothing.

A prickly feeling of desolation nips at my heels. I sense that there's no one here. The aqua trailer screams empty to me and after knocking once, I open the door and see that I'm right.

The inside of this dilapidated trailer is as it was.

There's a lingering smell of what Almay had been cooking but the pot is no longer there. How stupid of me, I think. Why hadn't I noticed the first time that there was no phone here? It's clear that wherever I'd reached her was not here.

I go back to the car and take out my list of Mcmanns, where Almay is on top, listed as *A*. The only address is the one I'd written down from her directions. I need to look at a phone book again.

I start the car and go back down the Krumville Road until I come to Route 209. From here it's only moments to the Lesbian Deli, as I now think of it.

I can't remember if they had a phone but it's hard to believe they don't. The parking lot is almost empty now. I don't see a phone, so I go up to the counter.

A large woman with kind blue eyes, wearing a T-shirt that advertises the deli, approaches, smiles. "What can I do you?"

"Do you have a phone?"

"Back through there, next to the rest rooms."

I thank her and follow her instructions. There's a pay phone but no book. I drop in my quarter and dial the number where I'd reached Almay earlier. Like some sort of creep I let it ring twenty times before I face that no one is going to answer.

Back at the counter I ask the same woman if she has a phone book anywhere.

"Would you believe somebody stole it?" she says.

This is nothing new to me living in New York City but I am surprised that it would happen here.

"Had to have been a weekender," she explains. "Locals wouldn't do that."

"Probably not," I say, feeling guilty because I'm a weekender.

A severe look replaces the smiling one. "No probablys about it."

"Right."

"Locals don't need to steal a phone book, they got one at home."

"Well, that makes sense."

She scrutinizes me with a gelid look. "You from the city?"

"Yes, I am," I say, trying to sound proud.

She gives an enigmatic slow shake of her head.

"I live in Greenwich Village. On Perry Street. In a brownstone." I can't stop. "I live there with my lover." I suppose I think this will endear me to her, but why I want this is another question.

"Greenwich Village, huh?"

"Yes." I want her to know we're both lesbians, and even though thousands who live in the Village are not gay or lesbian, it's still used as a code word.

"Lover? You own it with your lover?"

"Yes. She's a therapist."

I sense a slight recoil as though I've slapped her.

"You one of them ladylovers?" she asks.

Uh-oh. "I beg your pardon?"

"Je-sus," she says, the place is gettin' full up with your kind. Not that I give a damn, mind you. Don't understand it, but who says I have to, right?"

I smile weakly. All I want to do now is get the hell out of here but she's on a tear.

"Thing is, I just don't see what all the fuss is about. Never have. I says it to Jake, that's my husband, who gives a damn what people do in the privacy of their bedrooms? But people *do*. Beats me. I got more important things to worry about than whether two gals like each other better than they like some guy. Just 'cause I like one up the old flue doesn't mean everybody does. Long as nobody expects me to be . . . what do you call it . . . gay?"

I nod, still shocked from the "old flue" remark.

"Gay. Don't expect me to be gay, I won't expect you to be straight." She bobs her head, pleased that she knows the term for heterosexual.

"Right," I say.

"Tell me something, though, how come all you gals are buyin' houses up here?"

"I don't know. I'm here on a job." I dig in my purse and hand her my card.

She studies it as though it were an exam paper.

"Lauren Laurano, huh? I'm Midge Dexter."

We shake hands.

"Private investigator, huh? Now how did a little gal like you get into that?"

And I tell her.

"It's a long story but I'll give you the short version. When I was eighteen my boyfriend and I were parked in the local necking spot when two men attacked us. They shot and killed Warren, raped and beat me, leaving me for dead. I crawled to the highway.

"A recruiter got me into the FBI, I guess they thought I was tough, and when I graduated from college I became a full-time agent. I met my first lover there but we had to stay in the closet. Then, in a terrible accident, while we were on a case, I thought she was the perp and shot and killed her." I stop, remembering that moment when I killed Lois, and I'm filled with feelings of sorrow and melancholy, as if it had happened yesterday.

"That's terrible," the woman says. "You poor thing."

"Yes," I say. "It *was* terrible. I couldn't stay with the agency anymore so I quit, drifted around a little, until I met Kip, my present lover. It was she who suggested I go into this work."

"Makes sense."

"Well, that's it."

"So how long have you and Kip been together?"

"Fourteen years this fall."

"My God in heaven, don't know hardly any straights your age been together that long. Congratulations," she says, and sticks out her hand again.

Smiling, I take it and we shake.

Midge leans closer to me over the counter, her belly resting on some cellophaned cookies. "Was it the rape that done it, honey?"

I'm not at all perplexed by the question. I've been asked it many times by the uninformed. "Made me a lesbian? No. I had a boyfriend because that's what you did then. I didn't love him. In fact, I was madly in love with a girl in my class but that was in 1966 and things were different."

"So are you saying you were born this way?"

I shrug. "Who knows? I think it's like alcoholism. Part physical or chemical, part emotional. I think I was disposed that way and the combination of my parents solidified it."

"Now don't go blaming your parents, Lauren."

"I don't *blame* them. It's just the way it was. If anything I'm grateful."

Midge gives me a dubious look.

"Really," I say. "I'm very happy."

"Well, you *do* live in Greenwich Village. Guess you don't have trouble there."

I think of telling her about the rash of gay bashing but decide against it. I could be here all day and Midge doesn't really need a consciousness-raising session; she's doing damn well on her own.

"You lived here all your life?" I ask.

"Born and bred."

"You know the Mcmanns?"

"Well, honey, there're all kinds of Mcmanns around here. Which ones?"

"Almay?"

She thinks. "Nope, don't believe I know anyone with the name of Almay, Mcmann or otherwise."

"How about Susie?"

Something lights in her eyes. "You mean Susie Q? The one married Harold Black?"

My detective's heart gives Midge a tumble. "Exactly."

"Oh, my," she says, and a blush, like a rising sun, starts at her throat and travels up into her hairline. "Susie Q and I was best friends in high school."

I can't help questioning the nature of the blush, although I do it silently. Has Midge been so understanding because of her own feelings as a girl, or did she and Susie do some wicked boy-related teenage things together?

"Oh, I just loved that gal," Midge says. Then quickly, "Now don't go misunderstanding what I'm saying here. Not *that* way."

For all her openness and understanding, it's still there, the nasty prick of prejudice. Ah, well. "I didn't think that's how you meant it," I reassure her.

"Just so we understand each other."

"I think we understand each other perfectly," I say.

"Good. I near died when Susie married Harold Black. I knew it wasn't a love match, knew she was just doing it to get out of the house."

"Because her father wouldn't acknowledge her as his own?"

"Mmmmm."

But there's more. I can see it in Midge's eyes.

"What else?"

She shakes her head. I am, after all, an outsider, not privy to everything. Still, I can guess. Especially if her father didn't think Susie was his. I inwardly reel at the weight of incestuous cases as they pile up like bodies in a death camp.

"She was pregnant, though, and that was a terrible thing in them days. There was no legal abortion and a girl was shamed if she had a baby outta wedlock. So Susie married Harold."

"Was there any chance that it wasn't Harold's baby?"

"What do you mean?" Midge asks.

I hate to suggest this but I must. "Could it have been her father's?"

Midge lets out a deep sigh. "I'm not saying that Susie's father didn't sexually abuse her. Let's face it, if we want to believe all them talk shows, everybody and her sister had that going on. Anyway, Susie told me she knew it was Harold so I guess Bill Mcmann . . . well . . . didn't take any chances. Pig.

"Anyways, we give her a shower but she was depressed, hardly looked at the presents. And then she had the baby. A boy. Franklin, they named him. Then she was killed. Right out here on two-oh-nine. Semi hit her car and flipped it over like it was a pancake. The thing burst into flames in a second. Susie never had a chance." Midge's eyes are moist.

"The body?"

She presses her lips together, shakes her head. "Nothin' left. Bits of bone, is all."

"Then how did anyone know it was Susie Mcmann Black?"

"Her car. And she was gone."

"So no one could actually prove that she'd been the driver?"

Midge cocks her head to one side, stares at me like I'm crazy. "What're you gettin' at?"

It seems obvious to me but I tell her. "Someone else could've been driving that car, and Susie could have run off."

"Could, shmuud. I only wish that's what would've happened."

"Is it true that Susie wanted to act, wanted to be in the movies?"

This brings a smile to her tight lips. "That was just somethin' we daydreamed about, you know how young girls are."

"Sure. Well, why do you think her husband and his mother would tell me that she'd planned to run off before she was killed?"

"Couldn't say except they're crazy people. Always were. I never spoke to them again after Susie died so I wouldn't know."

I tell her about "Almay Mcmann," who she said she was and what she'd told me.

"Susie didn't have a sister. She was an only child."

I also tell her that when I returned to the trailer there was no one there, and I show her the list with A. Mcmann and the phone number.

Midge looks at the number, furrows her brow. "This looks like a familiar number. Oh, 'course it is. A's for Arthur."

"Arthur?"

"Yeah. Arthur and Anne Mcmann."

"Are they related to Susie?"

"Bud, that's Arthur, he's a cousin, I think."

"You know where they live?" I ask.

"Sure do. Want me to tell you how to get there?"

"Please." It's clear that this Anne Mcmann, for a reason I don't understand yet, pretended to be Susie's sister, Almay. At last I'm getting somewhere. Exactly where, I don't know, but *somewhere*.

Chapter

Eight

AFTER HAVING TRIED the Mcmann phone number
again to no avail, I decide to see former chief of police
Sidney Breese, who lives in Stone Ridge on a beautiful road with large upscale houses. Most of them are set
way back from the street and have wings, screened-in
porches, carefully manicured lawns. They are the kind of
dwellings that evoke a bygone era and for a moment I
wish I'd lived then. But it's only for a moment because it's
hard enough to live as a lesbian now. Idly, I wonder how
lesbians and gays who lived here then functioned. There
may not have been masses of them, like Midge says there
are now, but there had to be some. We've always been
everywhere.

I come out of a curve and see the name Breese on a
mailbox. The house is a rambling gray-and-white with
third-floor mullioned windows. I drive up the long pebble
driveway and park. When I get out a man calls to me
from the screened porch.

"Help you?"

"I'm looking for Sidney Breese."

"You selling something, I'm not buying," he states
flatly.

"Not selling anything. I'd like to talk."

He gets up from his wicker chair and walks to the screen, gives me a once-over. "Come round here," he says, motioning to a door on the porch.

Breese holds it open for me and I pass by him. As I do, I detect the piquant odor of raspberry and wonder if it's a soap, shaving lotion, or Breese's natural smell.

I hand him my card and while he reads it he gestures toward a white wicker couch with gingham pillows. After seating myself, I look up at him and see that he's smiling pleasantly.

"Private eye, huh? Thought about that myself when I retired but there wasn't much call for one around here."

Breese is a man in his eighties, I guess. His white hair is a curly band that runs from ear to ear. He has faded brown eyes, like fall leaves. His face is engaging with the expected crosshatches of wrinkles. A pair of khaki shorts show off surprisingly shapely legs and his light green T-shirt says DUMP DINKINS.

"Why do you care about Dinkins?" I ask.

"Don't. My daughter gave it to me," he says as though this is all the explanation anyone would need.

"Chief," I say, bringing a glow to his eyes. "I need your help."

"Wouldn't the present chief be a more likely candidate for helping?"

"I'm interested in something that happened in 1954." After I've said my piece, I ask him the most important question.

He says, "Thing was, there really wasn't much to identify."

"Teeth?"

He looks uncomfortable.

"It was Susie's car and Harold said she was skipping town."

"But there *were* teeth among the ashes?"

"Who'd you say you were working for?" he asks.

"I didn't. The teeth, Chief?"

After some throat clearing he says, "Frankly, we didn't see the need. But we were wrong."

"Wrong?" Tap tap tap goes my detective's heart.

"It wasn't Susie, after all. I sure thought it was at the time because who else would it be? Later, I found out it wasn't her."

"How?"

Breese splays his hands over his thighs. The fingers are long and well groomed. He stares at them for a long time.

"Chief," I urge.

He looks up at me, his face drained of color. "Anybody would've thought it was Susie."

"Chief, I'm not interested in that part of the story. You're right, everyone makes mistakes."

"It wasn't a mistake," he says forcefully, then backs down. "It was and it wasn't because there was no reason to think anything else."

"I agree. Now how did you discover that it wasn't Susie?" I'm careful not to use the word *mistake* again.

"I saw her in a movie."

"Susie? You saw Susie in a movie?" I can hardly contain my excitement.

"Yeah. This was years ago, mind you. The first time, that is."

"The first time?"

"She had a bit part but it was her, no doubt about it."

"What'd you do?"

"Do?"

"I mean," I say gently, did you tell anyone about it? Ask anyone if they thought it was Susie?"

He knits his brows together and looks angry. "Of course not. Didn't have to. I knew."

And had he mentioned it, he would've had to face incompetency charges, at the least.

"What name was she using?"

"I couldn't be sure. Not then. But over the years I figured it out."

"And?"

"She used lots of different names, at least six that I could figure. I suppose it's Franklin got you into this. I was still chief when he was in high school, that is, when he wasn't in jail, and he used to come over to headquarters least once a month trying to tell me his daddy killed his mama."

"What did you say?"

"What *could* I say? I did my best to disabuse the boy of this fantasy, even think I'd convinced him, until he turned up the next time."

"But you never told him or anyone else the truth?"

He shakes his head like a naughty child.

"So who was driving Susie's car?"

"I haven't the foggiest. I just know it wasn't Susie Black." He looks hurt suddenly, as though I'm trying to undermine his whole tenure as chief of police.

"Chief, you don't possibly remember the names Susie used, do you?"

"Sure do. Burned into my brain, so to speak. You know, considering."

"Could you give me that list?"

"Got a pad and paper?"

I dig them out of my purse and as he's writing I say, "Did you know Nicholas Parrish?"

"Sure I know him."

"*Know* him?"

"Well, I haven't seen him for years but . . ."

"You mean he's alive?"

"Sure. So is she."

"Who?"

"Rebecca, Susie's mother. After all that craziness they ended up together."

"I've been told he left the county."

"That's right. They live together in New York City."

* * *

I'm overwhelmed by the news of Parrish and Rebecca Mcmann living in the city and can hardly wait to interview them. But there's still work to be done here.

Armed with the list of names that Susie Black might've used, I drive to the tiny town of High Falls. It consists of a few stores, a post office, and, oddly, one of the best-known restaurants in the state: the famous DePuy Canal House. At Mohonk Road, across from a restaurant called the Egg's Nest, I take a right and pull into the parking lot of the omnipresent combination video store, deli, and pizza place.

Inside I go to the phone booth, dial again what I once thought was Almay Mcmann's number and what I now know is Arthur Mcmann's. This time a woman answers. I hang up. It must be his wife, the woman who, for some reason, represented herself to me as Almay.

As I'm leaving the deli my eye catches a box of frozen Snickers bars in the case. This is a new passion of mine. I buy one, get back in my car, strip off the paper, and leisurely nibble away. I stow the wrapper in my purse so Kip won't find it.

I leave the lot and go out to Mohonk Road. Following Midge's directions, I take my first left and journey along until I come to a mailbox that says Mcmann. Here I turn into a winding dirt road and drive about a mile until I spot a frame farmhouse surrounded by open fields.

A blue Toyota is parked near the house. I pull up next to the car and get out. There's no yellow dog to either greet or bite me.

I don't know what kind of reception to expect here, but as I walk up to the door, I open the flap of my pocketbook and slip my hand inside, where it rests on my gun. I use the brass knocker. In a few moments the door opens.

A woman in her fifties, who in no way could be confused with "Almay," dressed in tan slacks and an orange T-shirt, asks in a pleasing voice what it is that I want.

"Are you Anne Mcmann?"

"Yes." She sucks in her cheeks and looks at me suspiciously. "May I know why you wish to know and who you are, please?"

"I'm sorry. Of course." I show her my I.D., which she stares at an inordinately long time.

"Aren't you rather short to be a private investigator?"

"There aren't any height requirements," I say patiently.

She runs a hand through hair dyed the color of chocolate pudding. "Sorry, I didn't mean to be rude. It's surprising, that's all."

I nod as though it's perfectly understandable.

"Do you have a sister or cousin or any relative named Almay?"

"I certainly hope not," she says, slightly superior.

"How about Susie?"

"Susie."

I wait.

"Susie," she says again as though it's a remarkable name. "Mmmm, I may have heard that one but you have to understand, I'm a Mcmann by marriage. My husband, Bud, is the one you should talk to."

I pass over this for the moment. "I know this sounds strange but you didn't get a phone call from me today, did you?"

"Of course not." She sounds annoyed. "Unless you called about fifteen minutes ago and hung up."

"Not me," I lie. "Is your husband at home?"

"No."

"Can you tell me where he is?"

She glances at her watch. "Probably at the deli having coffee."

I remember that aside from the one where I'd bought my Snickers bar, there is another deli in town. "Which one?"

"Oh, the one next to the P.O." This is said as though the other dispenses diseases.

I thank her and go back to my car, knowing she's watching me. I hate mysteries. I particularly hate ones that make no sense . . . I *know* I called her number this morning and I *know* someone in her house answered it and told me she was Almay Mcmann, gave me directions to the trailer, and met me there. I'm not a crazy person.

The deli Anne has sent me to has its counter at the front, display case below with salads and meats, and in the back of the store several tables. Groups of men, ranging in age from early twenties to late seventies, sit at them drinking coffee and talking about whatever it is that men talk about. All wear billed hats in an array of colors with different logos. No one wears his backwards.

Which is Bud? I hesitate in my approach, as though I have no right to intrude here. And this, of course, is exactly the feeling they wish to convey, whether consciously or not, I don't know. I believe it's primal.

Nevertheless I have a job to do. As I get closer to the tables and it becomes obvious that I'm actually going to encroach on their territory, their talk becomes moribund and finally there is only silence. They all stare at me as though I'm a species they've never before encountered. I flash a full dimpled smile. Nothing.

"Excuse me. I'm looking for Bud Mcmann."

They stare at me, not one turning a head to look at Bud or anyone else. And then a big man, with arms like pot roasts, gives me a jaunty smile.

"You a stranger here, young lady?"

I imagine I hear the tune from *High Noon*. "Yes."

"Must be. Whatcha want with Bud?"

Another man, smaller but fit, says, "That's okay, Skeets. I'm Bud Mcmann. What's up?" His blue cap says METS in orange lettering. He wears a faded work shirt, jeans, and soft brown loafers, no socks, which seem completely out of place. He looks familiar but maybe it's just the type.

I dread having to say who I am in front of all these men so I try to finesse it. "Could we talk privately?"

Big mistake.

"Hey, there, Buddy boy, you old stud!"

"Keepin' secrets, huh?"

"Wait'll Anne hears about this, Budzer!"

"You dog, you!"

"Still waters!"

And assorted whistles, hoots, snorts.

"Chill out, guys," says Mcmann.

They continue to sputter and catcall as Mcmann walks over to me, takes me by the arm, and leads me outside.

"I'm sorry," I say.

"Hell, don't be. They're just having some fun at my expense. Yours too, unfortunately. Sorry about that. What'd you say your name is?"

"Lauren Laurano. I'm a private investigator."

Mcmann raises his eyebrows. "Hey now."

"How long've you lived in this area?"

"All my natural born days."

"Did you ever hear of an Almay Mcmann?"

"Nope."

"How about Susie Mcmann?"

"She was two years behind me in high school. I mean, I didn't know her well, but saw her around. She was a looker, I'll tell you."

"Then you're not related."

"I didn't say that. We're cousins somewhere."

I notice he doesn't use the past tense. "Did you know her husband, Harold Black?"

"Here's the deal. Black was a bit older than Susie, like maybe ten years, so I only knew *of* him. Saw him around town but didn't know him to speak to. What's this all about?"

"I'm trying to find her."

"Susie's dead." He looks sad but it doesn't seem real.

"You mean the accident?"

He views me with suspicion. "If you know, why're you asking me, why'd you say you were trying to find her, come to that?"

"I know there was an accident involving her car, but I'm not sure Susie was driving."

"Well, that's just plain crazy." He rubs his hands together as though he's washing them.

"What if I told you that I have it on good authority that Susie wasn't driving her car that night?"

Mcmann presses and unpresses his lips, says nothing.

"What if I told you Susie left town that same night and ended up in the movies?"

"Well, I guess I'd have to say you know quite a bit." My detective's heart rhumbas.

"Hell, here's the deal on that. Gal named Betty Rosner was driving that car. She was the one killed that day, not Susie. Susie'd left by bus and given her car to Betty."

"Didn't you tell anyone about Betty Rosner?"

"Nobody asked. Susie wanted to be gone so I figured, hell, let her *really* be gone. I knew she was never comin' back, and I figured it'd be easier on the boy when he grew up to think his mom died rather than up and left him behind."

"But what about Betty Rosner? Didn't anyone wonder what happened to her?"

"She was a gal on her own. Didn't have a family. Drifted into town that summer, nobody really knew her except Susie."

"And you," I supply.

A fringe of red around his neck like a collar expands and rises upward, flushing his face.

He leans toward me, whispers. "Here's the deal. I was a young pup and Betty, she was something. The kinda gal a boy dreams of, you know what I mean? Dreams of learning stuff from."

"Sex."

"Well, yeah. I lied to you a while ago. I *did* know Susie.

It was during that summer. She got to be friends with Betty and since I was seeing Betty, I saw Susie from time to time. Nice gal. Don't blame her for wanting out of the deal with Black, but I never could understand how she could leave the boy. Guess he would've just been an impediment or something. Still." He shakes his head as though this is one of the seven wonders of the world.

"Do you go to the movies, Mr. Mcmann?"

"Sometimes."

"Ever seen Susie in a movie?"

"Never did. Truth is I don't think Susie ever made it into the movies. In fact, I think she's probably dead."

"Why do you think that?"

"Well, she sent me her address from Hollywood and when I wrote her about a year later, it came back 'Addressee Unknown.'"

"That wouldn't necessarily mean she was dead."

"No, it wouldn't. But I heard, I don't know, somewhere, that she was dead."

Why do I feel he's making this up?

"You can't remember who you heard it from?"

"No."

"Perhaps your wife . . ."

"Look, here's the deal. I'd rather my wife didn't know anything about this. See, I was married when I was having my fling with Betty. You know how it is."

"Actually, I don't. How is it?"

"What?"

"Having an affair when you're married?"

A cold wrathful look comes into his eyes. "I don't know what your game is, but I think you'd better drop it."

"I'm not playing a game, Mr. Mcmann. Susie Mcmann Black didn't die in an automobile accident and you knew it and said nothing. I've been hired to find out what happened to Susie and I intend to do just that. And if I were you, I wouldn't go around making threats."

"Oh, hey, don't get me wrong. That wasn't a threat." He

is suddenly backpedaling, which only makes me feel he knows more than he's saying.

"I'm glad to hear it. Anything else you'd like to tell me, Mr. Mcmann?"

He stares at me for quite a while. It's not a comfortable feeling. Then he says, "Nothing," and turns his back to me as he enters the deli.

Chapter

Nine

═══════════════════

I AWAKEN TO AN INCREDIBLE DIN. In a moment I recognize the noise as New York City getting ready for another day. Even I have to admit it's worse than the resonance of birds and insects. But it's my kind of sound.

There are fifteen minutes before the alarm goes off so I lie still, not wanting to wake Kip. As I do each morning upon waking, I think of Meg Harbaugh. She's my first thought in the morning, my last at night. I idly wonder how long this will go on.

Meg, my oldest, dearest friend, has been dead, murdered, for almost two years. I miss her terribly. Even though I'd caught her murderer, who will be behind bars for a long time, there's no solace in this, nothing to erase the reality that I'll never see Megan again, never laugh with her or hear her call me Laur.

Time, everyone says. I suppose that's true. *"O! call back yesterday, bid time return."* This isn't what they mean when they speak of time, but it's the way I think about it. I am forever replaying the night of Meg's murder, creating new scenarios that will make her live again. This is a futile game and one I long to let go of, but can't seem to yet. Ah, Meg, I miss you so.

Kip rolls over, eyes open. She smiles sleepily. "I could sleep all day," she says.

Sure she could. Even on days off Kip has a hard time staying in bed, sleeping or not.

"Been awake long?"

"Not too." She takes in the street noise. "God, I loved the quiet this weekend."

"There were those birds," I say.

"Lauren, birds are not garbage trucks and police sirens and . . . what's that other sound?"

"I think it's the film company getting in place."

"Oh, that. When are they using the house?"

"Wednesday."

"I loved the weekend," she says. "I would've loved it more if you'd been with me more, of course."

I kiss her gently.

"Want to go there for our vacation?"

"And do what?"

"Sleep, read, lie around."

Even though Kip is a much more active person than I am and likes to exercise, bike, and stuff, vacations are another matter. It reverses then. I like to *do* something when I go on vacation while she's content to do nothing. Maybe this is because she can't ever do that at home. Last summer we went to France, my choice, and this year it is her turn to decide. I guess I know what it's going to be: sleep, read, lie around.

"You mean take a house up there?"

"Actually, I thought we might camp out."

I sit straight up. *"What?"*

"Gotcha," she laughs.

Camping out is my idea of a week of torture.

"Yes, take a house. We'd have fun. We'll explore. I promise we won't lie around all the time."

"Sure," I say, trying to sound enthusiastic.

"I love you. You're sweet."

"Sweet?"

"That is a bit hyperbolic. A nice young girl, that's what you are."

This is a phrase we picked up from a little old man in the neighborhood who always greets us by saying "Hello, young girls," which we are to him.

"Nice because I've agreed to rent a house for a month where there's nothing to do but watch grass grow?"

"Exactly."

"Can't we at least go where there's water?"

"You mean like the North Fork?"

"Why not? You could lie around on the beach and at least I would have water to look at and go into. Plus, we have friends there."

"Maybe that's not a bad idea." She puts her arms around me, pulls me closer, our bodies touching.

"How much time do we have?" I ask.

"Enough," she says, and we're kissing passionately.

I part her legs, stroke the soft flesh on the inside of her thighs, breeze through her hair, trace the tips of my fingers up across her belly, back down, and this time open her, touch her center. She shivers with delicious anticipation. No longer able to stand it, she gently shifts me onto my back, turns around, her breath warm on me. Perhaps for the trillionth time I discover the silken pink petals, the beauty that is Kip. Lips linger over lusher lips, tongues explore known territory, destined over time to thrill, conquer, rule.

In my office I look over the list of names that Sid Breese gave me.

Monica McCall
Elissa Laine
Miranda Sheedy
Pam Rice
Beth Davey
Betty Rosner

I'm struck again that Susie Mcmann might have used the name of her friend Betty Rosner. I wonder if she'd known about Betty's death in her car. It's the use of this name that makes me believe that Susie *did* go to Hollywood and, no matter what Bud Mcmann says, is perhaps still alive.

Chief Breese's memory of the films he'd seen her in wasn't quite as good as it was for the names he thought she used. Still, he'd remembered the last one, called *Dangerous Deceit*. Later, I'll check out the video stores and try to rent it. Breese has told me the part he *thinks* Susie played using the name Beth Davey.

I still have no idea why someone was pretending to be a sister of Susie or who "Almay" really was. Clearly there are people who want me to believe Susie Mcmann is dead. Why? I don't know. But it's this effort that makes me believe that Breese is right and Susie Mcmann is still alive.

I want to tell Boston Blackie what I've discovered. I know I won't have an easy time convincing him that his mother's alive because he so much wants to believe his father is a murderer. Still, I owe him a rundown on what I've learned so far. I punch in his number. There's no answer or machine. After taking a bite of something called a dream bar (a mixture of chocolate, peanut butter, and chocolate chips) and a sip of my coffee, I look up SAG.

"Screen Actors Guild East," a woman's voice answers.

"I wonder if you can help me."

"I wonder, too, dear."

I laugh. She doesn't. "I'd like some information."

"Tell me something I don't know," she says and yawns.

She's right, of course. Why else would I be calling if I didn't want information? "Uh, sure. I have a list of names and I wonder if you could tell me if any of them are SAG members?"

"Get real. You think I can stay on the phone while you

give me a bunch of names and then look them up? You're out of your mind, dear."

This is a very direct person and I always admire directness but I'd like to choke her. "There're only six," I say sheepishly.

"*Six?* Think about this, dear. I mean, seriously think about it. If everybody who called wanted me to look up six names, how long do you think it would take me? How long do you think I'd have this phone plastered to my ear like some sort of appendage? As it is I'm always on it answering some dumb question or another, but I'm not, *not* going to look up six, three, or one name. Got it?"

"Got it." I can tell she's about to sever the connection. "Please, don't hang up. Tell me what to do?"

"Oh, you're really asking for it, aren't you, dear?" She snickers.

"You know what I mean, dear," I say forcefully.

"You want to come in, you can check names in the book."

I take down the address and thank her.

"My pleasure, dear."

Suddenly it occurs to me I can do this with my computer and modem. I dial in to the Invention Factory and leave a message for David asking him to get on this for me. While I'm out pounding the pavement, David can contact his SAG friends and check it out. By the time I get back I'll have a message from him with all the info I need. I hope.

Childishly I want to call the woman at SAG East and tell her I don't need her but I know instinctively she won't care. This is part of what makes me a great detective, my intuitiveness.

I leaf through more papers and find the name of Nicholas Parrish, who supposedly lives on Central Park West with the mother of Susie Mcmann. This is again information from Sid Breese. I heave the phone book onto my desk and look up the name.

It's there. At least *some* Nicholas Parrish is listed. I write down the address and phone number. Now I have to decide whether I call before I go or not. The surprise element is always tempting. And although I don't like mysteries, I do like a surprise . . . especially when I'm the one who's springing it.

Outside the high humidity hits and wraps itself around me like a damp shroud. Sweat covers my body and I don't feel as if I'm glowing. What I feel is limp and miserable.

There are people sitting at the Riviera's outside tables and I wonder why anyone would do this if they could be inside in the air-conditioning.

I cross Seventh Avenue to the subway entrance, slowly make my way down the steps. Ahhh, that first warm rush of urine smell.

Actually, the subways aren't quite as bad as the media would like you to believe, because they've been spruced up, but it isn't like going to a party either. There's less graffiti, more cops, and the stations themselves have been given an overhaul, some of them restored to their original state. Still, I won't pretend it's fun. No matter what time of day or night you travel, THEY are present.

The wackos.

Today she gets on at Fourteenth Street and as I'm one of the lucky ones, she decides to sit next to me. There's nothing about her attire that would tip one off because she's neat and clean, wears a long-sleeved yellow blouse and a tan skirt, and carries a large straw bag with leather handles. She appears to be in her seventies.

What lets me know that she's almost certainly one of THEM is the hair.

It's red, and worn in corkscrew curls, a style that brings to mind the young Shirley Temple. And then there's the makeup. False eyelashes like the teeth of a rake, a heavy pancake base with rouged cheeks, and thick crimson lipstick that's drawn way above the upper lip.

These are, I believe, though I could be mistaken, clues to the mental state of my seatmate.

Right before we come into Twenty-third Street, she turns to me and says: "I haven't slept for the last twenty-five years."

"Really?"

"If I sleep I'll die."

I wonder if she's seen too many *Elm Street* movies.

"You want to guess how I stay awake?"

"You tell me," I say.

"Guess."

Oh, boy. "I'm not good at guessing games."

"You'd never guess anyway."

Why do people always do this? Not just loonies either. People are always asking you to guess and when you either refuse or take a stab at it, they tell you you'd never guess. What's the point?

"Should I tell you?"

"Please," I say, as we pull into the station.

"Not now," she whispers. "Too quiet."

I nod as if I understand that this is CIA stuff and we mustn't be overheard. We both face front until the train moves and the subway noises begin again.

"Are you ready?" she asks.

"Yes."

"Well, what I do is that I buy inexpensive clothing, usually from a thrift shop, for instance a skirt, and when I get it home, I turn on the radio — never look at TV — and then I find the final stitch and I unravel."

"Excuse me?" I don't know why I care that I don't understand what she's telling me, but the words are out before I have a chance to think.

She leans closer, whispers in my ear. "Unravel."

"Unravel?"

"I put on my glasses, get my magnifier, and find the very last stitch in the piece of apparel, snip it with my good scissors, and then I pull until the skirt, or whatever, is totally unraveled." She smiles proudly.

I can't help myself. "Then what?"

"Well, then I put it back together," she answers disdainfully.

"You mean you remake the skirt?"

"Exactly."

I debate with myself and lose. "Why?"

"So that I don't fall asleep. I thought I explained that part earlier," she says testily.

"Oh, right, you did."

"It's a longevity method I've been trying to patent but no one seems interested. Their loss."

"Certainly is. So you've been awake, uh, twenty-five years?"

"Exactly."

"You don't look tired." I cannot believe I'm having this conversation.

"Maybe I don't look it, chickie, but I'm exhausted."

The Thirty-fourth Street station appears through the windows.

"Must go now. Lots of good bargains around here. Nice talking to you."

I know it's impossible that the woman hasn't slept for twenty-five years but I believe that she believes it. And I also accept her story of unraveling and sewing.

As wacko encounters go, this was tame.

Central Park West is an elegant street and those who live here are usually well off. Living in one of these buildings, looking out at trees and bushes, you might be able to convince yourself that the park stretching before you is benign. But it's not. Not anymore.

I'm told there was a time when anyone could walk through the park at any time of day or night and be perfectly safe. It's hard to imagine an innocent period of history like this.

Now, especially at night, it's a treacherous place with predators lying in wait for any fool who enters. And even in the daylight it's been the scene of spectacular crime.

What would Peter Stuyvesant say?

The building I'm looking for is between Eighty-eighth and Eighty-ninth. When I find it there is naturally a doorman on duty. When are they going to stop dressing this way? It's demeaning for a man in his sixties to have to wear a purple suit with yellow braid and a captain's hat with a patent leather peak. Not to mention white gloves.

Before he gets a chance to ask me, I tell him whom I'm here to see and add that I don't have an appointment. He looks at me with incredulous eyes.

"No appointment?"

"I know," I say, "it's shocking."

"Huh?"

"Could you see if Mr. Parrish is in, please?"

"He's in."

"Well, then, could you buzz him and tell him he has a visitor?" I hand him my card, which he studies for six or seven hours.

I wait, prepared.

Grinning, he says, "A private investigator, you?"

"Yup."

He shakes his head, laughing. "Will wonders never cease."

I must say I don't expect this line and am at a loss for a response.

"What does the private investigator want with Mr. P.?"

"That's confidential."

"You don't say. He'll ask, ya know."

"Then I'll tell him. Could you please ring?"

He shrugs, turns to his board, lifts the handset, and presses 16P, which I assume is a penthouse. "Sarah, somebody here for Mr. P. A private investigator name of Laurano. Nope. Yup. Okay." He turns to me. "She's asking."

"Thanks."

While we wait he stares at me as though I'm some sort of specimen on a slide. "Catch a lot of crooks, you?"

"Thousands."

He weighs this and is about to comment when someone speaks to him through the phone.

"Yessir. Won't say."

"I'll say," I tell him, figuring out the question.

"Says now she'll say. Yessir, a girl."

I bite my tongue.

He looks at me. "So?"

"I want to speak to him about his daughter."

"He don't have no daughter, miss."

"Just tell him."

"You're not gonna get in on this kind of shenanigan."

"Tell him."

Shaking his head, he repeats what I've said. "Yessir. Okay." He replaces the phone, looks at me a little wide-eyed. "Says to come right up."

Chapter

Ten

===============

THE ELEVATOR HAS AN ELEVATOR MAN. His attire is as undignified as the doorman's and he's older by about twenty years. I give him the floor number and his hand shakes when he reaches for the gate handle.

"Sixteen," he says as we arrive with a slight lurch. "To your right."

I thank him and walk down a short blue-carpeted hall to an ornately carved door with a great gold knocker in the shape of a unicorn's head. There's also a bell, which I choose to use. I hear it chime.

The door is opened by a young woman with hair the color of canned peaches and a high-bridged nose that holds up round wire glasses. She wears a simple gray dress with a white collar, which may or may not be a uniform.

I tell her who I am and she ushers me into a lavish foyer. A fancy chandelier dominates and reflects in the mirrored walls.

"Follow me, please."

We wend our way through a carpeted corridor past many closed doors until she stops in front of one and knocks twice.

A voice from inside tells us to come in. The woman,

who I assume is Sarah, opens the door and gestures with her hand, as if saying *ta-da*, and my gaze follows to where a man sits in a wing chair.

"Come in, please," he instructs, in a hearty voice for one who looks so frail.

The door closes behind me as I cross the room. "Mr. Parrish?"

He nods, extends a surprisingly steady hand, and offers me a seat opposite him.

The room is massive, filled with bookshelves, plants, and bright modern furniture you'd expect to find in a contemporary beach house. Light pours in through unfettered windows.

Parrish looks good for his age, which is probably somewhere in his eighties. He has a full head of white hair with matching eyebrows like small flags. And there in his chin, just as "Almay" had told me, is a well-defined cleft. His neck is covered by an orange turtleneck. It's those crepey, wizened hands that betray him.

"How may I help you, Miss Laurano?" he asks robustly.

I hand him my card. He glances at it, then shrugs, as if to say this doesn't answer his question.

"I was hired to find Susie Mcmann."

His expression remains immutable.

"I was told that she's your daughter."

Something shows in the faded brown of his eyes, like a slide in a carousel clicking forward to the next, but he still says nothing.

"I've also been told that she's dead, that someone else died in her place, that she ran off to Hollywood to be an actress, and that she was murdered by her husband. Can you shed any light on this, Mr. Parrish?"

"Susie," he says, more to himself than to me. "If you don't mind, I'd like to call Rebecca in. Susie's mother," he adds.

"Fine."

There's a small intercom on the table next to his chair and he pushes down a tab.

The tinny sound of a woman's voice answers. He asks her to come down to the library and she says she will.

Parrish removes his finger from the intercom. "I don't suppose you'll tell me who your employer is?"

"I can't."

"Yes, that's what I assumed. She was a beautiful child, Susie. Good-looking young woman, too."

"Are you her father?"

"I believe so."

"You're not sure?"

Parrish smiles sweetly and holds out his left hand. There in the center of his palm is a purple birthmark shaped like a diamond. "I'd say this, which Susie also has, is almost conclusive."

I notice he says *has*. "Is she alive?"

As he starts to answer, a door opens, and a frail woman draped in green gossamer floats toward us. Parrish rises.

"Rebecca Mcmann, meet Lauren Laurano."

"How do you do," she says in a wispy voice.

Her hand in mine feels like a robin's rib cage and I'm careful not to apply too much pressure. Parrish seats her on a low white sofa.

I can't shake the feeling that I'm in the middle of a movie and keep expecting to hear someone call "Cut."

"Becky, this young lady wants to talk about Susie."

"Ah," she says, as though the one word conveys everything and perhaps it does to her.

"I'm sorry if this is upsetting," I say. "But I'm on a missing person's case. Your daughter is the missing person."

Her fingers flash in front of her face like a closing fan. "I'm not upset. Nicholas and I've been through much worse, haven't we, darling?"

"We have, we have."

They smile at each other as though they're new lovers

and I can't help being touched. Could it be that the lack of a formal marriage makes them more romantic? I've always wanted to be able to marry Kip, but marriage is a heterosexual privilege. Perhaps I'm better off.

Rebecca clears her throat. "Susie was my darling girl, but back in those days a mother didn't have the same rights she has today. I lost her because I wanted to be with Nicholas. I had to make a decision and I guess some would say that I abandoned my child. I don't see it that way. What I did was to give her a chance. Had I been unhappy, and I would have been had I stayed with Bill, I probably would have made Susie unhappy. I thought that leaving her with him she'd have a chance."

"And Almay?" I ask.

Rebecca glances at Nicholas, then back at me. "Almay?"

"Your other daughter."

Parrish coughs uncontrollably.

"Dearest?" Rebecca asks.

He holds up a hand as though stopping traffic. "I'm all right," he says, collecting himself.

She waits until she's sure this is true, then looks back at me, smiles, bewildered. "I only had the one child. Almay. Where did you get that name?"

I tell them my Almay story.

"Somebody's pulling your leg, Lauren," Parrish says sympathetically.

"Seems so. Whoever she was, she wanted me to think Susie is dead."

"And how did you find us?" Parrish asks.

"Chief Breese."

"Old Sid. How is he?"

"He seems fine. He believes Susie's alive. May I ask you a very personal question?" I say to Rebecca.

"You mean you haven't been?" When she smiles her face becomes a cascade of wrinkles but her beauty is still there. "Yes, you can."

"Was Bill Mcmann an abusive person?"

She looks at Parrish and even after all these years I see a look of humiliation cross her face.

"It's all right, Becky," he says.

"Yes," she says to me. "Bill often beat me."

"Why would you leave your daughter with a man like that?"

Rebecca looks down at her speckled hands crossed in her lap.

"I don't know if she should answer that," Parrish says sternly.

"No, Nicholas. It's a fair question. It's true that he was abusive to me. But he'd never touched the child and he never would."

"I guess one of the things I don't understand is why Mcmann wanted to keep Susie when he insisted that Mr. Parrish was the father."

"Oh, that's easy," Rebecca says. Her eyes reveal a cynicism I haven't noticed before. "It was to hurt me."

She doesn't have to explain this. "Mrs. Mcmann, it's been suggested to me that Bill Mcmann may have sexually abused Susie."

Rebecca gasps, puts an aged hand to her throat. "Oh, no."

"Does that mean you don't believe it?" I ask.

"I certainly don- . . . Oh, Lord. I don't *want* to believe it."

"You never heard any stories about Bill Mcmann sexually abusing Susie or any other person?"

"No, I really didn't. If I'd thought that. . . ." She trails off, the obvious unsaid.

"Did Susie ever try to contact you?"

"Never. I wrote to her but the letters were returned unopened. I'm sure Bill told her terrible things."

"Harold Black says she was killed in an accident and there's an obit to back him up. Another person thinks she was murdered and Breese says she went to Hollywood and got into the movies."

"We've heard all the stories including one that says she's really Debbie Reynolds," Rebecca says.

I laugh. "I haven't heard that one."

"You will," Parrish says. "Also Anne Bancroft, Lee Grant, oh, I can't remember the whole bunch."

"I've only heard that she became a bit player." I take out the list of names and hand it to Rebecca Mcmann.

I'm astonished that she doesn't put on glasses. The woman's amazing.

"The names don't mean anything." She hands the list to Parrish, who does put on glasses.

"No," he says, handing the paper back to me. "Don't recognize the names. What are they?"

"They're names that Susie might have used in her movie career."

Dreamily, Rebecca says, "We might have seen those names in a cast list, might have seen Susie but we'd never know it was her."

"Earlier, Mr. Parrish, you said Susie was a good-looking woman. How did you know that?"

Rebecca's head snaps around and I know that this is news to her.

Parrish looks uncomfortable. "Did I say that?"

"Yes, you did."

"I can't think why. Sometimes when you get old the mind plays funny tricks. I must have been imagining how she would've looked."

"Your mind never plays funny tricks, Nicholas," Rebecca says, and looks at him intensely.

"No, not usually," he answers, as though assessing her allegation.

I think he's lying.

I want to ask why she didn't try to see her child while Susie was growing up, but I don't wish to hurt this woman who believes what she did was right for her daughter. And then she surprises me as though reading my mind.

"You probably wonder why I didn't try to see Susie when she was a youngster."

"Yes."

"I did. I saw her only once, when she was in first grade. She must've told her father because after that the teachers were on the lookout for me. Police, too, and I couldn't ever get near her again."

"You tried, Beck," Parrish asserts solemnly.

"You think I get a lot of points for that, Nicholas?" She smothers a laugh as though it's unseemly.

"I think you did the best you could, Beck. I think we all did."

I think they probably did. "So, the truth is you have no idea if Susie's alive or dead?"

They both nod.

Parrish says, "I believe you said you'd heard someone *murdered* her?"

"That's true. My client believes this."

"And does your client know who did this or is that what he/she wants to know?"

"My client believes her husband, Harold Black, killed her."

"And what do you think?" he asks.

"First I have to find out if she's dead."

Rebecca says, "I remember Harold Black. He was an awful boy. Always torturing animals, pulling wings off flies, skinning rabbits while they were still alive."

These are shocking words and often the youthful profile of a sociopath. "Really?"

"I wouldn't make it up," she says impatiently.

"I'm sorry. Of course not."

"I was horrified when I heard Susie married Harold. I simply couldn't understand it. You see, I subscribed to the local paper and learned about it that way."

"Ah," Parrish says, holding up his hand, one finger pointed upward. "That's how I knew what she looked like."

I still don't believe him. But I don't know why he'd lie. "So, if you subscribed to the paper then you must've seen her obit."

"We did," Parrish says. "I'm sorry if you think we've been leading you down the garden path. I thought perhaps we could learn something from you."

This makes a kind of sense to me. "Then you're not convinced that she's dead?"

Rebecca says, "I suppose it's wishful thinking. And then, there are the other stories. It's confusing."

This might be the understatement of the decade.

"Your grandson's alive," I say, as though a ventriloquist forces my mouth to move and say the words.

"Yes, that's true, I suppose. I read she'd had a baby. I wonder where he is?"

"Would you like to see him?"

"Oh, yes, very much," she declares.

"Indeed."

I don't feel I've betrayed my professional relationship, because I haven't said, and won't say, how I know Blackie. "I'll have to see."

"You mean if he wants to meet *us?*" Parrish asks.

"Yes."

"What's he like?" Rebecca sounds as though she's asking about Santa Claus and sits forward on her chair.

"Let me find out if he wants to meet you," I say. I don't feel it's proper for me to give anything else away.

"Oh, Nicholas, wouldn't that be lovely. Our grandchild. And we'd have someone to leave our money to."

"Don't you have other children, Mr. Parrish?"

"I did. They're dead now. It shouldn't be this way. It's not the natural order of things. I should have died first."

"Don't say that, Nicholas. I couldn't live without you."

The odd thing is that they don't seem to accept or recognize how old they are. In some ways it's enchanting, in others, absurd.

"I'll see what I can do." What I won't do is tell Blackie

anything about the money. I also know there's no more to be gained here so I thank them, ask them to get in touch if anything occurs to them, and promise again to explore the possibility of bringing their grandson to meet them.

When I step out onto the street the weather is worse than it was. The air is thick, as though curtains veil my vision. I check the time and see that Kip's between patients. We often check in with each other during the day. After a ten-day search, I find a working phone and ring her.

"Thank God you called," she says.

"What's wrong?"

"You're not going to believe this."

"Try me."

"It happened on the set of Rick and Susan's movie. Someone was murdered."

Call me crazy, but I believe it.

Chapter

Eleven

IT'S A NIGHTMARE.

Or a daymare.

Police cars block the ends of Perry Street and the gawkers are four deep around the crime scene, which is roped off with the ubiquitous yellow tape.

As I try to get past, a cute young cop stops me.

"Sorry, lady, you can't come through here."

"Is Detective Cecchi here?"

"I don't know," the cop says.

I give him my dimpled smile. So what if I'm using an unfeminist technique. The way I look at it, men deserve it. "Could you find out, please, Officer?"

He doesn't tumble and I realize too late that he could be my son. I've got to start remembering my age and what will work on whom. I take a new approach.

"I work with Cecchi."

"I.D.?"

I hand him my P.I. license. He's going to love this, I know.

Cocking his head to one side, he says, "You gotta be kiddin'."

This could mean a myriad of things, so I ask.

"You're tellin' me a homicide detective works with *you?*"

"No. *I* work with *him*."

He stares at me. "Am I supposed to find a different meanin' in what you're sayin' here?"

"He'll want to see me."

"Just a minute. Kelman," he calls to another cop, who's even cuter than he is. She walks over to us and he asks about Cecchi, and sort of explains me.

"Cecchi's here," she says, giving me the once-over. Not that kind. I could be *her* mother, too.

Still, I try a nice sincere smile. "Would you ask him if I can join him?"

"Okay."

Kip didn't have any details of the murder like who, how, or where, so while she's gone I look around for Rick or Susan, but I don't see them. Nor is Cybill Shepherd, the director, or anyone else from the crew in evidence. But I do recognize someone.

Stan the Hat.

He is so called because he always dons one no matter what the weather. Today, it's a white cowboy hat made of some synthetic with a purple band circling the base of the crown. The brim's pulled down, shading his eyes. His long white hair hangs behind his ears and curls below his collar. He wears an electric-blue suit jacket, an oyster-white shirt with a string tie at his throat, a new pair of jeans, and brown highly polished boots. There are four shopping bags in each hand. Although I can't see what's in them, I know from experience that there can be anything from a toaster to a synthesizer. Stan the Hat is a portable store. None of my business.

"Hey, Stan."

"What a coinkadink," he says, sounding like Jimmy Durante.

"Not exactly. I live here." I point to our brownstone. "You know what happened?"

"A moider, I tink."

"You know who?"

"Somebody wit da movie peoples. A extra, I tink."

"Man or woman?"

"Got me," he shrugs. "Don't surprise me."

"How come?"

"Dere all nuts, dese movie types. What's a moider to dem?"

I don't quite get his reasoning but I know it would be futile to ask for an explanation. Just then Officer Kelman returns.

"You can come with me," she says.

"Thanks. So long, Stan."

"Gotta go myself. Gotta gig on Canal."

Whatever that means. I smile, wave to him, and follow Kelman, who leads me through the crowd to a humming trailer. She opens the door, and I climb up the stairs and go inside. I've never been in one of these things before. It's air-conditioned and the couch, chairs, and table are nice-looking pieces.

Cecchi, who's on a cordless phone, has set up a temporary inquiry room. As he paces, he waves to me. When he hangs up he says, "Hey, Laurano, what a mess, huh? And right in your own front yard. You didn't do it, did you?"

"Not this time. Who's the victim?"

"A bit player, name of Shelley McCabe."

The name's familiar but I can't place it. "M.O.?"

"Strangled. Unfortunately, in Ms. Shepherd's trailer. She found her."

"What was McCabe doing in there?"

"Good question. No answer. Want to see her?"

The usual. I do and I don't.

"Sure," I say.

We leave the trailer and walk down the block to the star's. When we enter I see that it's even nicer than the other one. This has a bar and a television, as well as better-quality furniture. In the kitchen area I note a blender and microwave.

"Over here," Cecchi says.

At the far right end of the trailer there's a futon in a frame. On the far side of it is the body.

She lies faceup, a wire around her throat. Her hair is short and curly, dyed a russet color like a winter apple. I'm grateful that her eyes are closed and wonder if someone closed them for her. There's something oddly familiar about the face, and even in death it's rather pretty: small nose, full lips, high cheekbones. The skin has a waxen quality so it's almost impossible to determine her age.

"What do you know about her?" I ask him.

"Not too much." He takes out his notebook, flips it open. "Like I said, Shelley McCabe. Age fifty. I think that's one of those creative ages, for work reasons. She's more like fifty-seven, -eight. Lives at Six-eleven East Sixth Street in New York, and Fifteen-forty Melrose Place in L.A. Single."

After a perfunctory knock, two men with a body bag come in.

"M.E. said we could take her now, Lieutenant."

"Go ahead."

We get out of the way and watch while the men carefully move the woman from her niche into a larger section of the trailer. One of them unzips the green bag, spreads it open. When they lift her, one arm drops downward, and that's when I see the diamond-shaped birthmark on the palm of her hand.

If there's one thing I hate more than mysteries, it's coincidences. What is the likelihood of my being hired to find a woman who has a diamond-shaped birthmark on the palm of her hand and then having her turn up dead in front of my house? I wouldn't want to take the odds on that one. Nevertheless, it appears this very thing has happened.

"You know her?" Cecchi asks.

My mouth must be hanging open. "Not exactly." I tell him everything I know about Susie Mcmann except for the name of my client and his relationship to McCabe. While I do this, the men zip the woman up in their green bag and carry her out.

When we get back to Cecchi's trailer I show him the list of names Sid Breese gave me. "Same initials," I say, while he reads. "Susie Mcmann, Shelley McCabe." We both know that people often use their own initials when changing their name.

"Yeah, this time. Wonder why she waited so long to use them? Well, hell, we don't know if this *is* the same woman for sure."

"No, not for sure," I say. But I *am* sure. It would be even stranger if she weren't the same person.

"I need somebody to I.D. this woman."

"All the people I've met haven't seen Susie Mcmann in years and years. She have an agent?"

He looks at his notes. "Her agent's name is Doyce Schroeder."

"Doyce?"

"What can I tell you, that's what it says. Doyce."

"Is this film shut down?"

"It is for now."

Poor Rick and Susan. "What's Doyce Schroeder's address?"

Cecchi runs two fingers down his aquiline nose. "Stay out of this, Lauren."

"But I'm already in it."

"Jesus," he says. "Well, will you keep me informed?"

I start to say *Don't I always?* but recall when I failed to do just that, in fact had lied to him. It took many months to regain his trust. "I promise."

"Yeah."

"I mean it, Cecchi. I'll never do that again."

"Okay."

"How about you? Will you keep me informed?"

"Yeah, sure."

"Doyce's address, please."

He sighs. "Four-three-two West Eighty-ninth, fourth floor."

I write it down. "Thanks."

"Get out of here, Lauren," he says good-naturedly.

I get.

Going from the air-conditioned trailer to the July street is again a shock. It's like a backwards sauna. I look around but still don't see Susan or Rick, so I decide to go into my house.

On the door to my apartment is a note:

We're all upstairs.
Rick

I go up to Rick and William's, knock once, then enter. They *are* all there. Rick, Susan, William, and Kip.

The apartment is a mirror image of our first floor but the furnishings are more eclectic.

"Can you believe this?" Rick says.

In imitation of an announcer, Susan says: "Nee, nee, nee nee. Nee, nee, nee nee. They were all there, ready to make a feature film. The writers, the actors, the crew. The director called 'Action.' The star screamed . . . and it wasn't in the script. There was a corpse in her trailer . . . and it wasn't in the script. The director called 'Cut' . . . and the film was shut down. Not coming to a theater near you . . . soon!"

"I'm sure it's not shut down for good," I say, slightly appalled by their focus but also understanding it. After all, they didn't know Susie Mcmann. Or did they? "Did either of you know the victim?"

Neither did.

William, Rick's lover, is lying on the couch. He looks better than he has in years. A while back he kicked a coke habit and has been attending N.A. for over a year. He's a gorgeous man and since he came back from a rehab called Hazelden, he's parted his wavy blond-streaked hair in the middle and cut it so it grazes his shoulders. He still has a beard and mustache but his complexion is wonderfully healthy, his blue eyes clear and bright. William is six five and his feet hang over the end of the couch. He wears a pair of green shorts and a gray tank top. Because he works out daily, the muscles in his arms are clearly defined, but not repulsive like some men's. He says in his incisive way, "They're completely overcome by the death of Ms. McCabe."

"Look, William," Rick says, "I'm not happy that this woman lost her life but it's a fucking nightmare for us."

"Our first feature," Susan says, not sounding too convincing. Her values are more developed than Rick's and the riff was more for the sake of being funny than her true feelings.

"I know all that but, in the grander scheme of things, what's more important? That your movie gets made or that a woman has lost her life?"

Susan and Rick glance at each other and say nothing.

William says, "What a team! Always thinking of the little people!"

"That's not fair," Rick says. "Suppose you had an article to write and . . . and. . . ."

"Precisely," William says.

"Well, it's not the same," says Rick.

Kip speaks with the discernment of a shrink. "It's perfectly understandable that Rick and Susan have one set of priorities while we, who aren't involved, have another."

I say, "Well, I *am* involved." I explain, although I keep the identity of my client and what his relationship is to the dead woman to myself.

Kip looks at me like I'm from another planet. "I *don't* believe this. Are you saying that the case that took us to Ulster County has to do with this murdered woman?"

"That's what I'm telling you. There's no positive I.D. but the person I was trying to trace was a minor actress and had a diamond birthmark on the palm of her hand. Did she have a speaking part, by the way?" I ask Rick.

"Speaking part. Hmmm. Susan?"

"I think so. Alixe Gordon did the casting."

"Well, Alixe Gordon isn't here. Would the director know?" I feel exasperated. "I mean, surely somebody on the set knows why this woman was here today and what part she was playing."

"I know," says a woman's voice.

We all turn and see Cybill Shepherd standing in the doorway. "I hope you don't mind, Rick. I didn't know where to go and the sign said . . ."

"Of course not, Cybill," Rick says, jumping up. "C'mon in. Sit down. Want anything to drink?"

"Thanks, something cold."

"Something to eat?"

"I don't want to bother you."

"Don't be silly, it's no bother," he says.

"Truth is, I'm one of your original chowhounds," Shepherd says.

Looking at that body this is hard to believe.

Kip clears her throat and Susan realizes that William and Kip haven't been introduced. She takes care of this and I wish she'd introduce me again because there's no way Cybill Shepherd is going to remember having met me before.

Cybill says, "Are you on this case, Lauren?"

This is a very unusual movie star. Once again I explain.

Rick brings out drinks and a plate of scones and sets them on the large coffee table in the center of where we're all sitting.

Cybill slides from her chair to the floor. "I'm going to sit down here closer to the food."

I love her for this. She digs right in. I wait to allow her

to eat and drink some, then ask what part Mcmann/
McCabe was playing.

"She was a waitress in the SoHo restaurant scene. We
were supposed to shoot that later. I guess we won't be
doing that today."

"Or ever," Rick the optimist says.

"Are you serious?" Cybill asks.

Susan says, "Of course not. Things will probably be
delayed a day or so, that's all."

"Good. Because I love this script." Shepherd reaches
for a second scone but stops, her hand in midair. "Oh,
God, that poor woman. Here we are talking about a
movie and a woman's been murdered."

I like her more and more all the time.

"Had you met her, Ms. Shepherd?"

"Cybill. No. I never saw her before . . . before I found
her. But I always know the names of everyone in the cast
and what part they're going to play when I work on a
picture."

"I'm sorry you're the one who had to find her," I say.

"Me, too." She hitches up her shoulders and shivers.
"But, hell, it was worse for her than for me. Poor thing."
Now she takes a second scone.

"May I ask you a question?" I say.

"Sure."

"The body was wedged between the wall and that futon at the far end of the trailer and you couldn't see it
from the door or until you got up close. How'd you happen to see her?"

Shepherd runs a hand over the right side of her long
blond hair and puts it behind her ear. "Yeah, that's weird,
isn't it? I'd lost an earring and I went back to the trailer to
look for it. I don't know where my assistant was. Anyway,
I was looking for my earring and I found her instead.
God."

"Did you find the earring?"

"No. I stopped looking when I found . . ."

"Of course," I say. I glance at Kip, who looks as though she's been devastated. "Kip, what is it?"

"What?" she says, sounding guilty and shocked all at the same time. Then begins to blush.

And that's when I realize what it is. She's smitten by Shepherd. The swine!

Chapter

Twelve

===============

AS I WALK DOWN TO SOHO I think about Kip's re-action to Cybill Shepherd and wonder if there's anything I have to worry about. Not that Shepherd is a lesbian, she's not, so nothing real would happen, but if Kip has this crush, or whatever it is, perhaps she's tired of me. Or is it simply lust in her heart, to paraphrase our last hon-est president, before this one?

I stop still, as though I've put on brakes, and almost tip over. I have some nerve! What about my own smitten-hood? Okay, so it's not a word. The point is, here I am worrying about Kip when I felt exactly the same way when I met Cybill. And what did it mean for me? *Nada.* Shepherd is beautiful (more so in person) and who wouldn't develop a little sneaker for her?

Kip and I have been totally faithful over the years, never once played around. Of course, I really only know that about me. And it's not as though I've never found another woman attractive since we've been together. The truth is I've found *several* attractive. All right . . . *many.* Big deal. But I never acted on these feelings. Neither has Kip. I'm sure I'd know. Wouldn't I?

Anyway, years ago we gave each other permission to have certain affairs: Kip said I could sleep with Barbra

Streisand and I said she could do the same with Michelle Pfeiffer. We both thought the largesse of this liberty staggering. However, at the time, neither of us thought we'd ever meet *any* movie star. And the truth is I'd be terrified to go to bed with Streisand, even if she begged. So would Kip with Pfeiffer. My guess is that the same fear would apply to Shepherd. I mean, let's say, for argument's sake, that Cybill was interested. I try to imagine it and the hot sweat that runs down my body from the weather immediately turns cold. No way. How would I look next to that body? Fantasy over.

I know that Kip isn't going to go after Cybill Shepherd, but what if this crush awakens her in some odd way and she starts looking at other, *available* women? What am I doing? In the fall we'll be together fourteen years. This is ridiculous.

Relieved, I continue down Sixth Avenue. Mrs. Field's Cookies has returned. I couldn't believe it when it closed. It was the last of the sugar gauntlet on the block between West Fourth and the Waverly movie theater at West Third. But then on a wonderful spring day Mrs. F. reopened. When I went in (well, I had to celebrate) the girl behind the counter told me there'd been a fire and they'd always intended to open again.

As I pass I take a deep breath and the fragrance of chocolate and sugar assaults my sense of smell. Oh, happiness. I would stop now for a white chocolate macadamia cookie if I weren't on my way to meet Blackie at Dean & Deluca on Prince Street.

I cross Sixth and traverse Third Street. Years ago this block was known for its jazz clubs. Now the big draw is a McDonald's. The Village is definitely not what it once was. I suppose everything, from television news to publishing, has turned into sleaze, even the eating establishments. Now I sound like Kip. Still, it's the truth.

I turn down MacDougal. The block between Third and Bleecker is pretty famous. From the days of Bohemians, to Beats to hippies, it's always been the street where things happen. I think comedy and Indian food happen here now, along with the usual shops and a few places that have been here forever, like the Caffe Reggio, Monte's, and the Derby. Gone are the famous artists' bars like the San Remo and the Kettle of Fish (although that's alive and well on Third Street).

On the southeast corner of Bleecker and MacDougal is a large coffeehouse that came and went and came back: the Figaro Café. Bleecker Street is a mess. There are still bars that feature folk and blues but mostly it's junky shops and more fast-food places.

The Bleecker Street Cinema is a murky memory and now houses Kim's Video, which has movies in categories like "Masters of Light" and "Set Design." I once complained that I couldn't find anything and was told by a particularly snotty young man that Kim's catered to a *different* kind of clientele. I told him to blow it out his ass. Kip was not amused.

Fortunately the turnover at Kim's (both clerks and patrons) is vast, so the man I offended is no longer there. I run down the steps into a non-air-conditioned store, thinking I might be able to pick up a copy of *Dangerous Deceit*. I can't bear to think of what category they might have it under. The safest bet is to ask a clerk to look it up, which is exactly what I do.

He types the name into his computer, waits, then says: "We don't have it. Are you sure it exists?"

The implication is incredibly annoying but the truth is I'm *not* sure. "Absolutely," I say.

"Who's in it?"

"I don't know."

The clerk, who has an underslung jaw, looks at me as though I'm stupid, insane, trash, or all three. "Then how do you know it exists?"

"I just know." I sound like a five-year-old.

"Well, just go know who's in it and maybe . . . maybe I can find it."

The phrase I'd used once before comes to mind but I

stop myself, actually thank the little weasel, and leave. Perhaps the movie is listed in one of our reference books at home.

I turn at the corner of La Guardia and Bleecker. I can't believe that the street peddlers are at their makeshift stores. Even this extraordinary heat doesn't stop them. How can they bear to stand there offering pottery, batteries, stolen books? I guess they have no choice. There don't appear to be many buyers out here. I can't imagine anyone stopping to look at a tie or socks.

My imagination must have sunstroke because two immaculately dressed, unsweaty women walk toward me, then stop at a table covered with sunglasses. It doesn't seem to matter that they already each wear a pair.

As I pass them by I overhear a fragment of dialogue.

"These would look perfectly wonderful on Tracy, wouldn't they, Eleanor?"

"Fab."

"How much?"

"Mumble mumble," answers the seller.

In a loud voice Eleanor says, "You know, if you want to do business in this country you should learn to speak English. C'mon, Althea, let's go."

"Fucking bitches," the peddler shouts distinctly.

I turn to watch the women race away as though they've been shot at instead of insulted.

The light changes at Houston and when I get to the other side, La Guardia becomes West Broadway and I'm in SoHo, which means South of Houston. Before the late sixties this area was devoted almost entirely to industry. Then the artists came in and turned the huge spaces into living and working lofts. By 1977 it was still cheap to buy here if you were a certified artist but by the second half of 1978 SoHo had become very expensive, chic, and mostly known for its art galleries. I have some friends who bought a thirty-six-hundred-square-foot loft on Prince in early 'seventy-eight for $70,000, put $55,000 into it, and could sell it, even in this market, for about $850,000. But as they say, where would they go?

The block between Houston and Prince is probably one of the most expensive and chichi in New York City. The restaurants are overpriced, the shops offer wares at price tags starting in the three-figure range, the art galleries show famous painters, and Rizzoli Books is here. But there's no getting around it, even in SoHo, New York in the summer smells like one huge urinal.

At Prince and West Broadway I turn east. The downtown side of the street is mostly taken up by a building that was once a bakery but is now a complex of galleries and shops. On my side, I pass the Meisel Gallery, cross Wooster, and finally get to Dean & Deluca in the middle of the next block.

Once this location housed the food emporium of the same name, but now that's on the corner of Broadway and Prince, and this spot has become a quasi coffeehouse/restaurant. No waitpeople.

I'm elated to get into some air-conditioning. The place is one huge room with white walls and high ceilings. Near the window the tables are high and round with white marble tops, the chairs black, like stools with backs.

I look around for Blackie but I don't see him, so I get on the self-service line at the front counter. What to choose? I particularly like the carrot cake here, but then carrot cake is what I have if Kip or some other cholesterol nag is with me. There are baskets stuffed with scones and muffins; gingerbread slices and tart trays; panniers displaying cookies of all types.

And there is blackout cake.

I order an iced cappuccino and a slice of gingerbread. Just kidding. When I'm served and pay the astronomical price for my coffee and blackout cake, I survey the room again and pick a table for two against the east wall.

I remove my stuff from the tray, return it to its place,

then sit where I can see the door and be seen by whoever enters. The first sip of my coffee is cold, revitalizing, delicious. I'm so thirsty I feel I could drink it down in one long swallow, but don't because I want it to last.

The place is buzzing, even at this hour. It's almost never empty and the weather has undoubtedly driven people from the streets to get somewhere air-conditioned. I actually know an adult person who went to a matinee of *Jurassic Park* to get out of the heat.

Behind me a couple are having a discussion.

"You've never seen film noir, that's what you're telling me? Is that right, Chasilee?"

"What I'm telling you is that I don't know?"

"How can you not know? Either you have or you haven't."

"The thing is, if I have seen it, I wouldn't know I'd seen it?"

She is one of these women who end every sentence like a question even when it's a statement. Kip's reading on this is total insecurity. I hope she's wrong because if she's right then many people under thirty are insecure. And it's mostly women. Sigh.

He says, "They're black-and-white films."

"I've seen those?"

"Yes, but they're not *just* black-and-white, I mean there are lots of B-and-W films that aren't noir. Noir is a style."

"Style is my life?"

"Right. But noir was a kind of film that . . ."

I don't hear the end of his explanation because Blackie comes through the door. He wears his New York black and the boots. I wave to him; he nods and gets on line.

"I don't like murder mysteries?" she says behind me.

"That's not what they are, Chasilee."

"But Steven, you just said they were crime pictures?"

"Look, we'll go to Kim's and rent some."

"I don't like watching movies . . ."

"Films," he corrects.

"I don't like watching *films* in the daytime?"

"Why not?"

"It depresses me?"

Blackie comes toward me carrying a cup of coffee. "H'lo. Glad to hear from ya, I was gettin' worried." He pulls out his chair and sits down. "So ya find out if he killed her?"

"I don't think he did," I say.

"Think?" He squints at me, his eyes like blue eyeliner.

"Why didn't you tell me about the obituary?"

He looks pathetic. "What would ya have done if I had, huh?"

We both know I wouldn't have taken the case. "Didn't you think I'd find out?"

"Yeah, but by then I figured ya'd be involved and all."

"Reading an obituary is a dead end. A wrap. *Finito.* In most cases," I add.

Blackie, who's been leaning back in his chair, jerks forward, his eyes ablaze with possibilities. "Whatcha mean?"

"I mean lots of weird stuff happened so reading the obit was not a wrap."

"Go on, sweets . . . I mean, Lauren."

I pretend I haven't heard. "Do you remember Chief Breese?"

"Unfortunately, yeah, I do. Why?"

"He told me the truth about your mother, that she didn't die in the accident."

"How d'ya know it's the truth?"

A good question. How *did* I? "Instinct," I tell him. This has validity because of what I now know. "I've tracked her down."

"You found her?"

Oh, boy. I hate this part. "I think so, Blackie."

"What's this *think* stuff again?"

As I deliberate on how to tell him, I sense the people

behind me stand, hear their chairs scrape against the tile floor. I look to my right, stalling and curious.

She looks sixteen, but is probably in her early twenties, long blond hair, pretty; and predictably, he's in his fifties, shorts, Gap T-shirt, paunch. Why? What does she want from this guy? And isn't *he* bored? He does what they all do, encircles her waist with a possessive arm: *I am a virile man and give her a good time, even though I'm old enough to be her father.*

Blackie brings me out of my ruminations. "Ya did or ya didn't find her?"

"I *think* I found her but I can't be sure."

"Dead or alive?" he asks.

"Dead."

"What'd I tell ya? Ya found the body, huh?"

"Yes. But it's not what you think. Strangely enough, this woman, who called herself Shelley McCabe, among other names, was murdered *today*."

"So she *did* dump me," he says sadly.

"I'm not clear on that. What happened to her exactly, why she left you with your father. If it's she," I amend quickly.

He lets out a hiss of breath as though someone's pierced him. "If?"

I fill him in on everything I've discovered, ending with the murder and the diamond birthmark.

"Yeah," he says.

"Yeah, what?"

"She had that. I should of tole ya that, I guess. I forgot. My father's mother tole me that's how they knew she was Parrish's daughter."

"Who would want to kill her now, Blackie?"

"Beats me. Hey, why're ya lookin' at me? I dint even know she was alive."

So he says. "What made you doubt that she'd been in that accident even though there was an obit?"

"I guess it was the way my old man talked about her,

hated her. I mean, why should he hate somebody so much that died in an accident? Jesus, I could've known her all this time. Maybe even . . . maybe if I'd a known her she wouldn't be dead now."

"Don't play those games with yourself, you'll drive yourself nuts."

"So who killed her?" he asks.

"I don't know. The police are working on it."

"Did she look like the picture I gave ya?"

How do you describe what his mother looked like dead? "The picture was old," I try.

He nods. "Yeah. Could I see her?"

I understand that he wants to go to the morgue. He won't be able to identify her, but I can't think of any reason he shouldn't see her if that's what he wants.

"I don't see why not. Want me to come with you?"

"Nah."

"You know where the morgue is?"

He nods. Of course he does. And I'm sure he knows the procedure. He doesn't ask me so I don't tell him.

"Her parents, your grandparents, want to meet you."

He touches his forefinger to his chest, raises his eyebrows.

"Yes."

"Hey, I dunno. I dunno what I'm feelin' here, ya know what I mean?"

"Sure. Think about it. Well, I guess that concludes our business." I can't believe how I sound. "I owe you some money."

"Hell no," he says. "Now you gotta find out who killed her."

"The police are . . ."

"Break," he says.

"Break?"

"Like, gimme one. It's shorter, more to the point, if ya get my meanin'."

I do and I like it. Break.

"I don't give a rat's ass if the police are investigatin'. I want ya to find the killer. Look how good ya done so far." He realizes the irony of his statement and gives a disconcerted laugh. "Ya know my meanin'," he states.

"Sure. Okay. I'll stay on it." I'm secretly delighted that he wants me to follow this one because I'm hooked. And, although I know Cecchi will do his job, it does affect Susan and Rick.

"You'll think about meeting your grandparents and let me know? They're very nice people."

"Must be old geezers, huh?"

"Pretty old. But very nice."

He bites a corner of his lip. "I gotta chew this one over."

"Right. Now, is there anything else that you might have forgotten to tell me, any little thing that might be of help?"

"Ya mean like the birthmark?" he asks sheepishly.

"Yes. But it could be even less important, I mean, you might *think* it is."

"Can't remember anything now. I'll chew on that, too."

"Did you ever hear of anyone named Almay Mcmann?"

"Nah."

"Betty Rosner?"

He shakes his head.

We finish our coffee and cake and leave D & D. Outside the heat bounces off the pavement like puffs from a fouled atomizer. Blackie is going in the opposite direction. I wonder if he's taking the subway at the corner of Prince and Broadway but somehow can't imagine him using this form of transportation. We shake hands, he promises to call me soon about his grandparents, and I promise to call him with anything new.

Since I'm in SoHo, I stop at the last bastion of the old-time neighborhood, Angie's. It's still got the original Formica tables and leatherette stools at the counter. Best of all, it still serves as a meeting place for some of the original residents of the area. The lunch crowd at Angie's has thinned out and only a few tables are occupied by neighborhood women having their third or fourth cup of coffee and waiting for Arnold, the bookie. Within half an hour it'll fill up again for homemade lasagna and spaghetti with meatballs at the lowest prices in town.

Angie's husband, Dario, died when she was thirty, leaving her with two kids, Trella and Dario Jr. She's been running the luncheonette for more than twenty years and made a decent life for both her kids. But Dario Jr. doesn't come around much anymore now that he's an assistant D.A. He's ashamed of his mother. I think she's tops.

Angie spots me as I come in the door and motions me to the back.

I follow her through a curtained partition to a small room with an old Naugahyde recliner, stuffing spurting from its arms like whipped cream from an aerosol can. There's also a card table and a folding chair. A bare lightbulb hangs from the ceiling but it isn't on at the moment. A snatch of daylight peeks through one small dirty window.

I turn to face her. She wears her hair in a pompadour, forties style. Her makeup is heavy-duty, the false lashes long and black against her powdered face.

"What's up, Angie?"

"Boy, am I glad you stopped by. Big Mar wants to see you."

We both know this is not good news.

Chapter

Thirteen

═══════════════════

BIG MAR IS MARIUS PETROCELLI, a capo in the Campisi family.

"What's he want to see me about?"

"I dunno, Lauren. Sonny B. came looking for you, said to tell you Big Mar wants to see you. Right away. Like yesterday."

Sonny B. is one of a dozen or so wiseguys who hang around the neighborhood always looking for an angle, running errands for the top guys. "Did he tell you where I'd find Big Mar?"

"The usual."

I nod. "Well, thanks, Angie." I start to draw back the curtain but she puts her hand on my arm.

"You'll be careful, won't you, Lauren?"

"I'm always careful."

"Big Mar's a little wacko, you know."

"Tell me something new," I say. Big Mar is no stranger to me. You don't work in a neighborhood like this without a dossier on the criminal inhabitants. "Don't worry," I say, and give her a peck on the cheek.

"Don't worry, she tells me." Angie shakes her head and long silver earrings jingle an atonal tune.

"Thanks for the info," I say, push through the curtain. "See you later."

Big Mar's "social club" is on Sullivan between Bleecker and Third. I don't like Big Mar. Not only is he wacko, he's mean. For instance, if I didn't show up within twenty-four hours he would send out some of his boys to bring me in, one way or another. I guess you could say Big Mar has an attitude. Worst of all, he gives Italians a bad name. I can't imagine what he wants with me. The Italian men of Big Mar's type usually have nothing to do with women except for sex. And I know that this is not what Big Mar wants from me. Hey, call me clairvoyant.

Near the middle of the block are two young women. One wears a fifties pink playsuit, red high-topped sneakers; the other, Hawaiian pedal pushers with a green tank top. She also has a full head of purple hair and bare feet. They whisper to me as I pass them.

"Smoke, smoke, smoke. Colombian Gold, twenty an ounce."

"Good blow, free taste."

I smile, say thanks but no thanks, and continue on my way.

The club is in a store. The window, trim, and door glass are painted a dark green. Chipped gold letters read Sullivan Social Club. The back of an air conditioner sticks out from above the door, its gurgling sound like a death rattle. At least I'll be cool. I knock.

"Who?" a voice asks.

"Lauren Laurano."

I hear a series of locks turn and Sonny B. opens up. He's short and his hair grows low on his forehead. A fat chin turns up, giving him a squashed look, as if his head has been put in a press. Sonny wears chinos and a black T-shirt, a pack of cigarettes tucked under the short sleeve of his left arm. A wooden match is between his teeth. He's like an escapee from a Scorsese movie.

"Come on in, girlie," he invites.

There's no point in correcting him so I count to three and step inside. The cool air hits me like the edge of a knife. Small groups of men sit at tables, playing cards, talking in Italian. All of them eye me. An elaborate espresso machine is on my right and a wiseguy named Pat is working it. Sonny closes the door and starts patting me down. I pull back.

"Gotta do it, honey. Rules is rules."

I know it's stupid to argue. Besides, I'm not carrying. "Keep it clean," I warn him as I raise my arms in submission.

They all laugh in a sniggering, lewd way and make remarks.

"Yo, Sonny, don't touch the tits."

"You got Anita Hill here, Son, so watch it."

"No sex harazzment, Sonny."

I wish I hadn't given my warning.

"She's clean," Sonny says to no one in particular.

"Where's Petrocelli?" I ask.

Sonny motions with his head toward the back room. He walks to the door, knocks twice, opens it, then waves me in.

Big Mar sits at a table by himself, a cup of espresso and a plate of cannoli in front of him. After all, Big Mar didn't get his tag by eating salads. He's large, maybe three, three-twenty. A fringe of gray hair rings his big head. He wears steel-rimmed glasses but they don't hide the flat cold look in his eyes. Above his thin lips is a small gray mustache. Hitler comes to mind. He wears a light blue silk suit, a dark blue shirt, white tie with a gold mermaid clasp. Chunky hands rest on the table, the kielbasa-like fingers tapping. On his right ring finger is a large diamond set in gold, on his left pinkie a black star sapphire the size of a Tokay grape.

"Miss Laurano," he says, giving me a smile with no feeling, "sit down, sit down."

I pull out the chair across from him.

"What'll ya have, my friend? Espresso? Cappuccino? Sumpin' stronger?"

"Nothing, thanks."

He pulls back his head, all three chins hide his neck. "Hey, *paisan*, ya don't wanna drink wit' Petrocelli?"

Big Mar always refers to himself by his last name. He doesn't like his nickname and this is a way to express his protest. If he catches anyone using the Big Mar handle he readily shows his disappointment in the person. A guy named Shifty Schneider had reportedly lost the middle fingers of both hands for committing such an offense.

"I just had some," I tell him.

"You could never have too much cap or espresso." He laces his fat fingers together and cracks his knuckles as if they are peanut shells.

"Not thirsty," I say. I have no desire to eat or drink anything Big Mar has to offer.

He frowns, the layers of loose skin that pile one on top of the other on his forehead giving him the appearance of a bulldog. "Hey, can't we be friends?"

I don't answer.

"Oh, yeah, I forgot."

I don't take the bait.

"You hate men, right?"

Here we go. Should I engage or not?

"Yer one of them lezzees, right?"

I can't help myself. "I'm a lesbian, if that's what you mean."

"Yeah, lezbian. And you girls don't like men, am I right or am I right?"

"You're wrong." Why am I letting myself get dragged into this stupid discussion?

"You telling me you *like* men?"

"Some men."

"Oh, yeah, like the faggoons, ya mean."

"Lesbians like some men, both homosexual and heterosexual. Why should *we* hate men? We don't have to sleep with them."

His mouth drops open. Clearly this is nothing he's ever thought about.

"So why did you want to see me?" I ask.

He shifts his bulk uncomfortably, then lights a cheroot.

"I hear some dame on a movie set got her ticket punched," he says dryly.

"You heard right."

"Word's out we done it. I don't like that. No way do I like that."

"Because you did or because you didn't?"

As Big Mar leans back in his chair, his belly spills over the edge of the table, nudging his crumb-filled plate. "Ya trying to bug me, lady?"

"Just trying to get the facts," I say amiably.

He grunts. "For the record, we didn't do it. We don't go round snuffing minor movie people for no good reason."

"How about major ones?"

"Huh?"

"Forget it. This rumor got started pretty fast, didn't it?"

"Ya know how it is. *They* like to dump on us any way they can."

They, I know, is the rest of the world, especially the police.

"It's the M.O., I guess . . . wire round da troat."

"So what's this got to do with me?"

"I wanna hire you."

I almost laugh out loud. "Hire me for what?"

"Ta find out who knocked off this broad, what else?"

"I'm not for hire," I announce.

"You ain't a private dick no more?"

"I didn't say that. I said I wasn't for hire." Even Big Mar should understand this.

"Ya mean you ain't for hire by *me?*"

"Right."

"How much you charge?" He blows a puffball of smoke in front of his face.

"Four thousand dollars a day."

"Four thousand . . . hey, *paisan*, you're a comedian, right?" His face fractures into a grin exposing tiny pointed teeth. Then he laughs as if he's got a sudden case of hiccups.

I say nothing. The hiccups change to gulps, the gulps to hyperventilation and then to wracking sobs. I've seen people go over the line from laughter to tears before, but this is something else. This is the wacko factor. I wait, drumming my fingertips on my knee. Finally he stops sobbing, pulls a neatly pressed handkerchief from his breast pocket, wipes his eyes, blows his nose, then drops it on the floor.

"So here's da ting," he says, as if nothing has happened. "We want you should find out who kilt this broad because we work wit' the unions, know what I mean? It's public relations."

I have to keep from laughing again. "Public relations?"

"Yeah. Image. I mean, what kinda image would we have if we went around knocking off broads like that one? And we want to keep the biz in town. We just got 'em to come back. You gotta keep up relations. So what d'ya charge? Two, three hundred a day?"

"Why me?" I'm genuinely curious.

" 'Cause you got access. Dis is a movie by yer friends, right?"

It gives me the creeps that he knows so much about me. I don't answer.

"And," he goes on, "yer on a connective case, right?"

This spooks me.

"Yeah, I know yer not gonna tell me, professional effects an' all dat. But we think yer in a good position to find the croaker on this one. Croaker? Huh? That's good. Rhymes wit' choker."

Fearing that the insane laughter will start again, I push back my chair and stand up.

"I'm not interested."

"Hey, wait a minute." Grunting, he struggles to his feet and brings his belly with him as if it's a separate person. "We'll make it worth yer while. Say, three-fifty a day."

"Plus expenses?"

"Sure, sure. What d'ya think, we're pikers?"

All I want is out of here. "I'll think about it."

"Dat's the girl."

He slams me on my back and I feel it on my chest.

"Hey, ya won't be sorry, ya know what I mean?"

I have no intention of taking the offer but it's important to stall him until the case is solved. I don't trust what he might do if I give him a categorical no.

"I'll see you, Big Mar," I say. Why can't I ever control myself?

His eyes narrow and his face looks like a popover ready to explode. "I'll pretend I didn't hear that," he says in a strained whisper.

"You do that," I say. I leave and walk through the front room. All conversation stops. Sonny B. stands near the door, feet crossed, arms akimbo.

"Come again soon," he says, as if I'd been to a tea party. He undoes the locks.

Hot as it is on the street, I'm glad to be out of Big Mar's social club.

When I arrive home Kip is with a patient. I go to my computer, boot up, get into my Winqwk program, and write David a letter. I've already written him about my case so there isn't much to fill in. But I *do* have a request.

```
Dear David,
    Guess what? I found the missing woman and I
found her dead. Guess where? On the set of a
movie in front of my house. I know, I know, but
it's true. And I need some help from you.
Since she turned out to be an actress, al-
though a minor one, could you try to trace her
acting history for me? The name she was using
on this film was Shelley McCabe. Maybe some-
one you know in the biz knew her, maybe you did.
Anyway, anything you can find out about her
would be of great help to me. I know you're
```

```
busy but as soon as you can would be great.
I'll check soon. Thanks and I hope Trin-
chieri's show went well.
```
Lauren

I exit from Winqwk, launch Unicom, and dial the Invention Factory. After I upload the letter to David I depart from the BBS. I don't turn the computer off because my screen saver will come on in three minutes so that I don't ruin my monitor. This week it's a bunch of floating fish. Sometimes it's Killer Crayon or Spirals. I like to change them now and then. I intend to call I.F. later to see if David's found anything, so this is why I don't shut down.

Kip and I finish at the same time and meet in the living room.

"Hello, love of my life," she declares.

Why is she saying this? "Hello."

She embraces me and I slide my arms around her waist without much enthusiasm. Pictures of Cybill Shepherd dance in my head.

Kip says, "Love me that much, huh?" She pulls back. "So, what's up?"

"I don't know what you mean," I lie.

"Really? I feel like I'm in the arms of a fish."

"Fish don't have arms."

"You know what I mean."

"I'm distracted by the case, I guess." What else can I say?

She releases me, plunks into a chair, puts her head back, and closes her eyes.

I know she's picturing Cybill. It doesn't matter that she often sits this way after a long day of patients. One thing has nothing to do with the other.

"Rough day?" I ask.

"Not especially. The usual assortment of neurotics and mass murderers. How about you?"

"I met with my client. He wants me to stay on the case." I sit on the couch.

"Well, that's good news, isn't it?"

"Who said it was bad news?"

She opens her eyes and looks at me. "No one. You're a little snappish, aren't you?"

"No." Now she's going to find fault with everything I say and do and think about how different it would be if she were with . . . Cybill.

"No? Sounds that way to me," Kip says.

"You always hear me wrong."

"I do?"

"Often," I amend.

"We sometimes hear each other wrong," she states sensibly.

"Don't," I say.

"Don't what?"

"Give me your sensible shrink voice."

"So now who's mishearing? What's the matter, darling?"

"Nothing. Forget it." I count to five. "So what did you think of Cybill Shepherd?" I try to sound casual.

"Seemed awfully nice."

"And beautiful, don't you think?"

"Well, sure, but that didn't come as any surprise."

"Your type," I state, remembering the blondes she was involved with before me.

"Hardly."

"What's that supposed to mean?" I ask.

"Lauren, you are not a tall blonde, in case you've forgotten."

"But the others were."

"Others?"

"Your exes."

"You're not jealous, are you?"

"Of course not." It does suddenly seem stupid.

"You *are*," she says. "You're jealous of Cybill Shepherd?"

"I said no."

"Yes, but you lied." She starts to get up.

"Don't."

She sits back down.

"Tell me the truth. Tell me what you *felt* about her," I ask.

"I told you. I thought she was awfully nice and different from what I'd expected."

"And beautiful," I repeat.

"And beautiful. A given."

"And you want her."

"Are you crazy?"

"Don't try the crazy offense."

"Lauren, this is ridiculous. First of all, the woman's heterosexual."

"Oh, I see," I say. "If she *were* gay then you *would* be interested."

"That's not what I meant."

"So what *did* you mean?"

"I'm not interested in anyone but you," Kip proclaims.

"Then what difference does it make if she's a lesbian or not?"

"It doesn't. It was a stupid thing to say."

What more do I want?

"Red rover, red rover, may I come over?" Kip asks.

"When you met me," I say, "I could've been anyone. It was a rebound thing and you know it."

"I don't believe it. Almost fourteen years later and you're still saying this."

"I could've been anyone," I repeat.

"Lauren, what the hell is wrong? You *couldn't* have been anyone because if that was true we wouldn't be sitting here today having this stupid conversation. Now stop it and tell me what's bothering you."

I think. "It seemed to me you were lusting after her."

"You're wrong," she says straightforwardly. "Totally wrong." She stays where she is but opens her arms to me.

To go into them or not? That is the question. If I go, I will have to give up the Cybill gambit. If I don't . . . nothing is gained and I end up feeling depressed and lonely and stupid.

I go.

After we reassure each other of our love I fill her in about the case. However, I don't tell her about Big Mar. This would frighten Kip. I don't recommend keeping secrets from your mate, but sometimes one has to, for peace of mind. Never mind whose.

Chapter

Fourteen

═══════════════

CECCHI HAS ALLOWED THE MOVIE to resume shooting. From my study I hear them unpacking gear while I dial the Invention Factory. I'm happy to see that I have mail because I'm sure it's from David.

After I download and sign off, I go into my mail-reader program and bring up his letter.

```
Dear Lauren,
    I've got a lead on the McCabe woman. But
you're off a little bit on the names. McCabe/
Mcmann did use a couple of them but someone
else used the others. And some are different
combinations. Got to run to rehearsal. More
later.
                                      David
```

More later? The little punk. What could *more later* possibly mean? David and I have never exchanged phone numbers so I can't even call him. Suddenly this whole idea of keeping our relationship strictly a computer one seems crazy.

I know where David rehearses. I could go there and find out what he's talking about. But this violates our agreement to never meet in person. Still. Life and death and all that.

Or is this an ethical matter?

And do I care?

How would I feel if David suddenly knocked on my door?

I would hate it.

I'll have to wait. Meanwhile I'll interview McCabe's agent, Doyce Schroeder, who should know a lot about her, including stage names, et cetera.

Though it's only nine in the morning the atmosphere is thick and sticky. There's not a trace of that thing called breeze. I imagine one of those big cartoon thermometers climbing steadily upward until it explodes. Night after night the frenzied television weather people behave as though we are all under a volcanic eruption. They love it. So we sweat a little; this is nothing compared to the rising of the Mississippi River.

The equipment trucks are lined up on the west side of the street. On the east side are the actors' trailers. The crew is setting up a shot. This will probably take hours.

"Hey, Lauren," a man yells.

I turn around. Across the street a guy who's come out of a truck waves at me. I don't recognize him but I wait while he walks toward me. When he's right up close, sticking out his hand, I see that he looks familiar. I still can't place him.

"Jim Daniels," he says.

I take a beat, then remember. "Jimmy the Snail," I say.

"The one and only," he laughs.

When we were growing up Jimmy was the slowest guy in our neighborhood, always picked last for any team. "How're you doing, Jim?"

"Hey, okay. I can't believe it's you. Don't tell me you live around here?"

"Right here," I say, pointing to my building.

"You got an apartment on this block?" he asks, impressed.

I hesitate but what the hell. "We own the building."

"No kidding." Daniels is big and has thick arms, large hands. The once full head of curly black hair has receded and gives the impression of a high forehead. His brown eyes are underscored by bags, like curtain swags. Still, he's good-looking and has a lopsided smile that used to get the girls. I wonder if it still does.

"What's he do?"

"Who?" I know who he means.

"Your husband."

"Jim, you're standing here with me but you don't ask what *I* do."

"Well, hey, I mean. . . ." He shrugs.

"How come?" I ask.

"How come I don't ask what *you* do?"

I nod.

"How come I don't ask what you do?"

"Right."

He shrugs twice. "I don't know. How come I don't ask what you do?"

"Because you don't think I do *anything.*"

"Hey, Lauren, don't break my chops here, okay? I just wanted to say hello. So, you a teacher?"

I hide my irritation. Teaching is the only profession that certain men think women can have. I lay it on him.

"I'm a detective."

"Must be interesting." He doesn't sound like he thinks it's interesting at all. "So, ah, what's your husband do?"

Daniels is a hopeless cause. "I don't have a husband."

"Oh, hey, so you live with the guy. That's okay. What's he do?"

"She's a therapist," I say.

"Cool," he says.

Though he doesn't take a beat, I know he doesn't think it's cool. He's not thrown by it, but he definitely doesn't think it's cool. Most movie people are homophobic even though their business would be nothing without us.

"I married Ceil Nardone," Daniels says.

She had been his high school sweetheart.

"That's nice." And it is. So few are still together.

"Yeah. We got four kids."

"Great."

"We live in L.A."

"So what're you doing here, Jimmy?"

"Working this picture," he says, as if it's something I should've known. "I'm head gaffer."

I know from my friends that gaffers are lighting technicians. But I'm irritated by Daniels's attitude and give him a dumb look so he can translate it for me, which is what he wants to do.

"Lighting."

I nod. Guess that showed him. God, I can be a jerk sometimes.

"So, you're a detective, huh?" He snaps his fingers. "You working on this?"

I tell him I am.

"Hey, big time, huh?"

I ignore this. "Did you know her?"

"Who?"

"The victim."

"Kind of. I mean, I been on other pictures with her. We didn't hang out or nothing."

"Can you tell me anything about her?"

He furrows his brow to prove that he's thinking. "Just between us, she wasn't much of an actress. In fact, I was always surprised to see her on a set. With so many others to pick from, bit players and extras, I don't understand how she got jobs."

"She was that bad?"

"Not bad, exactly. More like dull, nothing. Maybe she was sleeping with somebody significant."

For once I hold my tongue. "Anything about her personally that you can tell me?"

Daniels puffs up his chest like a pouter pigeon. "You gotta understand, Lauren, when you're working on a picture you don't have time to be watching extras. Being a gaffer is hard work."

"I'm sure it is," I say. "But I've noticed there's a lot of waiting time on a set."

"This is true. Lemme think."

Now that I've agreed how important he is, he seems more eager to help.

"Well, there was one thing that was sorta strange. Even though we didn't hang out, we'd schmooze occasionally. Sometimes if I'd reference a thing we talked about, maybe two pictures ago, she acted like she didn't know what I was saying."

"You mean she didn't remember that you'd discussed certain things?"

"Yeah. Right. Tell you the truth, Lauren, actors can be snobs. Even two-bit ones like her. Excuse me for putting down the dead. But it's the truth. That's why I don't get buddy-buddy with actors. They think they're better than everybody. Much worse than the directors."

"Did you ever call her on not remembering?"

"Nah. I didn't want to give it that much importance, make her think she was somebody and I was just this poor schmuck gaffer. Funny, though, that kind of thing could happen, like I just told you, then I'd see her on another set and she'd act like I was her long-lost cousin."

"Did she remember things you'd talked about then?"

"Oh, most definitely. I think she was maybe a little crazy."

"Anything else, Jimmy?"

"Nah. Like I said, I didn't know her too good, and didn't want to. Not that I'm glad she's dead or nothing. You got any leads?"

I shrug noncommittally.

"Privileged info, huh?"

"Right." I give him my card. "If you think of anything else give me a ring."

"Sure. Will do. Hey, I'm gonna be around here for a couple of weeks. Let's do lunch soon."

"Can we just *have* it?"

He laughs. "Don't mean to sound so L.A. Habit. But I mean it, I'd like to sit down, talk about old times."

"That'd be nice," I lie. "Got to go now. Say hello to Ceil for me."

"Will do."

We shake hands, and when I turn away from him I see Rick and Susan standing in front of a trailer drinking coffee out of Styrofoam cups and eating doughnuts.

As I approach Susan says, "It's the murder diet."

"Think there's a book in it?" I ask.

"Maybe a series," Rick says.

"You must be happy you're shooting again."

They nod.

"I suppose if William were here," Rick says, he'd call us heathens or something. I don't know, Lauren, ever since he cleaned up his act he's been Dudley Do-Right."

"William's always been an ethical person," I say.

"And we're not?" Susan asks defensively.

"That's not what I said, or meant. And there's nothing wrong with you being glad your work's back on track."

Rick asks, "You think this is an isolated thing, Lauren? Susan and I have visions of one actor after another getting killed. Maybe there's a crazy person connected to the picture."

"I suppose it's possible, but I doubt it." I'm convinced that even though it's been a coincidence in my case, it has nothing to do with their movie. Whoever killed Shelley McCabe was after Susie Mcmann.

"I'd feel a whole lot better if you were on the case," Rick says.

"I am."

They look at me incredulously. I explain that my client wants me to continue.

In her movie-promo voice Susan says, "She's just a small-time dick, but trouble is her business. When the big movie company comes to town and murder gets the spotlight, she goes after the killer bare-fisted. Lauren Laurano on the case. Coming soon to a theater near you."

"Go get the bastard," Rick says.

"I'm going, I'm going. See you later."

At the corner of Seventh Avenue and Grove Street the honey-roasted-nut man is setting up his cart. He's a new guy, hasn't been around for more than a year. Still, you never know who knows what.

The Nut Man is in his early thirties and has a beard with little shorn patches as if it has been badly mowed. He wears jeans and a T-shirt that says JUST DO IT. I've seen these around a lot and I'm not sure what the *it* refers to. The mind boggles at the possibilities.

I don't know his name but we're on nodding acquaintance. It's like that when you see the same person on the same corner day after day. Sometimes I even buy a bag of nuts. They're good. He'd started out with peanuts but recently added almonds and cashews. Weekends he does a helluva business.

I say hello.

"Not ready yet," he answers, but doesn't look up.

"That's okay."

"Take me another five minutes or more," he says pleasantly.

"I can wait."

He glances at me. "Oh, it's you. How's tricks?"

"Tricky. Mind if I ask you something?"

"Nope. But I bet I can guess what it is," he says.

"Really?"

"Sure. How'd you get into this business?"

I pretend he's right. "That's it."

"I went to Harvard," he says.

I laugh.

"You laugh. Thing is, I *did* go to Harvard, although not so I could sell nuts on the street corner."

"You graduated?"

"Sure. I don't like inside work. I don't like offices; they give me the creeps. Or maybe it's the people in them give me the creeps. But creeps are creeps."

"And you never run into creeps out here in the street," I put in.

"You want to know something? In a way, there's a better class of creeps out here. At least most of them know they're creeps."

"I suppose that's true."

"Anyway, it took me a while to figure all this out, that's what a Harvard education will do for you. You go from job to job for about six years until you crack the problem, which is that you don't want to do what you're doing. My dad was real pleased when I came up with this discovery."

"I'll bet."

"I like it out here. And you want to know something? I don't make what I could make stuck in some office doing *business*, but I do okay. Got a nice apartment on West Fifteenth, nice wife and two nice kids. We're happy. How many people can say that?"

"Not many."

"Right. You want peanuts, cashews, or almonds?"

What can I do? "Cashews."

You like your work, too, don't you? The private dick thing."

I'm surprised he knows this. "Yeah, I like it."

He smiles. "I make it my business to know what's going on around me." He extends his hand. "I'm Mike Farmer. You're Lauren Laurano."

I shake his hand and wonder if I've stumbled on some unexpected font of information.

"You know about everybody and everything in the neighborhood?"

"You mean like the movie murder on Perry Street in front of your building?" He coats the nuts, shakes, then bags them.

"Yes."

"Do I know who did it? No. Do I know the victim? Yeah." He hands me the warm bag of nuts.

"You do . . . did?"

"Yeah. She buys from me sometimes, we talk. Not like the other one."

"The other one?"

He looks at me. "This was Susie, wasn't it?"

"She told you her real name?"

"Sure. It *was* Susie?"

"Yes," I say warily. "What other one?"

"The sister. Not nice."

"The *sister?*"

"Susie was real nice, friendly. But the other one, phooey. A big snob. Wouldn't give me the time of day even though she always bought from me. Her name is Helga, calls herself Sharon. But this I got from Susie."

"Sharon who?"

"Sheedy. But she used other names like Susie did. Funny thing, even from a block away I could always tell which one it was."

My detective's heart sinks, then climbs like the sun behind a mountain. "Mike, what exactly are you saying?" I think I know but I have to hear it from his lips.

He looks at me, cocks his head to the side. "What part?"

"How about the you-could-always-tell-from-a-block-away-which-one-it-was part."

"Oh, yeah. It was the walk. Susie walked with joy and Sharon walked with sorrow, if you don't mind me sounding too poetic."

"Twins?" I ask, staggered.

"Yeah. Twins," he confirms.

Chapter

Fifteen

WORSE THAN MYSTERIES, worse than coincidences, are twins. I loathe and despise the twin gambit. There are twin movies and twin novels and twin plays. Recently, a Grand Master of Mystery Writers of America utilized this device. And, of course, even Shakespeare used the twin ruse. But he can be forgiven because it was new then. It's hard to believe that I'm involved in a twin case. Still, this explains what Jimmy the Snail said about Susie not remembering sometimes. If the Nut Man is right and the twin used other names, then she was probably an actress too.

I get the distinct feeling that this is going to be a good twin–evil twin ploy. The worst kind.

Did the evil twin (Sharon) kill the good twin (Susie)? I refuse to believe this.

Why has nobody mentioned a twin sister sooner?

And how can we be sure it's the good twin (Susie) who was murdered? Maybe it was the evil twin (Sharon) who was murdered, but not by the good twin (Susie).

Or maybe the good twin (Susie) *did* murder the evil twin (Sharon), which would make the good twin (Susie) really the evil twin (Susie), and the original evil twin (Sharon) now the good twin (Sharon). Good but dead.

I HATE THIS!

I go into the Waverly Place Luncheonette with hopes that I might locate Cecchi. Also, I know I'll find a phone book. Probably the only public one left in New York City.

In one sweep I take in the room. No Cecchi.

Ruby zips past me, a tray of breakfasts balanced on one hand. When she comes by again I stop her.

"Hi, Ruby. Seen Cecchi?"

"Not today." White shoes spirit her away with the silence only an older New York waitress can manage.

I go to the back, where the phone is, and pull out the Manhattan directory. No Sharon or Susie Mcmann or Shelley McCabe. There are many S. Mcmanns and S. Mc-Cabes, more than I want to deal with. None at East Sixth Street, where Cecchi said the dead woman lived.

Suddenly and shockingly, Ruby speaks to me of her own accord for the first time that I can remember.

"So you got a murder right on your own front stoop, huh?"

I nod, stunned at this unsolicited conversation.

"Which one of them was wasted?" she asks.

Obviously everybody knows about these twins.

"Susie," I say, as if the twin thing is old news, part of my history.

"Too bad. She was the nice one."

Here we go with the good and evil twins. I'm not sure I can bear it. "The other one?"

"*Farbissineh.* You know what that means?"

Yiddish, but I don't know the meaning and say so.

"Sour. Like a pickle. It was why it was easy to tell them apart. One sunny, one like a black cloud."

"Ruby, do you by any chance know where the sour one lives?"

"The exact address?"

"Yeah."

"I look like a Rolodex or something? I should know my customers' addresses like maybe they invite me over for cocktails and canapés? 'Scuse me, got work to do." Shaking her head, she mumbles to herself, but loud enough for me to hear: "I don't know what Cecchi sees in her."

I leave and stand on the sidewalk, staring into space, not sure what my next move should be.

"So where's your fucking cup? You don't have a fucking cup?"

It takes me a moment to realize that the woman is speaking to me. She's nicely turned out in a white linen dress, pearls, earrings that match, and a beauty salon perm.

"I beg your pardon?" I say.

"Your fucking cup," she says with an accent I can't quite place.

"Cup?"

"Don't you know you have to have a fucking cup? What's wrong with you?"

The language doesn't match the appearance at all and I'm fascinated by it. I don't even attempt to understand the content.

A leather purse swings on her right arm. She opens it with her left hand and takes out a pack of cigarettes, black holder, and lighter. After she's returned the items to her bag and taken a deep dangerous drag, she speaks to me again. "I don't know what this fucking world is coming to. Now you people expect us to supply the fucking cups as well. This is a fucking nightmare, is what it is." She blows smoke in the air, picks tobacco from her lip. "It should be easy enough to fucking get. Any fucking asshole could get a fucking cup. Well, this is your fucking problem, and I don't have fucking time to teach. I want vodka." She turns on her heel in a perfect swivel and sashays down the avenue.

It's only as I watch her go that I realize she thought I was a beggar and I didn't have my cup for her to put money into. Do I look this bad? Or was it her? I'll never really know.

I've come to a decision. Ethical or not, I'm going to find David because from what he said to me in his annoying little note, he probably has an address for the remaining twin.

David's theater, where the Nonsensical Nomads perform, is on Franklin Street. This is in Tribeca, which stands for Triangle Below Canal. The area has been steadily gentrifying for the last ten years. Those who can't afford or don't like SoHo are settling here. There are quite a few restaurants and clubs in the new region, and it also houses Robert De Niro's film complex.

David's company has been there for years. It was founded and run by his late lover, Ron Brooks, who died of AIDS two years ago.

Unlike Ron, David only directs so I've never even seen a photograph of him in the paper. The company has always done well but with the emergence of Tribeca it's blossomed into a highly respected theater company, garnering *New York Times* reviews. After Ron died, David wrote me that he was afraid the company would fold, but he's managed to keep it running smoothly, writing some plays of his own and receiving critical praise.

When Ron was running, writing for, and acting in the company, and before I knew David, I went with Kip, Rick, and William to see a show there which was a campy story about the Bakkers, Tammy and Jim. Ron played Tammy.

Practically panting from the hideous heat, I take a left at Franklin off West Broadway. The neighborhood hasn't changed much over the years, industry holding its own. In the middle of the block a blue flag bearing the white words "The Nonsensical Nomads Theatre Company" hangs above the doorway.

The entrance is unassuming. If it weren't for the flag you'd never know there was a theater in this building. I open the door and go into the tiny lobby. The box office is closed, which is why I didn't try calling David here. There are two doors off the lobby. Having been here, I know which one leads to the theater. My detective's heart is making a racket. I shouldn't be doing this. We swore to each other *never* to try to uncover the other person without agreement. I'm a total louse and I pray that David will understand.

The cool of air-conditioning envelops me when I walk into the small darkened theater. A rehearsal is in progress. The play they're doing is *Jurassic Pricks in the Military*. Destiny is playing Zsa Zsa Gabor, as one of the dinosaurs. I recognize Fritz Leslie as Colin Powell. They are talking to Sam Nunn, portrayed by Charles Loehman. The Nomads often combine things such as a movie and a political issue to make points. I stand against the back wall and listen.

ZSA ZSA

So, Colin dahling, is it true that you refuse to go into the park with Sam?

COLIN

How can I be sure he'll do his job? What if he refuses to protect me?

ZSA ZSA

And vy vould Sammy do that, dahling boy?

COLIN

He's a . . . a Jurassic Prick, and small at that.

SAM

I heard that, Colin. Lies. All lies. I haven't told and you shouldn't ask.

"Wait a minute, people," a male voice shouts from down front. "I think I have to rewrite this exchange."

"Why?" asks Destiny/Zsa Zsa. "It's good."

"No. It's not quite right."

This is obviously David and I feel as though I'm about to see a lover for the first time. My eyes have adjusted to the dark and I observe a small tonsure on the crown of his head.

"It's time for a break anyway. Houselights, please."

I hold my breath as the lights come up. The actors wander offstage and David hunches over in his third-row seat. Slowly, as if I were marching to the gas chamber, I go down the aisle and stop at his row. A few moments pass before he notices me.

"Yes?"

Of course he doesn't look anything like I'd imagined him. He's extremely good-looking in an unpolished way. The cut of his face is irregular and his gray eyes almost austere. His nose juts out as though the sculptor hasn't finished, and his mouth is large and lush.

"David?"

"Yes?"

All I want to do now is run. But this would be stupid. Still, I don't seem to be able to tell him who I am. He puts the clipboard he's holding on the seat to his left and rises. He's at least six feet.

He stares, says timorously: "Lauren?"

I'm stunned and frightened. "Yes," I whisper.

The rough-hewn face appears stony, then breaks into a jagged grin as he steps toward me and holds out his arms. I fall into them and am engulfed.

"You look just like I thought you would," he says.

"You don't."

"Did you think I'd be a screamer?"

I'm not sure if this is true. "I don't know."

He pulls back from me and we look at each other. "I can be," he says.

"You're not mad at me?"

"For what? Oh, you mean breaking our sacred trust?" He laughs deeply.

"I couldn't help it," I say lamely.

"Yeah? How come?" There's a teasing sparkle in his eyes.

"Because I'm a swine."

"The hell you are," he says reassuringly.

We look each other over. He wears jeans, a red tank top, and brown sandals. Black curly hair spills from his chest and one ear is pierced with a diamond stud.

"I can't believe I'm finally meeting you," he says. "C'mon, sit."

We take our places next to each other in the third row.

"You're really not mad?"

"Lauren, if you'll recall, I've wanted to meet you. It's been you that hasn't wanted to."

This is true. "I would've called but I know the box office isn't open and I never have known your home phone."

"I'm listed," he says.

"I never thought of that."

"Some detective."

"Well, it was kind of a spur-of-the-moment thing. I need some information and . . ."

". . . you needed it yesterday," he finishes.

"Right."

"Is it about the project you asked me to do a search on?"

"Yes. I need . . ."

Suddenly Zsa Zsa Gabor is hovering above us. "David," Destiny says, "I can't work under these conditions. I mean, I can't, I just can't."

"What conditions?"

"You promised me my own dressing room, dear, and I've yet to see it, let alone live in it."

"Des, I've told you, it's still under construction."

"Dig we must for growing Destiny, or what? How long can a frigging dressing room take to build? You using government inspectors to do it, or what?"

"I'd like you to meet a friend of mine, Des."

David introduces us. His/her hand in mine feels soft and creamy.

"Delighted, I'm sure," Destiny says.

I start to express *my* delight but Destiny interrupts.

"David, a person of my caliber should not have to share a dressing room with Sam Nunn. You know how he feels about me."

"No. I don't," says David.

"Think about it, sweetie. The point is *I'm* the star. I mean, am *I* the star of this cockamamie play or not, David?"

"You're the star."

"Then I should be treated like one. Either I get my own dressing room by tomorrow or I quit and that's final final." Destiny flounces off.

"Ah, the trials and tribs of a producer/writer/director. She won't quit. It's too good a part. Now, what do you need to know?"

I tell him about the improbable twin twist and ask who used the other names and whether he has an address for Sharon Sheedy.

"Sharon Sheedy is the one who used Miranda Sheedy, Beth Davey, and Pam Rice. And the address" — he flips to the next page — "for Sheedy is right near here, on Harrison Street. For McCabe it's Sixth Street."

"That one I know. I think she's the dead one. I have to talk to Sharon, who is really Helga if it isn't Susie."

"Huh?"

"Never mind."

He gives me the address.

"Well, David, I guess I can come see your play now."

"Great. Are you sorry we met? Will it be the same?"

I think about this. Now that I have a face to go with the letters, what will it be like? "I guess we'll have to see."

"Personally, I'm glad."

I rise. "I know you have to get back to rehearsal and I've got to find out which twin has the Toni."

He looks at me blankly and it's only then that I realize he's too young to know what I'm talking about. We've never told each other our ages and now I see that he can't be more than thirty.

"You're a child, aren't you?"

"I'm twenty-eight."

Could I be his mother? I wonder. I do a quick calculation. I could, but I would've been sixteen.

"You're not more than thirty-five, are you?" he asks. I adore this man.

"Yes, a bit. Do you mind?"

He laughs. "Hell, you could be in your forties for all I care." His big arms encircle me again and he gives me a gentle hug.

"I'm so glad you're not an ageist," I say.

We promise to keep in touch via modem and I thank him profusely for the much-needed information.

When I leave his building I head downtown for Harrison Street.

Chapter

Sixteen

I DON'T KNOW HOW MUCH MORE trudging around I can do in this heat. I wonder if it'd be cooler if I traveled on Roller Blades? I know I could take cabs and charge Blackie, but not all of them are air-conditioned. And even if I found one that was, it would probably take me months to get from one place to the other.

"Hey, what're you doing down here?" It's my friend Patty, walking her dog Lester.

"I could ask you the same?"

"I live here now."

I once told Patty that I thought she was beautiful, which I do, but prefaced it by telling her not to misunderstand, which she didn't. I feel that people are too afraid to tell each other things like that and we all should do more of it. I know I didn't regret telling her and I think it made her feel good.

Lester takes a nip at my ankle and I let out a pathetic little scream.

"Stop, Lester," Patty says, jerks his lead.

What is it with these lesbian dogs? This one is a Westie. I'm so glad we don't have one. When Kip and I decided to marry and live together we made an additional vow that we wouldn't have any animals or babies. Although the lesbian baby boom was not as prevalent then, we knew some couples who had children. Why do they always have boys?

"It's okay," I say stupidly. It's definitely *not* okay that Lester makes me his lunch, so why am I saying this? It's some kind of reflex response as though Lester is Patty's child and I don't want to insult her. This is absurd.

"So, I repeat," Patty says, tucking a maverick wisp of brown hair into her ponytail. "What are you doing in this neighborhood?"

"It's not as though we're bumping into each other in Toledo," I say.

She laughs. "I don't know why, but I never picture you leaving your house."

"Patty, do you know what I do for a living?"

"You're a detective."

"Then how could I never leave my house?"

"Nero Wolfe didn't."

"Wolfe was a character in a book." Is this more merging of life and art?

"I knew that," Patty says, smiling. "Not." Patty is a "Wayne's World" fan.

Lester moves dangerously close to my feet and Patty pulls him back.

"Do you know where Harrison Street is?" I ask. "I thought I knew but I can't find it."

"It's a funny little street and if you don't know where it is, you don't know where it is." She gives me directions. "Are you on a case?"

"Yes."

"Can I come with you?"

"Of course not."

"Gotcha. Even if you were Lew Archer I know I couldn't come with you."

"Patty, has it occurred to you to read some contemporary detective writers? Maybe even some women?"

"I've read them all. See you, love to Kip," she says as she rushes off.

Harrison Street is short. On one side are several

restored brownstones and on the other are high-rises. Chanterelle, one of the most expensive restaurants in New York, occupies a corner. The De Niro building is nearby and I vaguely wonder if I might run into Bobby. Just kidding. Although I used to know his father because he lived across the hall from Jenny's mother. I guess that's not really knowing a person.

Number 25 Harrison is a redbrick, three-story house. I climb the steps and look at the one bell. It says "Sheedy & Collins." I ring and in short order, through the intercom, a woman's voice asks who it is. I tell her my name and she tells me to wait.

The smell almost knocks me over when the door opens. There's no doubt in my mind as to what it is. Cats.

The woman who stands in the doorway is tiny. She has sheer skin with blue veins like delicate strings in an egg-shaped face. Her pink scalp shows through unstyled vestiges of white hair. An orange-and-white cat, with long hair and a bushy tail, is in her arms, and around her feet swirl several others of different colors and sizes. A steady sound, like people praying, comes from inside the house. But I know it's cats mewing.

"What is it you wish?" she asks in a wavery voice.

"Are you Sheedy or Collins?"

"Collins."

"Is Ms. Sheedy at home?"

"No, she isn't."

"I'd like to talk to you about her."

"Oh, dear," she says enigmatically.

"Is there a problem?"

She shakes her head. "Come in." The cat hisses at me.

"Toto," I say aloud. "I don't think we're in Kansas anymore."

"Kansas?"

"Nothing," I say.

She looks to either side of me. "Who's Toto?"

"No one."

"I don't believe I have a cat named Toto."

"Probably not."

I follow her and six cats down a hallway. The smell of cat urine makes me want to gag. We go into a living room that is furnished with what had once been good pieces but are now in various states of devastation. There are other cats in the room, too many to count quickly. I have to ask.

"How many cats do you have, Ms. Collins?"

"Oh, dear," she says, and I realize this phrase is routine. "So many darlings, so many."

It is clear she has no idea how many she has.

She strokes the orange cat, then lets it jump from her arms. "Gus," she says.

"Gus?" The cat clamor is louder here and I have to shout.

"His name," she explains, pointing at the retreating animal. "They're so dependent, so needy, sometimes I don't know what I'm going to do. You can't love them all the same no matter what anyone says. Some are simply nicer than others. Take Taj, for instance. She's grumpy most of the time and it's hard to show her love and compassion. On the other hand, Phoebe's a delight. Well, you know what I mean, don't you, dear?"

"Absolutely," I say seriously.

"And then there's Sontag and Annie, who won't have anything to do with the others. Very snooty, those two. Sit down, if you can find a place." She leaks a smile.

Gingerly, I sit on the edge of the ravaged couch. Ms. Collins continues to stand, now holding an all-black cat.

"This is Wally."

I nod. "Ms. Collins, when did . . ."

"Call me Win. It's Winifred but everyone calls me Win. My parents called me Fred but I didn't like that." She wrinkles her nose as if the name Fred is equivalent to the odor in the house.

"Win. Okay. When did you last see Sharon?"

"You know, it's funny that you ask. I haven't seen her for about five days. She's working on a picture, I think."

"Weren't you worried when she didn't come home?"

"Oh, no. We lead very separate lives. Often she'd stay out all night. But I have to admit she doesn't usually stay gone this long."

"How long have you two lived together?"

"Oh, dear. Quite a while. Eight years, perhaps."

"Do you by any chance have a photograph of Sharon?"

"Why would I have a picture of her? I hope you don't think we were, you know." The wrinkled nose again.

To start up or not? That's the question. Do I have to be a defender of the realm all the time? I decide to give this a pass unless there's another reference made.

"Surely she had pictures of herself. All actors do."

"Had?"

"I beg your pardon?"

"Had. You said 'had.'" Her faint blue eyes appear alarmed and when the cat jumps from her arms, her hands go immediately to her skimpy white hair, the tiny fingers twisting and turning as though she were trying to make curls.

"Yes," I say softly. "I think she's dead. I mean, it could be either she or her twin, we just don't know yet."

"Twin?"

"You didn't know Sharon was a twin?"

"Sharon isn't a twin. Oh, dear. No. Sharon's not a twin. Where did you get that idea?"

"It's been established, Ms. . . . uh, Win."

"Established? What does that mean? Established by whom?"

Win is agitated, speaking very quickly. I understand her confusion. It must be terrible to live with someone for eight years and not know a basic fact like this.

"Try not to be too upset. How did you meet Sharon?"

"I placed an ad. She answered it. But, oh dear, Sharon is not a twin."

"Perhaps you didn't know," I suggest gently.

"I know. She isn't a twin. Sharon's a triplet."

BREAK!

This cannot be real.

"A triplet?"

"Yes, dear. Sharon, Susie, and Samantha."

"Samantha," I say, stupefied. I feel like I'm trapped in a soap opera. "Does any of them have amnesia?"

"No, I don't think so," she answers seriously.

More than coincidences, more than mysteries, more than twins, I hate triplets!

"Is Samantha an actress, too?"

"I don't believe she is. Don't know what she does. Never met her."

"Then how do you know she exists?"

"The other girls, Susie and Sharon, talked about her. They told me."

"But they didn't say what she did or where she lived?"

"Not that I can remember."

"Win, could I please see Sharon's room?"

"Oh, dear. I don't know if I should do that. Privacy and all."

As delicately as I can, I explain the situation again. Reluctantly Win gives in and takes me down a long hallway to Sharon's room.

Inside the smell of cats is fainter. I notice bottles of deodorizer on many surfaces. It's a fairly spartan room; there's a bed with a tan chenille spread, a chest of drawers, a small bookcase, a night table, and a wooden chair with arms that doesn't look at all comfortable.

On the night table is an empty glass, a small enamel box with a picture of dancing pigs on the top, and a book, *Divine Victim*, by Mary Wings. There is a Three Lives bookmark at page 89. Was Sharon Sheedy a customer of the Js? I write this in a notebook.

Inside the box are earplugs rolled into neat little balls like wax marbles. It occurs to me that they might have fingerprints on them, should any be needed.

"I'd like to take these."

"Oh, dear. What will Sharon say when she comes back and finds them gone?"

Win, I think, is in deep denial. I'm not sure how I should play this. I can try to explain again or . . . it's going to be or.

"I'll take full responsibility, Win."

"But why would you want to take her earplugs? I hope she has more."

"I'm sure she does. Most people have more than one set of earplugs."

"What if she doesn't?"

"It'll be all right," I assure her.

She nods faintly and I'm not confident that she understands but I press on. "I'd like to look through her drawers."

Win's hand flies to her lips and muffles a gasp. This seems too much, dear, much too much."

I see that it's necessary to explain again. I add that I'm going to turn over any information or pertinent things I find to the police.

"Police?" She sounds alarmed.

"Yes. And I'm sure they'll be coming here as soon as . . . ."

"Coming here? Oh, dear. No. They can't come here. I won't let them in."

"Are you afraid of police, Win?"

She whispers as though there's someone else in the room. "Cats. The cats."

"Oh, they won't care about them. Really."

"People . . . horrible people have complained."

"Still, it's not something the police are interested in."

"Are you sure?"

"I am. Now may I look in the drawers?"

She gives me permission. I find what I'm looking for in the top drawer. The actor's photograph. A stack of them. As I flip through I see some have the Sheedy name, some Davey, some Rice. But they're all the same picture. I take the top one.

The rest of the drawers yield nothing special as they're filled with clothes. But it makes me wonder.

"Win, do you remember what Sharon was wearing the last time you saw her?"

"Oh, dear."

I realize that Win is the kind of person who probably doesn't notice much of anything about other humans.

"Maybe," she says, "if I looked in her closet."

"No. It's what she was wearing when she left here last."

"I know that," she says irritably. "If I look in there I might see what's *not* there, if you see what I mean?"

I do and I apologize for being patronizing.

We open the closet door. There's not a whole lot. Three dresses, two skirts, four blouses, a pair of jeans.

Win stares and stares as if reading the closet like another might read tea leaves or tarot cards. And then she claps her tiny hands together and turns to me, a smile cracking her tender face.

"A dress. Oh, dear. Yes, I'm sure. It's not here and I know that one."

"Which one?"

"The white one. White with lots of little blue horses on it."

My detective's heart does a double axel. I know I've seen a dress like this but where? It's not what the body in Cybill Shepherd's trailer was wearing. And then I remember.

The woman in the Dumpster on Eighth Avenue and Twelfth.

Chapter

Seventeen

RAFFAELLA'S, ON SEVENTH AVENUE across from Tenth Street and two blocks away from Three Lives, is a spot that's been around for a couple of years. There are times when I like a *real* coffeehouse, times when I can't face Ruby Packard's animosity, times when I can't stand to be in a cop hangout.

I'm meeting Cecchi there in five minutes. I walk up Seventh Avenue, still stunned by the encounter with Winifred Collins and the probability that the woman in the Dumpster is Sharon Sheedy, which might mean that the woman in Cybill's trailer is a person named Samantha and that Susie Mcmann is somewhere else.

Triplets. It boggles the mind.

So why did Rebecca Black tell me she had one child? Surely, even if no one else knew, she would. Unless . . .

" 'Scuse me, lady." He's dressed in a suit and tie, hair combed and clean. A map in hand, a tourist.

I stop.

"I wonder if you would mind giving me some directions?"

I smile. "If I can." I'm not great at this. I almost always have to ask Kip what subway to take and I never know north and south if I'm in an area I'm not familiar with.

"Can you tell me how to get to State Street?"

I feel very dumb. State Street? I've never heard of State Street but before I can tell him this he says:

"You know, 'State Street, that great street.'"

Uh-oh. "You mean in Chicago," I say, quick on the up-take.

"Yes. 'I saw a man there who danced with his wife,'" he sings, and smiles genuinely.

How can I tell this man he's in New York? I guess I can try.

"Sir, you're not in Chicago. You're in New York."

He looks at me with shock, and his mouth falls open. "You must be mistaken," he says.

"No. I've lived here for a very long time." I'm always amazed when they're clean, well dressed, and crazy.

"But last night I was in Chicago," he says forlornly.

And then it dawns on me. "Where were you in Chicago?"

"The Parker House. I'm here . . . there . . . here on business."

"Did you have a cocktail or anything like that?" I ask, as delicately as possible.

For a moment I can't tell whether he's offended or frightened.

"A cocktail," he repeats.

"Maybe a few," I suggest.

"Oh, my God," he says.

And I know for sure that he's been in a blackout. "Do you know what day this is?"

"Of course I do," he says indignantly, straightening his shoulders. "I don't know why you people in Chicago have to be so damn rude." He whips around me and marches down Seventh. This phenomenon is not strange to me because, although my mother has never ended up in another city, both in person and on the phone I've had conversations with her that she later can't recall. And I've come to understand that she's been in a blackout. I feel sad as I turn and watch the man walking away from me. I know he'll undoubtedly go through remorse and guilt and pledge never to drink again. But unless he gets help the next stop could be Rhode Island or the Fiji Islands.

When I get to Raffaella's, Cecchi is waiting at a window table.

"I ordered for you," he says as I sit down.

I pray he hasn't ordered me anything of the chocolate variety. I pray he has.

Streisand sings "Have I Stayed Too Long at the Fair?" in the background. One of my favorites. The waiter arrives and puts an iced cappuccino and a huge piece of chocolate cake in front of me. I look at it and then at Cecchi.

"What?" he says.

I've never seen a slice this large.

"It's after noon, what's wrong?"

He knows I try not to eat chocolate before midday. He's refused to take my cholesterol seriously. Perhaps this is my fault. I haven't made a big thing about it.

"You want *me* to eat it?" he asks, grinning.

"That's okay. I'll manage."

"So what's up?" he asks.

I hold up one hand as I take my first bite. Is this better than sex? I wonder. Close.

"Have you identified the woman in the Dumpster?" I ask him.

"No."

"I think *I* have."

He throws up his hands in amazement. He both likes and dislikes it when I get him information. "How can this be?"

"It's a fluke, Cecchi. I think her name was Sharon Sheedy. Just tell me one thing."

"Just tell her *one* thing. What?"

"Does she have a birthmark on the palm of her hand in the shape of a diamond?"

"You mean like the one on that actress, Shelley Mc-Cabe who was Susie Mcmann?"

"Yes, except I don't know if she was really Susie Mcmann."

"What?"

"You're not going to believe this, Cecchi."

"You're absolutely right. I'm not."

"First tell me about the birthmark on the Dumpster woman."

"None."

"Oh." I'm disappointed.

"None because there wasn't anything left of the palms. So I don't know."

"Do we know yet how long she'd been dead?" I ask.

"About three or four days."

"Funny nobody found her with all the homeless looking for stuff in garbage cans and Dumpsters."

"Oh, probably more than one of them found her before we did. Nobody wants to get involved, you know that. So tell me what it is I'm not going to believe that I *am* going to believe," he asks.

In between bites of cake I tell him what I know.

"Triplets?" he says. "This has got to be a joke."

"I wish it were. I mean, it seems like a soap or something."

"Like a De Palma movie. Twins I could almost live with."

"Me too."

"So how many names have we got?"

"Real names or actors' names?"

He groans.

I say, "The triplets seem to be Sharon, Susie, and Samantha."

"But why would the mother lie to you, say there was only one child?"

"I've thought about that and I think there's only one answer. That's what she believes."

"Huh?"

"Nicholas Parrish was and is a very rich man. He was the father and as we all know, money actually does talk. He was married, she was married, and at the time of the birth he didn't think he and Rebecca were going to get together. Anyway, back then they didn't always know ahead of time if a woman was going to have triplets or the baby's sex or anything. I don't know this for sure, but I bet Nick was at the hospital when the babies were born and I think he must've paid off some people to put two of the three up for adoption or something."

"Wait a minute. You mean this Parrish guy paid off a whole hospital?"

"Maybe. Or maybe just the nurses and doctor who were directly involved."

"And then what? They grew up and all ran into each other at a party?"

"I don't know about that part."

"So the mother, Rebecca, thinks she has one daughter?"

"Right."

"And two of these triplets have been murdered?"

"Yes."

"Why?"

"I have no idea."

"Great. We can't even be sure which ones are dead, right?"

"Right. Well, I think Sharon is the Dumpster woman."

"And Samantha?"

"Maybe the actress."

"So the one you were originally looking for, Susie, she's still alive?"

"I don't know. I think so. I'm on shaky ground here."

"Tell me about it, Laurano."

I reach into my purse, take out the box with the earplugs, and give it to Cecchi. "Fingerprints," I say, as he opens the pig box.

"Huh. Yeah, I guess there were fingers left intact. Nice

work. Give me the address of this woman, the Parrish guy, and anything else you have."

I do. We finish our coffee and cake, pay the check, and leave.

"Where you going now?" he asks me.

"To Three Lives," I say innocently.

"You can read when this mishmash is going on?"

I shrug.

"So let me know if you find out anything else. And thanks, Lauren.

"Right."

As he turns away I hear him murmuring "Triplets." I cross Seventh again and walk down Tenth on the north side of the street. At the corner of Waverly is the durable bar called Julius'. It's been in New York as long as I have and before. I used to go there for their hamburgers, which were served on toasted bread with lots of pickles. Basically it's a gay bar, a bastion of the old guard. It's the type of place that people in Iowa think of as the typical Village hangout: sawdust on the floor, a long wooden bar with a brass rail for one's feet, scarred tables, and a smell that's a cross between stale beer and male sweat. I glance in and even at this hour men are drinking. At night they are often three deep at the bar, along with tourists who wish to gawk and feel superior because they're heterosexual. I cross Tenth and go in the bookstore.

Jenny, Jill, Hilary, and Theo are in residence. Several customers float around while Jill keeps an eye on them. Thieves have managed to cut into their profits and Jill is furious. Her special interest has always been art books, but they can only afford to carry a third of what they used to because of the peddlers on Sixth Avenue who offer the same, stolen books for half the price.

I've long ago stopped buying from these people, even Richard, who claims his books are used. It's a terrible problem and one that the police do nothing about. The street booksellers enjoy complete freedom, it seems.

I exchange greetings with my friends, give Theo a pat.

Their staff has been cut down because of the economy but Hilary is still the manager for the Js. She's blond, and this year she's wearing her living sculpture, her hair, the same length on both sides. Blue eyes like pool water shine intelligently.

"Hi, Lauren," Hilary says from behind the high wooden counter.

I say hello. The place is, as always, cozy and wonderful and like no other bookstore in New York because Jenny designed and built it herself. You feel like you're in an English bookstore, which was exactly the effect she wanted.

"I read something you're going to love," Hilary says. "It's called *Was* by a man named Geoff Ryman and it's about . . . no, I'm not going to tell you. Trust me."

"I always do," I say. "Is it out?"

"Right here."

She hands me a trade paperback and I look it over, remember that when it was published in hardcover and was reviewed I added it to my must-read list. "Put it on my account," I say.

"You've got it. Want a bag?"

"No. Hil, do you know of a customer named Sharon Sheedy?"

"Oh, sure. Very nice woman."

Jenny comes over. "I don't like her."

"You don't like anybody," Hilary says.

"Not true. But Sheedy has the look of smell."

Hilary and I glance at each other. Jenny's always coming up with these interesting forms of description. It may be offbeat but I know immediately what she means.

"Kathleen Turner has it, right?" I say.

"Perfect," Jenny answers.

And then we get on a roll and before too long we're all laughing and screaming out names of regular people as well as celebrities who qualify.

"Mickey Rourke!"

"Jack Potter!" A customer.

"Ann Flocks!" A customer.

"Al D'Amato!"

"Norman Mailer!"

"Shelley Winters!"

Suddenly Jill shouts, "OH, NO YOU DON'T." And she's out the door. The rest of us, including Theo, who's barking, run outside and we watch Jill gallop down West Tenth Street toward Sixth Avenue in pursuit of a man in a raincoat that flaps behind him.

When the man hits the middle of the block near the Ninth Circle Bar he has to veer around a group of men.

Jill shouts, "Stop him! Thief!"

Jenny says, "Oh, God, it scares me to death when she does this."

The men look at Jill, then at the thief, and begin their own pursuit.

The thief trips in front of the big white brick building on the corner and flies headlong through the plate glass window. We can hear the crash of glass from where we are. Using the door, Jill disappears inside. While we stand in front of the bookstore a lot of shouting and yelling is heard. In a moment or two, Jill comes out of the door carrying an oversized book, which I guess is one of the expensive art editions.

As she walks back the owners of other stores, standing in their doorways, applaud her, as we all do.

"Goddamn bastard," she says, out of breath, red in the face but looking satisfied. "I hope he bleeds to death."

"You don't mean that," says a woman walking by.

"Oh, yes I do," Jill says. "This is a seventy-five-dollar book." She holds it up, still in its shrink-wrap and spotted with blood.

We all come back in, Theo barking.

"Theo, stop," Jenny says.

"I need a rag to wipe off the blood on this book."

The wail of an ambulance siren goes by. We glance out

and see one pull up where the thief dove through the window.

"He's never gonna do that again," Jill says proudly. Then softer, "There *was* an awful lot of blood. I think he might've cut an artery."

Jenny says, "What do you care? You hope he bleeds to death."

Jill looks slightly chagrined. "You ever hear of the heat of the moment?" With this her face drains of color and she turns white as a peeled mushroom. "You should've seen him. His whole leg. Jesus. I think I'm going to be sick."

"Put your head between your knees," Hilary instructs.

"That's for fainting," I say.

"Come on, Jill," Jenny says lovingly. "Come behind the counter and sit. Theo, stop." Jenny gently guides Jill to a chair. She still clutches the book.

We all crowd around the counter so we can see our hero, Jill. I for one am incredibly impressed at her speed, audacity, and persistence.

"Theo, stop."

Jill says, "The goon didn't want to give up the book. Can you believe that? There he is, lying on the floor in the lobby, blood pouring from his leg, and he's still gripping the book like it's his passport to heaven or something."

"Don't talk about it," Jenny says.

"Why not? I got the little bastard, didn't I?" Her green eyes light up, and her normal color comes creeping back along with a smile that rivals that of the Cheshire cat.

We all congratulate Jill, and Hilary finally gets her to let go of the book, which she takes away to clean.

I'm aware that their minds are on the attempted robbery and Jill's heroism, but I have a pressing need to know. I suppose one could call this a defect of character. "About Sharon Sheedy," I say.

"The look of smell," Jenny says automatically.

"Right. Aside from that?"

Hilary says, "Sometimes she has money and buys hardcovers, sometimes not, but then she buys paperbacks. She's a good customer, always buying something."

Why does this conversation seem familiar? "Has she been in recently?"

Jenny says, "I haven't seen her for a while."

"It's been over a week, which is odd," Hilary says. "She's a two-, three-times-a-week customer."

"Have any idea what the last book she bought was?" Now I remember why this feels like déjà vu. There's a scene in the movie very much like this.

"I do," Jill says, looking more like herself. "I recommended it and I think it was the last time she was in here, if you say you haven't seen her for more than a week, Hil."

"What was it?" I ask.

"Mary Wings's new book."

"*Divine Victim*," I say.

"Right."

"Did any of you ever notice anything unusual about her?"

They look at one another, shrug.

"Look of smell," Jenny says.

"Besides that, Jen."

Jill says, "She's a fairly ordinary-looking person, Lauren. Unless you mean the diamond-shaped birthmark on her hand."

Chapter

Eighteen

WITH JILL'S REVELATION that Sharon Sheedy did indeed have a diamond-shaped birthmark, it's pretty certain that she *is* the woman in the Dumpster.

I make a call to Cecchi with this information, then take an incredibly hot but uneventful subway ride uptown. *Uneventful* means that I was only hit up three times for money and that no one tried to grope or rob me. Why do I stay here? I definitely know I don't want to live upstate full-time. Or even part-time. Still, as much as I love my city it gets harder and harder to live here. I suppose that Kip and I need to explore alternatives.

Now I have to find out whether it's Samantha or Susie Mcmann who was the dead actress known as Shelley McCabe. Aside from the fact that I've been hired by Blackie to find her, or her murderer, I worry that if she's alive, her life is in danger. Somebody wants the Parrish triplets dead.

During the greedy eighties, the Upper West Side tried to duplicate SoHo. It didn't work. Some of the same shops are here but the ethos is different, as if only the facade has changed. The area used to be devoted to the old and now the young are here as well. Even so, it brings to mind prayer shawls and Kaopectate.

I've come up to this part of town to see the agent, Doyce Schroeder, who I hope will shed some new light on all of this.

Doyce's building is one of those potbellied apartment houses, and the nameplate shows he lives on the fourth floor. I push the bell. A faint voice responds and after I identify myself she buzzes me in. I climb the three sets of stairs and when I get to 4G, a chain is across the partially opened door.

I can see an eye and part of a nose. Is this any way to do business?

"How do I know you're who you say you are?" she asks.

I slip her my I.D.

She gives it back to me, closes the door, undoes the chain, opens up again, and lets me into a dark hallway. It takes about eight weeks for my eyes to adjust.

The woman is shorter than I am, which always makes me nervous because I'm so used to looking up. I guess that she's in her fifties. She wears a simple green sweater and skirt. Her face is long and thin; narrowed blue eyes give me the once-over.

I ask her her name.

"Marissa Anders."

"Beautiful name."

"Don't bother."

"Don't bother what?" I ask, genuinely confused.

"Trying to get around me. I'm immune to flattery so you might as well know that right off the bat."

"I meant it."

"Inconsequential. You want to see Mr. Schroeder?"

"Is he in?"

"Maybe yes, maybe no."

Why is it that I never come across *normal* secretaries? But what's normal, after all? "So which maybe is it?"

"You don't tell which one when you say 'maybe yes, maybe no.' That's the whole point. Didn't your mother ever say that to you? Mine did all the time. And then you had to wait to see which one it would be."

"Right. What do I have to do to find out?" I almost dread the answer.

"State your business."

"My business is with Mr. Schroeder."

She looks at me as though I haven't understood the protocol here. Perhaps I haven't.

"In other words," she says, "you won't tell me why you wish to see him?"

"That's right."

A slippery smile creases her face. "You're an actress, aren't you? Don't deny it. I know what I know. You think I've been his secretary for twenty years for nothing? Oh, I know all the tricks, sister. Telephone repair men, census takers, delivery boys and girls. Still, I have to admit this is a new one. Pretty good too. A detective. Probably would've gotten past most with that one."

"Why did you let me in if you think I'm not who I say I am?"

She sighs. "*He* insists. 'You never know,' he says. Follow me."

We walk down the dark hallway, which opens into a surprisingly light and cheerful living room that doubles as Ms. Anders's office. The walls are hung with photos of men and women I assume are Schroeder's clients. Glancing quickly, I don't recognize any of them.

"So you want to fill out a form and leave your pictures?" she asks.

"Ms. Anders, I'm not an actress. I'm a detective and I need to ask Mr. Schroeder some questions about a client."

"For real?"

"For real."

Anders ponders this. Finally, she says, "I'll see if he's in. Give me your card. And who do you want to see him about?"

"Susie Mcmann."

Anders raises her thin eyebrows. Then she slips sideways through a door. As I walk around the room, I carefully look at the black-and-white photos. Only two look vaguely familiar. They are both women.

There's something about the eyes of one, who appears to be in her thirties, that haunts me, as if I've seen them before. The other is younger but the photo is older, taken perhaps in the fifties. Could this be one of the triplets? She slightly resembles the picture of Sharon, but only slightly. Still, it's an old photo.

The fact that I can't identify any of these clients by name is odd, because I'm a movie buff and used to go to the theater all the time before tickets cost seven hundred dollars a seat.

Anders slithers back into the room.

I point to the younger of the two women in the pictures. "What's her name?"

"Allison Mayer."

"She looks familiar."

"Why not? She's an actress."

"But I don't know the name."

"So who are you, Pauline Kael?"

I ignore this. "It's an old picture, right?"

She glances up at it. "Now that you mention it, yeah, I guess it is. I don't know why we don't have an up-to-date."

I'm about to ask her the name of the other familiar-looking woman but she cuts me off.

"He says he'll see you."

"Good. Thank you."

"He'd see Godzilla," she mumbles, as she leads me to the door, knocks once, and opens it. I go in, she shuts the door behind me.

The room is an office and dominating it is a huge walnut library table that doubles for a desk. Schroeder's not behind it. When I look to my right I see him and almost gasp, but catch myself in time.

He sits in a wheelchair swathed in blankets, his head and arms the only parts of him showing. The arms are covered by a brown sweater but the hands are shriveled, the fingers attenuated. The face is what is so disquieting.

Because he's so clearly ill.

"I'm not gay," he says.

"I'm so sorry to hear that," I say. I can't help myself but I know why he's made this announcement before saying anything else like hello, and it irritates me even if he is sick.

"I didn't get it because I'm gay."

He's talking about AIDS. He knows he has that unmistakable wasting look of the disease and wants to set some sort of record straight with me, God knows why.

"Mr. Schroeder, I'm really sorry you're sick but I'm not interested in your sexual orientation."

"You met my wife, Marissa," he says, as if this is incontrovertible proof that he's heterosexual, which of course it's not.

"Yes, I met her."

"We've been married twenty-two years."

"Congratulations."

He squints at me through wireless glasses. Small tufts of hair sprout from his head like burgeoning weeds. There's no way to tell what he once looked like because now his features are exaggerated, his skin a grayish color. I think of Tom and what Kip and I have agreed to, then quickly expel it from my mind.

"I'm not a drug user either," he says.

"Did you share a shower in the military or something?" I know I shouldn't do this but his attitude is enraging.

"Military?"

"How did you get the disease? A blood transfusion?" I doubt this.

"No. A whore."

Is this supposed to make him more macho to me? Am

I to feel differently about him because this married man contracted AIDS having sex with a whore?

"Goddamn fucking bitch."

Mr. Schroeder takes no responsibility and I'm not at all surprised.

"I hope she's dead by now," he says, bitterly.

"She probably is."

"Good. Just as long as you know what's what."

"That you're not gay," I say.

"Right." He swipes at dry lips with the tip of his tongue.

Should I or shouldn't I? What's the point? This homophobe will be dead soon. My response is callous but the world is asking for it.

"Mr. Schroeder, I'd like to ask you some questions about a client, maybe more than one."

"Confidential," he says importantly.

"Susie Mcmann," I say.

"Yeah, she's my client. Didn't jump ship like a lot of them when this. . . ." He waves a puny hand over his body like a wand but nothing changes.

"You mean when your clients learned you were ill they went elsewhere?"

"I told them I wasn't gay."

"Perhaps that wasn't important to them."

"So what about Susie?" he asks.

"Do you happen to know where she is right now?"

He ignores this question and says, "I'm the one got them all together."

My detective's heart two-steps.

"What do you mean?"

"Amazing story. You wanna sit?"

He gestures toward another chair.

"You won't believe this," he says, and smiles like the flash of a scalpel.

"Try me." I *know* I'm going to believe it.

"When Susie came to me I almost fell over because I already had a client who looked just like her."

"Sharon Sheedy."

"Yeah." He sounds disappointed. You know the story, why bother me?"

"I don't know the story. I know they were sisters."

"Twins," he says. "Least that's what I thought at the time. But Susie says she doesn't have a twin. I take out my Sharon file and show her a picture. Susie goes all white, almost faints. Christ, I remember it like it was yesterday."

His eyes become flat and I know he's lost in the past. I wait.

"Time's a funny thing," he says.

"How so?"

"I spent a lot of my life wishing time away, thinking if I could get past this or that, then it'd be different. I kept waiting for my life to begin and now it's almost over. Thing I didn't know was that it *had* begun. Don't wish time away," he admonishes.

"I try not to," I say honestly.

"Good. Where were we?"

"Susie and Sharon."

"Oh, yeah. Well, I make a date for them to meet and when they see each other they know it's true. That they're twins. Except they're not." He raises his eyebrows as if to make what he's said a mystery. I decide to let him blow me away.

"They aren't twins?"

"Nope. Well, they think they are but then one night they find out different. They're in this restaurant when guess who comes flouncing in?"

"Who?"

"Another one. They're triplets."

I give an appropriate gasp.

"Yeah. I know. It sounds like a B movie or something, doesn't it?"

"Now that you mention it."

"But this one isn't an actress."

"Oh." I get a sinking feeling. That will mean that Susie is dead.

"At least she wasn't when they met her. She was a graphic designer or some such. But those girls talked her into coming to see me and she became an actress too. Funny thing was, this Samantha, she'd always wanted to be one, never had the guts before the other two got hold of her."

"How long ago was this?"

"Let's see, maybe eight, ten years ago."

"And are you telling me, Mr. Schroeder, that these women didn't know that they were triplets, all had names starting with *s,* and all became actresses?"

"Yes and no. They didn't know they were triplets, I'll get to that in a minute, and they didn't all have *s* names to start with except Susie, who became Shelley. I named Sharon but that was pure accident. Her real name was Helga Wertham. Now anybody'd know that wasn't a good name for an actress."

"And how'd you happen to name her Sharon Sheedy?"

"Nice ring to it, don't you think?"

I nod. "Did Susie tell you about Parrish?"

"Parrish? Who's Parrish?"

"I think he was the father of the triplets."

"Nah. The father's name was Burke. Susie figures out the whole thing. It seems their real father was somebody named Burke and he being a rich son of a bitch must have paid off hospital people and put Helga up for adoption. The same thing with Samantha, who was really named Nora Kassenbaum. When she became an actress she took her adoptive mother's maiden name, Wilson. Samantha Wilson. I gave her the Samantha and the girls thought it was fun that they all had *s* names."

I could be reeling but I'm not.

"I tried to get them some work as triplets but there wasn't any call for it. Not even a goddamn commercial."

"Do you know where any of them is now?"

"Sure. I still work for them."

"You have their home addresses?"

"Naturally. Still, that's confidential."

"Mr. Schroeder, two of the triplets have been murdered."

"Jesus God Almighty. Which two?"

"I'm not sure which two. I think Sharon and Samantha. You said you still work for them. Did you place any of them on a film recently?"

"Samantha. Shoots down the Village."

"Is the film called *I'll Be Leaving You Always?*"

"Yeah, that's right."

I'm relieved that Susie's not dead. I guess it's for Blackie's sake.

"Bound to happen," Schroeder says cavalierly.

"Excuse me?"

"A whole lot of money's involved. When there's a whole lot of money, murder doesn't come as a big surprise."

"Do you know who, when, where about the money?"

"Maybe."

Oh no. Does he want me to pay him? "What does *maybe* mean, Mr. Schroeder?"

"I've got a lot of hospital bills."

"I'm sure you do and I'm sorry about that but I can't offer you more than fifty."

"I'll take it," he says, holding out a trembling hand, palm up.

I give him the money, mentally noting to add this to Blackie's bill. "So, you were saying."

"What I know is the following: Susie was brought up by her father 'cause her mother ran off with Larry Burke. She didn't know she had these sisters but she did know that Burke, her real father, was rich, rich, rich. And that her mother, Harriet, lived with him."

Burke and Harriet? Who are these people? What about Parrish and Rebecca? Something is definitely not adding up here.

"Did she ever confront . . . Burke and Harriet?" I remember Parrish's saying Susie was an attractive young woman, then stumbling around as to how he'd known this.

"Sure. Susie went to see them on Central Park West."

At least that fits. For some reason Susie didn't want to use real names, tell Schroeder that Rebecca and Nicholas were her real parents.

"They told her everything they had would be hers someday."

"What about her sisters?"

"Susie didn't mention them to the Burkes. She told me she figured if the parents got rid of them at birth, well, then, that's how they wanted it."

"Why did she tell *you* all this?"

He looks at me as though I'm crazy. "An agent, at least *this* agent, is like a father to his clients. She knew I wouldn't tell the other two. *Entré nous,* you know?"

I don't correct him. "But didn't Sharon and Samantha have any desire to meet their real parents?"

"Susie told them they were dead."

Chapter

Nineteen

TO SAY THAT I'M DISCONCERTED by this news is
an understatement. The facts that Susie told her sisters
that their parents were other people and that they were
dead, that now both of these women have been murdered, and that Susie had been promised the inheritance
lead me to the worst conclusion. Susie Mcmann Black
could be the killer.

Schroeder has given me an address for her. She lives
downtown on Broadway, between Washington Place and
Eighth Street.

But first I have a hair appointment. Yes, detectives get
their hair cut just like anyone else. When I get out of the
subway at Sheridan Square a man with a long beard says
to me:

"Spare some change so I can buy some pot."

I have to admit this is an original approach, but in
good conscience, I can't contribute to the buying of
drugs.

I avoid Greenwich Avenue whenever I can because it
makes me think of Megan. But Rose and Margie have
opened their own shop here, so what can I do?

The XLS Salon is on the second floor above an ever-
changing store. At the moment it's a framing shop. Rose is

the only one who can cut my hair the way I like it. Finding the right haircutter is like finding the right therapist.

When I enter the shop Rose and Margie shout hello to me. They are both from Puerto Rico but have lived here for quite some time. Rose met Margie when she was her student in hairdressing school. They were both adults, although Margie is the younger of the two. Rose was divorced and thought she was straight until Margie stole her heart. I know the whole story of their courtship and lots of other stuff. They've gone from being owners, to working for others, and now back to owning.

The place is one big room lined with mirrors, the usual hairdresser chairs, heat lamps for perms, and lots of plants.

Margie, who is the shorter of the two, has a square build, a pretty face with rich brown eyes, and a curly cap of black hair. She always sparkles, no matter what is going on.

"How's Keep?" Margie asks.

"Kip's fine."

"Give her my love."

"I will."

I go off to have my hair washed by one of the workers. I liked it better when Rose washed my hair but it wouldn't be seemly for her to do it now. When this is over, the young woman wraps my hair in a towel and leads me to Rose's station.

"How are you, Lauren?" Rose asks.

I tell her I'm fine. She's in her fifties and is a grandmother who is going through change of life. She also has black curly hair but highlights what I suspect is the gray. Both she and Margie are on perpetual diets and there's always some new crisis going on in their lives.

"How's Kip?"

"She's fine." They both adore Kip.

She leans down and whispers in my ear. "What's she like?"

"Kip?"

"Cybill Shepherd."

"Why are you whispering?"

"Well," she says, looking at me in the mirror, "you know."

Rose whispers a lot. I think it comes from years and years of keeping secrets from others as well as herself.

"She's very nice. Down-to-earth," I tell her.

"Oh, I just love her. Me and Margie, how we loved that *Moonlighter*. And I heard about the murder," she whispers. "Did you know her, Lauren?"

"No."

"We did."

I grab her hand just as she's about to take her first snip. "You knew Samantha Wilson?"

"All of them, the triples. They all came to Rose. One thing, Lauren. Are the other two twins now?"

I feel terrible having to tell her. "Two of them have been murdered."

She gasps, puts her hand over her face. "No," she mumbles. Which ones?"

"Sharon and Samantha, I think."

"Oh my God. Margie, come here," she calls.

Margie comes over and Rose tells her. Margie's brown eyes grow round and wide, like a cartoon. "I knew it," she says.

"Knew what?" Rose and I ask in unison.

"I know what I know," she says cryptically.

Rose and I glance at each other in the mirror. She gives me a look as if to say *What can you expect from this one*.

"Margie, don't be that way. You know something, you tell. Lauren is a dick."

"I thought she was a dyke," Margie says, and laughs hysterically.

"Both," Rose says.

"Right," I concur. "So you know something, Margie?"

"Susie, she didn't like the other ones. She told me they were . . . inferior actresses, is how she put it."

My detective's heart is sinking. I don't want Susie to be the killer. I don't want to have to report this to Boston Blackie. Not that I think anyone would kill somebody for lack of talent. Well, come to think of it . . . no, it would be the other way around.

"What else did she say?" I ask.

"About what?" Margie stuffs a cigarette between her lips.

"Not in here," Rose says, holding up one finger.

"I'm not lighting it."

"Don'."

"I'm not."

"Well, don'."

I continue. "Margie, did Susie say anything else to you about . . . well, about the other two?"

"Only thing she says is that someday soon she's gonna go to Paris, France."

"Why?"

"'Cause, she says, someday she's gonna be real rich."

Oh God. "Did she tell you how?"

"Yup. She says she has very rich parents and she gonna inherit."

Rose asks my next question. "And what about Sharon and Samantha."

"Nope."

"What does *nope* mean?"

"Nope means nope. The other two wouldn't be gettin' any."

"She tell you why?"

"She just grins when I ask. Hey, maybe she killed them both."

"Don say that, Margie."

Margie shrugs.

"She's so bad," Rose says to me about her partner. "She says anything she wants, anytime, to anyone." It's as though she's speaking about a child.

"Who knows, Rose. Anything's possible, right, Lauren?"

"Yeah, anything," I say. Hairdressers are known for their wagging tongues and I wonder about this with a question. "You never mentioned this to Sharon or Samantha?"

"Mention which?" Margie asks.

"Anything Susie said."

"No, I never did. You wanna know why?"

"Yes."

"Because the other two, they never speak of the parents. In fac', they say their parents are dead, so I know somethin' out of the extraordinary's goin' on and I don' wanna create dilapidation in their relationships."

Rose says, slightly annoyed, "Why didn't you ever tell me?"

"I don' know." Margie's unlit cigarette bobs in her mouth and she looks genuinely puzzled. Then she grins sheepishly. "I think I forgot."

"How could you forget such an important thing, Margie?" Rose asks.

"I got other things on my mind more fabulous."

"Like what?"

"Like you," Margie says and gives her a seductive look, a fast peck on the cheek and wanders off.

I feel lousy with this new information about Susie, but for the moment there's nothing I can do except to settle in to have my hair cut.

The day grows hotter as I walk from Greenwich to Sixth Avenue. I wish I were on the beach. I hope I can talk Kip into going to the North Fork in August. I have to work on this.

Peddlers, from Eighth Street to as far as the eye can see, are doing a smashing business. I don't get it. You'd think that the Dalton's people would object to someone selling brand-new books in front of their store that were probably stolen from them. But nothing is ever done about it.

Outside Blockbuster Video there are two tables with books that have just come out. I know I shouldn't. I don't have the time. I won't get an honest answer anyway, so what's the point? It's an exercise in futility. Why bother?

"Excuse me," I say to the woman behind the card table.

"Yes?"

"Where did you get these books?"

"Say what?" She looks at me as if I've asked her something about quantum physics.

"These are all *new* hardcovers. Some of them are barely out. Where'd you get them?" Why do I do this?

"Let's see now, you want to know where I get these hardcover books, that it?"

I nod.

She takes a long brown cigarette from a pack in the pocket of her turquoise T-shirt, taps it on the table, tucks it between her lips, lights it with a kitchen match she's ignited on a bright red nail, inhales deeply, blows smoke into the air above her.

"So," she says, "you want to know where I get these books. Well, I'll tell you. I got this friend who got this friend who got this friend who knows a man who knows a man. Follow?"

"Sure."

"And that man, that last one I mentioned, *that* man, he knows a woman who knows a woman who knows . . ."

"Never mind," I say.

"No, you wait. You want to know, I'm trying to tell you."

"I changed my mind." All I want now is to get away from her but she reaches out and clamps her hand around my bare arm, the nails digging in like Lilliputian lances.

"Yeah, but *I* didn't. Change my mind, that is. I decided to give you an answer and I'm giving it."

I hear her and continue to feel the nails in my arm.

"So, as I was sayin' . . ."

I can't believe it but she starts the whole thing over again from the first friend. Finally she's back to where I'd cut her off.

". . . a woman who knows a child. That child's got a good friend who works in a warehouse. A *book* warehouse. And *that* friend, in the warehouse, he sells the books to the child, who . . ."

And she goes all the way through the list again but backwards. I'm not positive, because I can't actually remember, but I think it's exact. When she's finished she smiles at me angelically.

"Thank you," I say.

"Anytime." She lets me go.

We both know I won't ever ask any of these people again. I leave and I hear her giggling behind me when I turn east on Washington Place. As I walk I find that I'm getting angrier and angrier.

Okay, so I've been humiliated by a thief.

Big deal.

So why am I so mad?

Because I did a stupid thing. And she bested me.

The fountain in Washington Square Park spurts as if it has the hiccups. A few kids run under the wispy water and many people sit around the edge, sunning themselves, drying out, generally taking it easy. This makes me madder.

Question: Why don't these people have to work?

Answer: Because they're smarter than I am.

Now I'm really pissed off. By the time I hit Washington Place and Broadway, I feel like I could tear the head off someone. So what do I do? I act out, as Kip would say.

A few feet down from Shakespeare's Bookstore there's a table of three-card monte. A big man stands behind it giving his spiel, moving the cards around. In front of the table are a number of people: a woman, two men, and a boy about seventeen who's the mark. He's about to place a hundred-dollar bet.

"Don't do it," I yell to the boy. No one pays me any attention, particularly the boy, so I start uptown on Broadway. When I look back over my shoulder, I see the boy reaching out, ready to part with his money, and I can't stand it. I turn around. A large man blocks my way.

"Why don't you just mosey on the way you was goin'," he says to me.

"What?"

"Mosey on the way you was goin'."

"What are you talking about?"

"You know what I'm talkin' 'bout."

This man has a shiny bald head, bushy eyebrows, and reddish skin, as if he forgot to turn off the sunlamp. He wears a tank top and the muscles in his arms are nasty-looking. But do I stop? No. I somehow get past him and back to the table, where I shout again to the boy to save his money.

This time, a woman turns around and grabs me by my collar, twists, puts her black face right into mine. "Get the fuck outta here, babe, 'fore you sorry."

"Let go of me," I say.

"Go." She lets me loose, backs off slightly.

My fury mounts and I touch the dealer's arm.

He whirls on me.

"Yo, don't you go touching me."

I point to the woman. "She touched me," I say lamely.

"You better get 'cause nobody touches me."

I notice that the boy has withdrawn his money at the same time the dealer does. "Just a minute, son, pay no attention to this crazy."

The boy looks at me, his billed cap on backwards. I shake my head no. The dealer speaks low and his spittle sprays me.

"You wanna live, stupid, you turn around and start up this street."

I believe him and I do. But I'm so angry I start looking for a cop. Do I find one? Of course not. At Astor Place, blocks past where I want to go, I see a phone and decide to call the police but I don't have any change. And then I start to calm down.

Am I crazy?

These are dangerous people. After everything that's been written and said about this monte scam, who am I to try to save that boy his cash?

I AM A NUTCASE.

Whoa. Okay. I cool down. At least inside. I'm dripping wet from anger and the heat of the day. I stop, stand still, look around. This part of Broadway is a mess. In between the Wiz, McDonald's, other fast-food joints, Reeboks, et cetera, are apartment buildings. Many of them co-ops. People have paid good money to be on this noisy, disordered street.

Seven twenty-two is the address I look for. I find it wedged between two stores. It's a narrow building with eight floors. I look at the list of names. And there it is: Susie Mcmann.

Simple as that.

Chapter

Twenty

WITH NO REAL HOPE I push the fifth-floor bell. Almost immediately there's a response. From the speaker a woman's voice asks who it is and I give her my I.D.

She rings me in.

The lobby is small. Beside the mailboxes, there is one elevator that waits on this floor. I jab the black button. Nothing happens. A moment later it moves upward until it stops at five. I can hear the door open, close, and then start down. When I check out the elevator button again I notice that there is a lock under it. Tight security in this building. Usually you can get on in the lobby and then the tenant rings you up. Here, there is a different method.

The elevator opens and I get in. I don't bother to push five because I know it's controlled from above. Slowly, it rises. I feel distinct excitement to realize that I'm finally going to meet Susie, the person whom I was hired to find.

She's standing there when the doors open. There's no mistaking her, because she looks like her sisters, and even resembles the old picture of her that Blackie showed me.

"I've been wondering when someone would come," she says in a mellifluous voice. "But of course I expected the regular police."

"Why haven't you contacted *them?*"

Susie smiles charmingly. "Why make it easy?"

After this interview I intend to call Cecchi with Susie's address. I step off the elevator into a hall.

"How do you know about it?" I ask.

"Winifred Collins, for one. And the murder on the movie set has been in all the papers. Think I don't know my sister's stage name? I guess I'm next."

"You don't sound as if you much care."

"Want to come in?"

I follow her to the right. She wears a peach-colored Gap pocket T-shirt and lightweight tan slacks. Although she's in good shape she can't hide the slight middle-aged spread.

Susie opens the door to her apartment. The living room is large and airy. Green plants are everywhere, set off by white furniture. She steers me toward a sailcloth-covered couch.

"Want something to drink?"

I decline and she shrugs, sits in a white wing chair, a huge black marble table between us. Magazines are fanned so that you can see each name, and a Sue Dunlap novel has a bookmark near the middle. I wonder if she bought it at the Js.

"You read her?" Susie asks, noticing me staring at the book.

"Matter of fact, I do. And so does President Clinton."

"Yeah, that's what made me try her. She's good. You're a detective and you like reading mysteries?"

"I like reading anything."

She smiles. "Me too. Used to read the back of cereal boxes when I was little. Raised by a father who thought reading was similar to devil worshipping."

"And your mother?"

Her eyes become sad and she ignores my question. "When I got to school you couldn't stop me. I was always bringing books home from the library. I think reading saved me."

"Saved you from what?"

"A mental death . . . no, a spiritual death."

"How so?"

Susie cocks her head to one side, stares at me. "C'mon. You're a detective, you probably know all about me."

There's no point in equivocating. "I know some things about you, not everything."

"But you know about my background, right?"

"Some. I don't know anything about your father."

"Real or step-?" she asks.

"Step-." I realize my lack of knowledge about this man for the first time. "But you thought he was your real father, didn't you?"

"There was always talk. In a small town you eventually hear everything. But my stepfather raised me, the bastard."

"Why do you call him that?"

"Because that's what William Mcmann was. Oh, he didn't do anything to me like incest or any of that. He was just about the nastiest, meanest man you'd ever want to meet."

"Why'd you keep his name?" I ask.

"What name should I have used, Parrish?"

I let this pass for the moment.

"I certainly wasn't going to use Black and mostly I've used my different acting names. But hell, Mcmann is my legal name. I'll tell you what was wrong with Mcmann, the same thing that's screwed up the world forever. Religion. William Mcmann was *religious*." She rolls her eyes heavenward.

"I think I know what you mean."

"You probably do. These real religious types base their lives on hating. Not all, of course. Lots of good people are religious. And then there are the ones like Mcmann. What a piece of work he was. Anybody or anything different from him was wrong. He was sort of early Pat Buchanan."

We both laugh.

"Why am I laughing?" I say. "Buchanan scares me to death."

"Because you're a lesbian?"

This jolts me momentarily since I haven't told her and I don't think I look stereotypical. "Yes. Do you care?"

"That you're a lesbian? No. Should I?"

"No. But some people do."

"Idiots."

"How about Sharon and Samantha? Would they've cared?"

"No. At least I don't think so. Anyway, sometimes I wondered what was going on with Sharon and Winifred. On the other hand, the pussies they were interested in seemed to have four legs." She roars with laughter.

I'm slightly shocked by this vulgarity and I wonder if I'm a prude at heart or simply delicate. I try to imagine someone describing me as delicate and fail. Which means I'm probably a prude. Is this being like Buchanan?

Susie reads me. "You think that's crude, huh?"

"No, of course not, I . . ."

"Sure you do. It is. Sometimes something comes over me and I blurt out stuff like that. I can't imagine where I got it from. Certainly not from William Mcmann."

"Maybe your *older* sister," I try.

"What older sister?"

"Almay."

"Who?"

"There's a person in Stone Ridge who says she's your sister, Almay Mcmann."

"I never heard of her."

"I thought you'd say that." I tell her about my meeting with the specious Almay.

"Somebody was pulling your leg."

"Clearly. But why?"

"You're the detective," Susie says as though she's the first to make this comment.

"I'm beginning to think this impersonator was not looking out for your best interests."

"Sounds like a safe bet to me," Susie says.

"Who *actually* knew, in the Ulster County area, that you were triplets?"

"Well, my father and the hospital personnel he paid off at the time of our birth."

"How could he keep a whole hospital quiet?"

"He was a rich and powerful man and it only involved the delivery-room people, from what I understand."

"Did Parrish tell you this?"

"Yes."

"And Rebecca . . . your mother, didn't she know that she gave birth to triplets?"

"In a word, no."

"He kept the birth of two other children from her?" I find this astonishing and manipulative.

"Rich and powerful," she says again with a trace of scorn. "And my father and I couldn't see much point in telling her at this late date."

"Especially since she might want to see them and you'd told Sharon and Samantha they had different parents who were dead," I say.

"Yes, that, and the fact that I never let on to him that we three met."

"Was it because of the money, your inheritance, that you kept them from knowing one another?"

"Why not?" she asks defensively.

If Parrish didn't know, why would Susie have to kill her sisters? For a moment I think this takes Susie off the hook, but then I realize leaving them alive could be risky. But Susie said she feared for her own life.

"Who stands to gain if you die?" I ask her.

"Don't know how the will's made out."

I remember Rebecca's saying to Nicholas that they'd have someone to leave their money to when I brought up Blackie. "What was it like to meet your mother after all those years?"

"I haven't. My father and I have kept my existence from my mother."

I'm stunned. "You mean you meet with your father secretly?"

"Yes. It's a very clandestine relationship," she mocks me. "The truth is, I've only seen *him* once."

"Why?"

Susie rises, walks to a window. With her back to me she says, "I guess I can't forgive him for farming out my sisters. And I can't forgive her either, that's why I didn't want to see her."

"Forgive her for what?"

She turns around. "Leaving me with Mcmann. If she'd hadn't left me with Mcmann I never would've married Harold."

"So when Doyce brought you together with your sisters you knew about them from Parrish."

"That's right."

"But you told your sisters your parents were dead?"

"Yes."

"They believed you?"

"Why not?" She shrugs.

"Is it possible that one or both found out you were lying?"

"I don't see how. I told them we were born in Connecticut and that we were all given up for adoption. Our real name was Burke, mother Harriet, father Larry, that I'd traced them and they were dead. Killed in an auto accident."

"What about your son?" I spring on her. "Where is he now?"

"Why don't *you* tell *me?*"

Smart cookie. "What makes you think I can?"

"A process of elimination. If Harold's still alive I don't think he'd bother hiring you, my parents didn't hire you, and. . . ."

"I thought you'd only seen your father once."

"That's right. I talked to Nicholas on the phone."

"Why?"

"He called me to tell me about your visit. He was concerned about me."

"Is that all he told you, that I'd come here asking questions about you?"

"Yeah. He said he didn't know who hired you. I knew even then but I didn't say anything to him. He also said you'd offered to see if their grandson would meet them. Franklin would be a grown man by now so it has to be him. Guess you think I'm scum abandoning him like that."

"I try not to make judgments."

"*Try?*"

"It's not always possible," I admit.

"I guess I could say you had to be there. I had to get out and I knew I couldn't take care of the kid on my own. As rotten as Harold was to me he loved that kid. I thought he'd do better with him."

"Just as your mother thought about leaving you with William Mcmann?"

She looks at me, presses her lips together. "That's lousy."

"I'm sorry. I didn't mean it to be. I thought it was something you hadn't given any consideration, and maybe you could understand her better if you made the analogy."

"*You* made the analogy."

I sigh because she's right.

"Let's get back to your sisters. What if somehow, recently, the other two discovered the lie, found out their parents were alive *and* wealthy. Then what?"

"No way, José. I hate to say this about my own flesh and blood but the girls weren't that bright, know what I mean?"

"I hear you," I say.

"Trust me. Samantha was brought up by morons and Shelley by cretins. And wouldn't you know it, they both grew up in New Jersey."

I decide not to tell her that that's where I'm from. I have my own reasons for not liking N.J. but I feel defensive when someone else denigrates the state. So I play dumb.

"What's that supposed to mean? The New Jersey part."

"You ever been there?"

"As a matter of fact, I have. There are a lot of nice, smart people from Jersey." I can't believe I'm defending N.J.

"Name one."

"Thomas Edison."

"An aberration," she asserts.

"What's this problem you have about New Jersey?" If Kip could hear this she'd be hysterical.

"It's not a problem . . . I just hate that state."

"Why?"

"You ever smell it?"

"Never mind," I say, realizing her feelings about N.J. are irrational. "You don't seem very broken up over their deaths."

"So now you're the grief guru?"

She's right. Everyone mourns in different ways. I think immediately of Megan. There's no reason that Susie has to grieve the way I do and I have no idea what she feels inside. Perhaps this carapace of indifference is a defense.

"How *do* you feel about their murders?"

"Bad."

"Did you kill them?"

"Yes."

"What?"

"Gotcha," she says, laughing.

"I don't think this is funny."

"Truth is, I don't either. But you have to admit, that's a stupid question."

"No, I don't have to admit it," I say. "It's asked all the time. In fact, it's incumbent upon me to ask it."

"Maybe, but it's still stupid. If I *did* kill them, would I tell you?"

"You might."

"You've seen too many movies," she says, and laughs

again. "I told you I'm scared. I think I could be next. Fact is, I'm *sure* I'm next."

"Why?"

"Why would anyone want to kill Samantha and Shelley and not kill me?"

"They wouldn't."

"Right. Hey, you're not a bad dick after all."

"Do you think it's possible that someone found out who you all were and is trying to get rid of you because he or she will inherit if you're all dead?"

"In a word, yes."

"So who would that be?"

"My older sister Almay?"

"You said you had no older sister."

"Maybe I'm wrong," she says.

"You're not. I've checked."

"I don't get it. Why would someone pretend to be my sister, or the daughter of my mother, for that matter?"

"I'm not sure but I'm beginning to think the Almay person might be the key."

"To what?"

"The murder of your sisters. It was Betty Rosner in your car when it crashed, wasn't it?"

"That's right," she says, only mildly surprised that I know. "She borrowed it that night to go see Bud Mcmann, her lover. Bud was married but he and Betty were crazy for each other that summer. On the way to meet him she had the accident. They all thought it was me in there so I figured it was a good time to blow Stone Ridge."

"Bud Mcmann knew it wasn't you."

"Guess so."

"Where were you?"

"I was having my own rendezvous. Betty'd dropped me off right before it happened."

"You mean you were having a love affair too?"

She nods. "We made plans to meet here in New York City, then go on to Hollywood. Never showed up. Guess it was too hard, too scary to leave the family."

"Who was he?"

"She." Susie smiles. "Anne Mcmann."

Chapter

Twenty-one

AFTER I CALL CECCHI with Susie's address, I walk home, running over in my mind what Susie has told me about everyone, especially her affair with Anne Mcmann. I can understand why Anne lied about knowing Susie; she obviously is still terrified that her affair with another woman might be exposed. Did Bud know about Susie and Anne? If he did he gave no indication of it to me. But why would he? I can't believe it but I'm going to have to make another trip upstate. A day trip. Alone this time.

Now that I've found Susie I should tell Boston Blackie. He's my employer and I've done my job. On the other hand, he's a likely suspect. If the triplets were dead, wouldn't he be next in line to inherit? But how would he know about the triplets?

Will Susie tell her son that she's a lesbian? If so, how will he respond? I can't imagine him taking it in stride. A tough little guy like Blackie will probably be horrified. Still, you never know. He might even be a closet liberal.

When I turn into my street I see that there are no trailers or movie people in place and remember that they're shooting on St. Luke's Place this afternoon. I feel relief that they're gone, as if my home has been returned to me.

Kip is reading the paper when I come into the kitchen. I pray there won't be a rant. As the ethnic cleansing continues she heats up.

"Want to guess what's on *Oprah* today?" she asks.

"I'm sure in my wildest I couldn't."

"Premature Oedipus complex and the afterlife damage."

"You're not serious? What does that even mean?"

"No. I'm not serious." She laughs. "Gotcha."

"Actually, you didn't."

"Sure I did."

I look at her. "Kip, you only *get* a person when they fall for it. I didn't."

"Don't be so literal."

"That's not being literal. Well, it is, but that's what gotcha means." Suddenly, the way Susie said 'Gotcha' after I asked whether she'd killed her sisters resonates. "Isn't that what gotcha means?"

"What are you talking about?"

"If I asked you if you'd done something that you'd done and you answered yes and I believed you, would that be a gotcha? A real gotcha is when one person tells the other something that's *not* true and the other one falls for it, right? I mean, if you'd really done it, admitted it, and then said 'Gotcha,' that would be a way of confusing the questioner, wouldn't it?"

"I have no idea what you're talking about."

Neither do I but Susie's gotcha bothers me. It was inauthentic in some way. "You see, your gotcha was . . ."

"Oh, please, Lauren."

Uh-oh. What's this about? "Something wrong?"

"Why?" she asks innocently.

"*Why?* Because of the way you just said 'Oh, please, Lauren,' that's why."

"Don't start."

"Don't start what?"

"Hearing things," she says.

"You don't know how you said it."

"Here we go. I say it one way, you hear it another."

"I didn't hear it another," I say.

Kip says, "This always happens. We mishear and then we're off to the races."

It's true that this happens a lot. Both ways. We misinterpret a tone or an inflection but today, even though I might have overdone the gotcha thing, I'm convinced that there really is something else going on. "So nothing's bothering you?"

"Nope," she says in a false spirited way.

Now I know I'm in for it. But I honestly can't think why. I'll let it go until she's ready to talk . . . surely I've learned this in all these years. "What is it?" I can't stop. "What did I do?"

"It's more like what you *don't* do," she says sotto voce.

"What don't I do?"

She puts down the paper. "Have you any idea what our health insurance is going up to?"

MONEY!!!

I should've known. This is a real issue between us although most of the time we can deal with it. The simple fact of the matter is that Kip has money and I don't. Nothing new. We can go along for ages without it interfering in our lives and then, suddenly, something gets to her. Today it's health insurance.

"Because we're self-employed it's going to cost us about eight thousand dollars a year . . . apiece. That's sixteen thousand a year, Lauren."

"I can add."

"It's not funny."

"I'm not laughing."

"Do you have any idea what the monthly expenses are? Just the mortgage on this house alone is enough to make one shudder."

"Kip, you wanted to buy this house. You knew I couldn't afford it. I give you what I can." I try to keep my voice even.

"Has it ever occurred to you that you might get a *real* job?"

"As what?"

"I don't know. Didn't you learn anything in college?"

"That's so ridiculous. I'm forty-five years old, who the hell is going to hire me?"

"Why can't you get a job in publishing? You were an English major."

"First, at my age no one is going to hire me at an entry-level position, and second, don't you think there are loads of people out there better qualified than I am? And third, I'm a detective, a private investigator. That's what I do, Kip."

"And you make very little money at it."

"Sometimes. Some years, that's true. But I do other things."

"Like what?"

"Like everything around this house."

"Oh, really. May I remind you we have a maid."

"With the exception of cleaning, I do the laundry, the food shopping, most of the cooking, make phone calls dealing with things like insurance rates or IRS stuff, get plumbers or electricians, just generally everything, Kip. What do you do?"

"Pay."

It's so rotten I can't think of anything to say. And then I do. "If we were heterosexuals, would we be having this conversation?"

"We're not and I don't know."

"It's not like I lie around reading and eating bonbons all day. I do my best when it comes to making money. I'll never make as much as you and that's something you knew when we got together. In fact, Kip, you were the one who suggested I become a P.I."

"I had no idea then it would be like this."

"Like what?"

"Like me paying for everything."

"Kip, that isn't even true. You paid for the house and it's *your* house, as you take every opportunity to tell me and . . ."

"When do I do that?"

"How about when we're having a fight and you say 'Get the hell out of *my* house'?"

"You know I don't mean it," she says.

"How do you think it makes me feel?"

"You should be used to it by now."

"I'm not." Nothing novel is going on here. These wrangles happen at least four or five times a year, and they always make me feel like hell. "Kip, if there was something else I could do for income, I'd do it. But, what do you want me to do, work at McDonald's?"

"You're overqualified and besides the salary's too little."

"Exactly. I pay for half the phone and lights and . . ."

"How can you possibly know what you pay for?"

"It was your idea that we put our money together," I counter.

"Actually, it was William's idea."

"And you thought it was a good one." We were married eight years at the time and he pointed out that it looked like we were in for the long haul, so why have separate accounts, split the bills?

"Well, maybe it wasn't such a great idea," Kip says crisply.

"You mean you want to separate our money again? Now? We're going to be together fourteen years in the fall."

"I think you should do something to supplement your income."

"Like what?"

"That's not my problem, Lauren."

I hate her guts. I get up, start for the door.

"I suppose now you're going out for a doughnut or something?"

"That's not your problem, Kip."

"You're right. If you want to clog up your arteries and die, it's *your* problem." Suddenly she puts her head on her arms on the table and sobs.

Kip doesn't use ploys like this. She's not manipulative this way. I take only a second to go to her.

"What?"

She mumbles something into her arms.

I kneel and turn her toward me, put my arms around her. Although I'm still hurt and angry, I know that something bad must have happened. "Tell me," I urge.

"Tom," she wails.

"What about him?" I ask, frightened.

"Oh, Lauren," she says, looking at me. "Sam called this morning. They're flying in today to take him to the hospital here."

I feel like I'm falling. "What does it mean?"

"He's very bad. Sam said Tom wanted to come home."

As San Francisco has been home to Tom for a long time, wanting to be here must be a signal that Tom feels he's nearing the end. It's been three years since he was diagnosed, longer since he was infected. We've known this time was coming but you're never prepared.

"Oh, God, Kip." It's all I can say.

"I can't believe this is happening, Lauren."

Neither can I. "We'll get through it."

"Yes, but *he* won't. I'm so scared," Kip whispers.

"There's a lot to be scared about."

"What if, when he asks, we can't go through with it?"

"Do you want to call another meeting?"

"We've agreed. There wouldn't be any point," says Kip despondently.

"Nothing's written in stone. And Tom has always said that any of us could change our mind at any time."

"I've never believed that he really meant that," she says.

"I know." It's true. In the beginning, when the nine of

us had agreed to help Tom die, he'd told us he wouldn't hold anybody to the promise we were making then. And although none of us has expressed it, I'm sure none of us believed this was a real option, believed that Tom would expect any of us to back out. I'd always felt it was something Tom thought he *should* say.

"When are they arriving?" I ask.

She looks at her watch. "In about an hour. They're going straight to Sloan-Kettering."

"And then?" I know there's no way we'll be able to do this in a hospital.

"I suppose after tests and things, after there's nothing else they can do, they'll release him and they'll go to their apartment." She stands up, wipes her eyes on her sleeve. "I said we'd meet them at the hospital. Okay?"

"Of course."

The case will go on hold.

Tom looks terrible. This is the worst I've seen him. I feel if I touch him he'll break, or at the very least it will hurt him. His eyes are sunken, and appear huge in his ravaged face. Still, his sweetness shines through.

Sam, who stands on the other side of the bed, holding Tom's bony hand, looks almost as bad. But it's clear his appearance is not from the disease, but rather worry, fear, dread.

No one in authority has surfaced since Tom was admitted two hours before. It's typical and we're annoyed, but not surprised. We've all come to know hospitals well during the plague and agree that they might be all right to visit but you wouldn't want to stay there. Having learned that even tantrums get you nowhere, we will wait.

Sam says, "Do you want something to drink, Tom?"

"No, thanks." His voice has lost the euphony it once had and sounds high, tinny.

"I'd like a Coke," Sam says. "Want to come with me, Lauren?"

"Sure." I know at once that Sam needs a break and also wants to give brother and sister time alone.

We don't converse as we walk down the hall; our sneakered feet make a pocking sound on the tiled floor. Sam's shorn his long black hair and now has a crew cut. I wonder if he's done it to show oneness with Tom, whose hair has vanished during chemo, but don't feel right about asking. They're entitled to privacy about their personal choices; so little privacy in other areas is afforded them now.

On the elevator we continue our silence, listen to others.

He: Look, Bruce is going to get the house and there's nothing we can do about it.

She: It's not fair.

He: Since when does fair mean anything?

She: But you're the oldest son.

He: Bruce is the favorite.

She: That's not true.

He: Then why is Bruce getting the house?

She: He's the favorite.

He: It's not fair.

We reach our floor. When the elevator doors close, Sam and I look at each other and burst into laughter. He throws an arm around my shoulders and, still laughing, we enter the cafeteria. I pick up my brown tray (why are they always brown?) and go directly to the dessert section. Okay, so it's not Dean & Deluca, but I actually *like* hospital food. It's comforting to me in some way I've never understood. For instance, there's nothing quite like hospital meat loaf and mashed potatoes. The same can be said for tapioca, chocolate, and bread puddings, although it's no place to have cake of any variety. In deference to my cholesterol count I choose the tapioca, eschewing the other puddings. They're probably equally high but I feel that in a hospital I must make some obeisance in the direction of health. I also get a cup of coffee, pay the cashier, and find a table against the wall.

Sam joins me with chocolate pudding and a soda. Eyeing his pudding, I know I've made a horrible mistake. I'll have to live with it. I taste my tapioca: it's somewhere between paste I used in the first grade and marbles I played with in the third. In other words, excellent.

"How's the pudding?" I ask.

"Perfect." His blue eyes try to sparkle but lack legitimate luster.

"You look like hell," I say. We've never pulled any punches with each other.

"That's how I feel. Like I'm *in* hell. Is that awful to say?"

"No."

"You can't imagine what we've been through, Lauren."

It's true, I can't.

"A to U. Acupuncture to the urine of pregnant women."

"I thought that was for dieting," I say.

"It probably is. It sure isn't an **AIDS** cure. One crazy thing after another, the wait and then the disappointment. Talk about your roller coasters."

"And now?"

"And now it's a matter of getting the final and official 'nothing more we can do' prognosis." Sam slams against the chair back, his face parallel with the ceiling. "God, I'm a shit. I'm really a fucking shit," he declares.

I think I know but I ask anyway. "Why do you say that?"

He levels his gaze to mine. "I want it to be over. Not all the time," he adds hastily, "but a *lot,* Lauren, a whole goddamn lot."

"That doesn't make you a shit; that makes you human."

Quietly, he cries and tears course down his cheeks. I reach across the table, put my hand on his, wait.

Too soon he pulls out a handkerchief, wipes away the evidence. "This isn't the time or the place," he says stoically.

"I can't think of a better place than a hospital," I observe.

He gives me a wan smile. "It's the goodness of people, the understanding, that gets to me, I think."

Perhaps.

"And God I'm tired."

Yes.

"I love him very much. You know that."

"Of course."

"It's so awful to watch this once vibrant, active man just fade into, I don't know what, a zombie sometimes. So hard to know he's not interested in anything anymore but his disease. Sometimes I start to tell him something I've read in the paper about Clinton, Bosnia, or Dole and then I see him looking into the middle distance, realize he isn't listening, couldn't give a damn, and who can blame him? But it gets lonely.

"You remember Tom and movies? I don't think he's seen one all the way through in months. I go to the video store and spend hours looking for one I'm positive he won't be able to resist. Finally, I think I've found the perfect, perfect flick and twenty minutes into it, he goes to bed, or falls asleep, if he's already there. So I feel like this incredible failure. And I know it isn't about me, Lauren. I honestly know this. But everything gets so screwed up and things that never were important suddenly are and vice versa. Jesus, it's a mess. I'm a mess."

"Sam, why wouldn't you be? It's been going on for a long time and you're the one who sees it all, has to deal with everything."

"We saw *Angels in America* when it was there last year and afterwards we couldn't say a word to each other and we both knew why. He wondered if I wished I'd gotten out when he was diagnosed and I wondered if he knew what I was feeling. I don't wish I'd left, by the way."

"I know you don't."

"But I do want it to end, Lauren."

"It's going to."

"Yes. And then I'll want him back, regret all the time I wished him dead."

"Probably."

"Will you remind me of this conversation if I need you to?"

I promise.

"You don't think I'm a monster?"

"No, not at all. I think it's great that you can admit to it. Great that you could tell me."

He smiles. "Funny. I mean, I love you, but we're not as close as I am to some other friends and I couldn't tell them."

"We're family," I say.

"Yes, that's part of it. But I think I knew you'd understand, not judge me."

Now *I* want to cry. It was only a few years ago when Sam had seen me as quite judgmental.

"You've changed," he says, as if reading my mind.

"I think that's true. Megan's murder made me examine a lot of things about myself."

"Why does it always take a tragedy to make us grow?"

"I don't know. God's little joke, I guess."

"Funny guy."

"Funny gal," I correct.

"Whichever," he says, smiling.

We finish up our food, dump our garbage, replace our brown trays, and head back to the elevators.

It will probably be a long night.

Chapter

Twenty-two

WHEN DR. CALHOUN finally made his appearance at ten o'clock last night we were all exhausted and angry, yet none of us expressed it. Certainly it was Sam's place, not ours, but he chose to remain silent. There's always a reluctance to declare displeasure for fear of retaliation: complete neglect of the patient. Sure, it's paranoid, but one doesn't want to take chances.

When Kip and I got home we fell into bed without saying much. So at breakfast (if you can call an ounce of Grape Nuts with skim milk that) we review the night before.

"Arrogant," Kip says of Dr. Calhoun.

"What's new?"

"Why are they like that?"

"Sharon isn't." Sharon Lewin's our doctor and she's almost perfect. She'd be total perfection if she'd stayed on Eleventh Street instead of moving uptown . . . Still, we go to her, which shows how good she is.

Kip says, "Sharon's a woman."

"You're not really saying that only male doctors have the God complex, are you?"

"Of course not."

I know she is but I don't want to pursue it . . . now. "I didn't think so."

"Anyway, Calhoun was typical," Kip says.

"Yes. But at least he isn't homophobic."

"True."

She stops eating her granola and looks at me. "Tom looks awful, doesn't he?"

"He's been looking bad for a long time, Kip."

"But now . . . I don't think he'll make it to Christmas, do you?"

I'm stunned by this calculation because it's clear to me that Tom won't make it through the summer. *Denial.* Kip's in denial. Who am I to jolt her out of it if she's comfortable there? That's what denial is for. She's not ready to face the truth. Fine.

"No, I don't think he'll make it to Christmas," I say, comfortable with my deceptive reply.

As though I'd pronounced a death sentence, she begins to cry. I put my hand on her arm so she knows I'm there. When she's through I take my napkin, wipe away tears, then kiss her gently.

"Thanks, honey," she says. "Let's talk about something else."

She's a typical therapist — they never want to talk about *their* feelings.

"What's happening with the case?"

I fill her in. "So, I think I'd better go upstate again."

"When?"

"I was thinking about today."

"Today?" she says, alarmed.

"What's wrong?"

"What about Tom?"

I look at her quizzically.

She says, "We don't know anything yet."

"And we won't for a few days. That's one of the reasons I thought this would be a good time to go."

"Sure. Of course. You're right. Anyway, you can't stop working just because Tom's in the hospital."

"I think you know if I'm needed I'll be here, Kip."

"My God, Lauren, what would I do without you? What do people do who're alone? I couldn't handle it."

I could tell her that she would but what's the point? That's not what she needs or wants to hear now. Instead, I kiss her eyelids, cheeks, lips. We hold each other for a long time.

I tried calling Blackie but all I got was his machine. Now, as I walk across Perry toward the dock where we park the car, I run smack into the film company. And Susan. And Rick. And Cybill.

Susan immediately senses something wrong. "What's up, Lobes?"

I tell them about Tom. They all make sympathetic sounds but no one ever knows what to say and why should they . . . there's nothing anyone *can* say. I change the subject to the film.

"How's it going?"

Cybill says, "I just love playing this part. 'Course it would've been a thousand times better if they'd let me be a lesbian. I'll just never figure out what they're afraid of."

"Who?" I ask.

"Anybody. But I meant the powers that be in Hollywood. God, I think it would be great to see two forty-something women up there on the screen making love, don't you?"

What does a person answer to this? The best I can do is nod.

Cybill continues. "They are so dumb. That's all I can say about them. Dumb, dumb, dumb."

A young man approaches our group. "You're wanted on the set, Ms. Shepherd."

"Honey, how many times do I have to tell you? Call me Ishmael."

"Huh?"

We all laugh.

"I'm coming," she says to the confused man. Then to

me, "Good to see you again, Lauren. You getting anywhere with the case?"

"I have some new information," I say.

"And I have to act. Hell. Tell them so they can tell me,
okay?"

"I will."

She waves good-bye.

"What?" Rick asks.

I tell.

"Triplets?" they both yell.

"I know, I know."

"Hold everything," Susan says. "Nee, nee, nee nee.
Nee, nee, nee nee . . . She wasn't a woman alone, but she
wasn't married. She didn't have a boyfriend, but she was
surrounded. What was she? *Triplets,* coming to a theater
near you. Soon!"

Rick says, "How can this be, Lauren? I mean, we
wouldn't *write* something like that . . . I wouldn't even do
that to Nickelodeon, and you know how I hate them." Rick
had a bad experience with a sitcom at that network.

"Would I make this up?"

Susan and Rick look at each other and in perfect unison say, "You might."

"Well, I'm not. I wish I were. I'm worried about Susie,
the remaining triplet."

"Follow the money," Susan says wisely.

"Or the sex," I answer, equally wise.

The good thing about the trip to Ulster County is that
there's very little traffic. I arrive at the Mcmann house at
one-fifteen. When Anne Mcmann sees me she's not a
happy camper.

"I thought I told you that I don't know any Almay or
anything period."

"Actually, you didn't say the anything period part."

"Very funny."

"Sorry." I take a good look at her this time and I can

see that even with the dyed hair she's an attractive woman. "I want to talk to you about Susie," I say.

She blinks. "Who?"

"Susie Mcmann Black."

"I told you, I'm a Mcmann by marriage."

"Yes, I know. I didn't say you were blood relatives. But I think you knew Susie a long time ago."

"Well, you think wrong." She starts to shut the door but I get my foot in, just like they do on-screen.

"Mrs. Mcmann, I'd like to talk to you about the summer of 'fifty-four."

She blinks again. "Wasn't that a movie?"

Everyone is obsessed with movies. "That was *The Summer of 'Forty-four,* I believe."

" 'Forty-two, actually."

"Right."

"But then they made a sort of sequel and that was 'forty-four."

I can't believe we're having this conversation. "I guess."

"They did." She's adamant. "Want to know who starred in it?"

"No. I want you to let me come in and I want you to talk to me about Susie Mcmann Black and the summer of 1954."

"What if I tell you that I don't have any idea what you're talking about?"

"Then I'll have to call you a liar," I say bluntly.

She stares at me, saying nothing, as if she's weighing whether being called a liar is important or not. Finally, she opens the door wider and steps aside, allowing me to enter.

The walls of the living room are painted pale peach. On them are paintings and prints of dead animals. A stuffed yellow bird is perched on a shelf, eyes glassy like burnished stones. The furniture is circa 1960, everything covered in flowered prints. An anemic brown rug is wall-to-wall. Thin gauzy curtains cover the windows. I find it a particularly depressing room.

"Do you wish to sit down?" she asks in a tone that conveys her hope I don't.

"Thank you," I say, and sit on the sofa.

Reluctantly, Anne Mcmann takes a chair opposite me. "Well?" she barks.

"You *did* know Susie, didn't you?"

"Why do you believe that?"

"Because she told me you did."

"That's ridiculous. Susie died in 1954. A car accident. You can read about it in the paper."

"I have."

"Well, then?"

"We both know that it was Betty Rosner, not Susie Mcmann, who was killed in that accident."

"But there was a service, they buried her," she says solemnly.

"Did they?"

"Well, not really. She was burned in the car. It was just a service."

"You knew that wasn't Susie."

I don't know what you're talking about." She sucks in breath like she's suffocating, then says, "Where is she? Susie?" Two spots of color dot her cheeks like dabs of rouge.

"She lives in New York City."

A hand flies to her lips. "Is she a . . . ?"

"What? Is she a what?"

She shakes her head as though trying to rid herself of the unasked question.

"A lesbian?" I say.

"Oh, don't." She squeezes shut her eyes; a moue of disgust twists her lips.

So here I sit opposite a genuine homophobe. Definitely not a first, but still a feeling I don't like. "Don't what?"

"That word." She purses her mouth as if she's tasted a bitter vetch.

"What word would you prefer, Mrs. Mcmann?"

"I wouldn't prefer *any*," Anne says honestly.

"Well, she is," I say. "A lesbian."

"Why do you keep saying it?"

"Because it's true."

"Susie was married and had a son."

"Please. That's meaningless. For that matter, you were married too. Susie told me about your relationship."

"What relationship?" Fear and anger lace her question.

"During the summer of 1954 you and Susie Mcmann Black had a lesbian relationship, Mrs. Mcmann."

She jumps up. "How could she say such a thing? How can *you?* Why should I believe anything you say?"

"Would you like to see her?"

"NO," she shouts. "I think you'd better leave."

"Why?"

"Because, because. . . ." Anne bursts into tears, her hands cover her face.

I feel sorry for this woman. She must be so confused. Slowly, she gropes for her chair as though she's arthritic or blind or both, finally sits, still crying, but softly now.

I wait.

"What's this all about?" Anne asks.

Would that I knew! I stall. "Meaning?"

"Why are you here?"

"Two people have been murdered," I tell her.

"Who?"

"Susie's sisters." I cannot bring myself to say . . . what *do* you say? If she had had a twin I could say Susie's twin. But how do you refer to two of triplets?

"Sisters?" Anne looks puzzled. "Susie was an only child."

"No, she wasn't." I explain, and in doing so have to use the word *triplets,* which doesn't trip lightly off my tongue.

Anne looks at me as if I'm insane.

"I know how it sounds but it's true."

"Is Susie in danger?" she asks, alarmed.

"Probably. That's why I need your help."

"I don't see what I have to do with it."

"Somehow I think the answer to this case is rooted in history. And you're part of that history."

She sighs deeply, a sound of resignation. "Because of my relationship with Susie?"

"Yes."

"It was . . . it was a crazy thing. I never have before or since."

As she can't bring herself to say the words I help her out. "Had a relationship with a woman?"

"Yes."

"And you were married during your affair with Susie?"

She winces at the word *affair* but nods.

"Did anyone know?" I ask.

"No," she says resolutely. "And I don't want anyone to know now."

"What possible difference could it make now?"

"This is a very small town, Miss Laurano . . . and it's not liberal country. It was dangerous then and it would be dangerous now for anyone to know."

"Including your husband?"

"*Especially* my husband."

"You think he'd hold it against you after all this time? I mean, you've been married what, something like forty years?"

"Time, years, they have nothing to do with it. Abnormal things are not overlooked easily. Don't misunderstand, we're all aware of the gays and lesbians who have houses here and who come for summers, but that's different."

"How?" I ask.

"Well, they're outsiders. We don't care what they do. We wouldn't socialize with them, particularly, but they can do what they want as long as they're discreet."

I mustn't let this get to me. "You can say this even though you participated in a lesbian relationship, discreet though it may have been."

"It wasn't a *lesbian* relationship."

"Oh? Really. What was it, then?"

"Why must we label it?"

"Mrs. Mcmann, what kind of relationship do you have with your husband?"

"What kind? I don't know what you mean."

"It's a heterosexual relationship, isn't it?"

She looks at me blankly as though she doesn't understand the word. "It's normal," she says annoyingly.

"Heterosexual," I repeat.

"If you *must* label it."

"That's what it's called. And what you and Susie had together . . ."

Anne shouts at me, "You have no idea what we had together."

"You're right. Why don't you tell me?"

"It was beautiful," she says softly. "I loved her. We loved each other. But we both knew it was wrong. We knew it had to end."

"Are you telling me that you didn't have a plan to meet again?"

"We were saying good-bye that night."

Why had Susie lied to me about this? Was it only a fantasy she'd had? Or was Anne lying? If so, why lie about that now?

"Because everyone thought it was Susie in the car instead of Betty I was able to mourn her. I knew she was alive but for me she might as well have been dead."

"How did Bud take it?"

"He seemed sad. You say she's in New York City?"

"Yes. Would you like to see her?" I ask again.

"Yes."

"I'm sure that can be arranged."

"Oh, I don't know," she says, fussing with the fabric of her skirt. "What would be the point?"

"Think about it and let me know if you want to." I give her my card. If I can get them together at least I'll know who's lying. "Where can I find your husband? At the deli?"

"No. He's gone into New York today."

I experience a frisson of fear. Does he go in often?"

"Now and then."

"For what reason?"

"I don't know," she answers irritably. "He likes to."

I ask her if he'd been in New York the day Sharon was killed and she doesn't remember. The same with the day of Samantha's murder.

I need to find out.

Most of all, I need to get back to NYC as fast as I can.

Chapter

Twenty-three

IT'S STILL LIGHT at almost eight-thirty when I reach the city. I drive directly to Broadway and look for a place to park near 722. At this time of the evening it's not hard to find a spot.

Why, I continue to wonder, would Susie lie to me about the end of her affair with Anne? Perhaps she was trying to make herself more sympathetic, knowing I was a lesbian. The more I think of this, the more it seems to fit. Anne, after admitting what she did to me, would have no reason to lie about that part of the story.

It seems Anne never got over Susie, and might have had a happier life had she allowed herself to be who she really was. She seems the epitome of someone who's remained in a joyless relationship because of what others think. But there are thousands of women who live like this.

It's true that some women have that one lesbian liaison for one reason or another, maybe experimentation, then are heterosexual from then on. But there are many other types. Some of them come out after the children are grown, and for the second half of their lives are able to enjoy being themselves. Some have secret romances with other women, stay married, and lead a double life;

and some, like Anne, have one relationship, then live a pretend reality until the day they die. This is a desolate existence and it makes me angry at a society that refuses to acknowledge and accept those who are different. Ah, hell.

I ring Susie's bell. There's no answer.

My detective's heart sinks.

Has something happened to Susie already? Maybe she's just out.

With or without her there, I want to get into her apartment, but it's much too early to try anything. A few doors away is a McDonald's. The thought of spending hours there isn't appealing. What would a P.I. do in a movie? I wonder this because I feel my life has become a movie. So why not act as if I'm in one?

I go to Astor Place, where there was a working phone booth yesterday. Amazingly, it's still operable and I punch in Cecchi's home number.

Annette answers. "He's not here, Lauren. He's working."

"Have any idea where he might be?"

"I don't. But you have his beeper number, don't you?"

"Right."

"How's Kip?"

"She's fine."

"Let's get together soon, it's been too long."

I agree and we hang up. I punch in Cecchi's beeper number, then realize I can't tell him where to call me because there's no number on this phone. Miraculously, I get my quarter back and begin a search for a phone with a number on its face.

After half an hour I determine that no such public phone exists any longer. I suspect this is no accident. The wonderful world of telecommunications doesn't want people called back on pay phones. You can't blame them, but I do.

Before I leave this area I return to 722 and ring Susie

again. There's still no answer, so I drive across town to Perry. They're doing a night shoot and the street is completely blocked off.

I finally find a place on Eighth Avenue, across the street from the mystery bookstore Foul Play. I have to confess, occasionally I buy books here. I don't know what the Js would think so I don't tell them. Since Foul Play is a specialty bookstore, they often have books the Js don't carry. Also, I like both John and Ann, who work here, and sometimes I stop in to say hello. But I never buy a hardcover because the Js can always order that for me. The truth is, my book buying has diminished like everyone else's, because I can't afford it.

Where Perry and West Fourth intersect, I encounter a man with a walkie-talkie. Instinct tells me he's waiting to keep me from going home. I can't believe I have to go through this again. Rather than explain I flash my P.I. license.

"No," he says flatly.

"No *what?*"

"You're not Cybill."

"Of course I'm not Cybill! When did I say I was?"

He points at my I.D. "She's playing that part."

Oh, no. "I'm not playing a part," I say carefully. "I *am* Lauren Laurano."

He laughs. "Cybill's five ten, eleven . . . you're a shrimp. Pardon me, but it's a fact, kiddie."

"I'm almost five two and my height has nothing to do with Cybill's height."

"The woman's playing a P.I., kiddie. P.Is are not five two."

I do not enjoy being called kiddie but this seems the least of it now. "What's your name?"

"Ed."

"Look, Ed, you know Susan and Rick?"

"No."

"The writers."

"Writers? Why would I know the writers? Why would anyone know the writers?"

Now I appreciate what Rick and Susan are always complaining about.

"The point is I'm real and Cybill isn't."

"You don't know Cybill, then, kiddie. She's the most real person I ever met."

"That's not what I meant. Listen carefully, Ed. *You* are part of a team making a movie."

"No shit."

"Just listen, okay?"

"Sure, kiddie."

"Good. *You* are making a movie. Cybill Shepherd is the star and she's *playing* the part of Lauren Laurano, a P.I. who lives on Perry Street. *I* am the *real* Lauren Laurano, a P.I., no matter how tall I am, who this movie is based on and I want to go to my house and there are triplets!" I lose it because I can tell Ed's not buying any of this.

"Triplets?"

"Forget the triplets."

"What triplets, kiddie?"

"Just forget them, pretend you never heard of them. Okay?"

"Maybe they have triplets on daytime but not in a feature. Maybe even a made-for-TV movie but that's not what this is. We don't have triplets in theatrical releases, kiddie, okay?"

"Fine."

"You gotta be kidding with the triplets."

"I wish I were. But, hey, listen, I agree . . . no triplets anywhere, except in my weird life."

"That a sitcom?"

"What?"

"My Weird Life."

"No. It's *my* weird life."

"Oh. *Your* weird life."

"Right."

"You're a triplet?" Ed asks.

"Please. I beg of you: forget the triplets."

"But it's interesting, kiddie. Never met a triplet before."

"Ed. I want to go to my house."

"You say you live down there? Right where they're shooting, kiddie?"

"Yes. Can you call someone on that?" I ask, indicating the walkie-talkie.

"Why would I have it if I couldn't use it?"

"You wouldn't. So use it."

"For what?"

Exasperation is not the word for what I feel. "To check my credentials, Ed. To see if it's all right for me to go home."

"Oh. Okay."

He brings the walkie-talkie to his lips, presses a button. "Yo, there's this triplet here wants to come down the street. Says she lives at the address where they're shooting. Right." To me, he says, "What's your name?"

"I told you. Lauren Laurano."

He laughs. "Nah. Your real name, kiddie."

"That *is* my real name," I say through clenched teeth.

Into the walkie-talkie Ed says, "Says her name is Lauren Laurano. There is? No shit. Right." He signs off. "Beau says you're real."

"Thank God for that. I was beginning to think I was an android."

"That some kind of triplet?"

"Good-bye, Ed."

"Better hurry, kiddie. They're about to start shooting."

I make my way through the tangle of wires and people connected to the shoot.

Jimmy (the Snail) Daniels, my gaffer acquaintance, calls to me. "What about that lunch, Lauren?"

"Soon."

"CeCe says hello back."

His wife, Ceil. "Great," I say.

Rick and Susan are huddled with the director. Susan looks up. "Hey, Lobes," she calls. "The very person we want to see."

Somehow I find this hard to believe.

"You were serious about the triplet stuff, weren't you?"

I say that I was.

"We need the remaining one," Rick says.

Barry Berry says, "So we don't have to reshoot. You see, dear girl, the one who was murdered had another scene." He smiles at me as though I'm his new best friend.

Berry wears his same outfit, but because it's night he's draped a safari jacket over his shoulders like a cape. The ever-present brown cigarette hangs from his mouth.

"And," he continues, "these lovely writers have told me that there's a bloody triplet, which you now seem to be confirming."

"Yes, that's right."

"Do you know where she is, pet?"

"I know where she lives but I don't know where she is."

Berry says, "Let's take that one from the top, dear girl."

I explain.

"I see. Well, we're not going to shoot her scene until tomorrow. Will you have her by then, love?"

"Have her?"

"Located her," he rectifies impatiently.

"I hope so."

"Good. Tell her to be at Three Lives Bookstore at seven A.M.," he says. "Do you know where that is?"

I nod. I knew there was going to be a scene there but not when or who was in it.

"Good, dear heart. Do you happen to know if she's SAG?"

"I'm sure she is. Look, what if I don't contact her by then?" I have no intention of telling bloody Barry Berry my worst fears.

"You simply have to, pet. We're on a schedule." He

looks at me condescendingly, turns away, and hurries down the street.

"Just what is he supposed to be?" I ask Susan.

"He's supposed to be an English director but we happen to know he's from Peoria," she says. "You think you can find this woman?"

"I'll try."

"Quiet on the set," someone yells.

"I have to get inside. See you later."

Kip is sitting in the living room watching a baseball game while she simultaneously reads *Newsweek*. She looks up.

"You're back."

"A clever deduction, Watson." I bend over and give her a kiss. "Magazine and television, huh?"

"I'm trying to distract myself."

"How is he?"

"The same. How'd it go for you?"

"I'll tell you in a minute." I reach for the phone, punch in Cecchi's beeper number, then my number, and hang up. I sit next to her, take her hand in mine, and tell her about my interview with Anne Mcmann and my suspicions about Bud and worries about Susie.

"So you're going to have Cecchi help you?"

"Yes."

"I'm glad. I always feel better when he's with you."

"That's so sexist, Kip."

"I'd feel the same way if Cecchi were a woman. It's the professional aspect I'm referring to."

"I'm a professional," I say, insulted.

"Please, no technical. You know what I mean."

We've decided to call these little word disagreements *technicals*.

"Right," I say. "What else is new?"

Kip says, "A new recovery group has been formed for people who've been on talk shows."

I laugh.

"Really. There's also going to be a Recovery channel on cable."

"You go too far."

"*They* go too far. I'm not kidding. I just read about it. Do you realize, Lauren, that everyone is now supposed to be in recovery?"

"Recovery from what?"

"Whatever. Everything. Anything. It's grotesque."

I say, "There's really a recovery program for people who've been on talk shows?"

"I swear."

"So who makes them go on in the first place?"

"Do you think I have a sensible answer for this? Anyway, while you're waiting for Cecchi to call back I have something else I want to talk to you about."

This sounds ominous.

"I don't think we're *real* lesbians, Lauren."

"Obviously you need a recovery program," I say, laughing.

"I'm not fooling around now. I've given this a lot of thought and I don't know how else to put it. We're not *real* lesbians."

I can't begin to imagine what this might mean. "Is it something we eat or don't eat . . . no, never mind, that doesn't sound right. Okay, why aren't we *real* lesbians?"

"It's something we don't *have*," she says.

"Kip, I hate to destroy your illusions, but *real* lesbians don't have that. Even fake lesbians don't have it."

"What are fake lesbians?"

"I have no idea," I say, feeling a bit desperate.

"But you said 'Even fake lesbians don't have it.' "

"I know what I said. It was just . . . I was only . . . Kip, do you realize that when you get into one of your things you completely lose your sense of humor?"

"What things?"

"One of these serious 'I've discovered something important about life' things."

"Are you mocking me?" Kip asks.

"*Moi?* No. I'm pointing out a facet of your personality, that's all."

"Thank you very much. But that still doesn't tell me what *fake* lesbians are."

"I don't know what they are . . . there probably aren't any. I mean, why would anyone want to fake being a lesbian?"

"I can't imagine. That's why I'm asking," she says.

"Why don't we just get back to why we're not *real* lesbians."

She sighs. Weighs her options. Considers her alternatives.

"Okay. We're not *real* lesbians because we don't have any animals."

"Are you serious?"

"Very."

"Have you forgotten our pledge?"

"What pledge?"

"You *have* forgotten," I say.

"I guess I have."

"When we agreed to be together. We made certain pledges. Like not having to be thought of as a couple."

"That one really worked, didn't it? What else?" Kip asks.

"No animals."

"We *never* said that."

"We did. We said that lesbian couples all had cats and dogs instead of babies and we weren't going to do it."

"Yes, but that was years ago and now they *do* have babies."

"They had them then too, it just wasn't as prevalent."

"Mostly then they had them because they'd been married. Now they have them together. I mean it's planned, worked out and all that."

"Is that what this is *really* about?" I ask.

"What?"

"You want to have a baby?"

"Christ no. I have you. Just kidding."

"Laugh riot."

"Anyway, we're both too old," she says.

"Actually, we're not."

"Of course we are."

"Not true," I say.

"Well, I don't mean that it's not physically possible, it's that it would be risky at your age," Kip says.

"*My* age?"

"You *are* two years older, darling."

"So you never fail to mention. Wait a minute, what is this? Too risky at my age but not yours?"

She lets out a long breath. "Risky at mine, too. Anyway, if I wanted a human child I'd adopt. There are millions of kids out there who need homes. I can't see the whole egocentric thing of having to reproduce yourself when there are starving —"

"Armenians?" I supply.

"Who?"

"Armenians. Didn't your mother always say that when you wouldn't eat your spinach or mushrooms or whatever? Mine always said, 'Think of the starving Armenians.' "

"Mine were Hungarians," she says.

"Right. What the hell does this have to do with anything? I mean, what the hell are we talking about Armenians and Hungarians for? I never understand how our conversations get like this."

"Like what?" Kip says.

"You can never stick to the point."

"You're playing the blame game, Lauren."

"I thought you really wanted to know how our conversations get like this."

"If it's anyone who doesn't stick to the point, it's you," Kip says.

"I think you said . . ."

"Technical," she says.

"But I . . ."

"Don't. Just don't go back over the whole conversation to prove to me that I'm the one who goes off on a tangent, okay?"

"Okay." I want to so much it hurts.

"Let's start over," she appeals.

"Okay. You want a baby."

"No. I don't want a baby. A baby is the last thing I want at my age. I want a cat."

"A cat?"

She nods, bats her eyes at me.

"Not a dog?"

"Too much trouble."

"A cat," I repeat.

"A kitten, to be precise."

"What kind?"

"What do you mean?"

"A certain breed or an alley cat?"

"How did you know?" Kip asks, beaming.

"Know what?"

"That I wanted a certain breed? You see, this is why I love you, this is why we're together after all these years, you read my mind, you know me better than any other living human . . ."

"What breed?"

"A Persian."

"You're kidding," I say.

"No. Why?"

"Plate faces?"

"That's cruel," Kip says.

"Have you ever looked at their profiles? They don't have any."

"I love the way they look."

"But they have this humongous hair," I point out.

"It's gorgeous."

"It has to be brushed all the time or it gets mats. Who's going to groom this plate face?" As if I don't know.

"Stop calling her that."

"*Her?*"

"Or him," she says, not looking at me.

"Kip, you said *her,* as if you already had someone, I mean, some *animal* in mind."

"We wouldn't want a boy, would we?"

"Why not?"

"I thought you might not like a boy cat," she says.

"That's ridiculous. Why would I care what sex it is?"

"So then you don't care if it's a girl?"

The phone rings. It's Cecchi. I tell him to hold on and put my hand over the mouthpiece.

"I care, Kip. I care because I don't want either one, girl or boy."

"But Lauren . . ."

"Continued later," I say to her, and go back to my call, relieved that this crazy conversation is over.

Chapter

Twenty-four

CECCHI AND I sit in the Waverly Place Luncheonette. It's 2:00 A.M. Ruby's not on duty at this hour. Instead, there's a surly waiter and a sullen counterman. I long for Ruby.

I've brought Cecchi up-to-date. His head spins with the ridiculous nature of this case. Nevertheless, he agrees that Susie might be in danger. We haven't any idea where to look for Bud Mcmann and can't put an APB out on him because we have no hard evidence that the man's done anything. Earlier we went to Susie's apartment house but still no one answered. We have also phoned every half hour to no avail.

Cecchi says we have no legal right to go into her apartment and we certainly can't get a warrant on what we have so far, which is basically conjecture. So he agrees to my plan that we break in. This is one of the major reasons I love this man: he *doesn't* go by the book.

Cecchi often says: "They have pages and pages of rules and I have none." I worry that someday he's going to get into trouble and I pray that it's not on a case with me when it happens.

I take a sip of my five hundredth cup of coffee. Cold. I

wave to the waiter for fresh. Scowling at me, he pours the dark liquid that's beginning to look like beach tar. I try to see things from his POV. That's point of view, in movie parlance.

This is what the surly waiter sees: A man in his forties with a woman in her forties (or maybe even thirties . . . no, the light's bright in here) drinking cup after cup of terrible coffee. They both wear wedding rings, although not identical, therefore they're married to other people. So they must be deciding where to go; where to sleep together; or *if* they should sleep together. In other words he sees two cheats!

"Cecchi, do you think the waiter thinks we're lovers?"

"No."

"Why not?" I tell him my scenario.

"First, he doesn't give a rat's ass, and second, he doesn't give a rat's ass."

"What about the rings?"

"He hasn't noticed them, Lauren. He's a waiter, not a detective."

I hadn't thought of that. My mental movie melts. "Kip wants to get a cat."

"I thought animals were a definite no-no."

"So did I. But tonight she said she wanted a female Persian."

"How come? Things okay with you two?"

"Sure. Fine."

"So what's going on that's different?" he asks.

I smack my forehead. How could I be so dumb? Tom. I tell Cecchi.

"Sounds right. Annette got the dog when her mother died. You want a cat?" He wrinkles his nose.

"I like cats okay."

"Hate 'em."

"Why?"

"They stink up the place."

I think of the cats at Winifred Collins's house. "Not one cat. Not if you take care of the litter."

"I thought Kip had allergies."

"She does but she's been taking shots."

"For cats?" he asks.

"Mostly for other things, but I think the cat shots are mixed in."

"Sneaky," Cecchi says.

"You think so?"

"I've always thought so."

I'm shocked. "Really? How come you've never mentioned it before?"

He looks at me, his dark droopy eyes heavy with sleep. "Why would I?"

This is true. Still, you'd think it might've come out before this. "I know it's not an easy thing to say about somebody's mate but . . ."

"Whoa. Hold everything. What are you talking about?"

"You said you thought Kip was sneaky."

"I *never* said that."

"Cecchi, you just said it."

"Get a grip, Lauren."

"Sneaky. You said she was sneaky to mix in the cat shots."

He laughs. "No. All I said was 'Sneaky.' I meant cats."

I could feel like a fool but I don't. "Well, that's not true either. Cats have a bad rap."

"So, you gonna get one?"

"She just sprang it on me tonight. But if you think it might be related to the inevitable loss of Tom . . . well, I guess so. I mean, why the hell not?"

"Yeah, why the hell not if it helps?"

"Right."

"Okay, let's go. It's late enough for a weeknight," he says.

We pay up, make one more phone call to Susie with no luck, and get into Cecchi's car, parked out front on Sixth Avenue. It might be a weeknight but Green-wich Village doesn't know it. There are lots of people walking the streets, hawking wares as though it's high noon.

And the same is true of Broadway when we get there. Don't these people ever sleep? Or are there different shifts of street vendors? We park.

When we cross the street McDonald's is lit up and jumping with customers who are not quiet. It sounds like a party's going on inside and people spill out onto the sidewalk. Vendors are selling incense, candy, socks, jew-elry, books, and cassettes. These are only the ones I can see — others line the street stretching from Astor to Houston, but the biggest proliferation is right where we want to go.

"What'll we do?" I ask Cecchi.

"Nobody'll notice or care."

We go to 722 and ring Susie's bell one last time. Nothing. Cecchi takes out a bunch of keys and begins trying them in the front door. I stand guard, my back to him, facing the street like a lookout. For what? Po-lice?

"Got it," he says.

We go in.

We're confronted with that locked elevator. Now it's my turn. I take out my special set of picks and go to work while Cecchi plays lookout. Fifteen minutes later the door opens. We get in. But, of course, floor five is in the locked position. This is the trickiest part of all. If anyone who lives in the building wants in or out, we've had it.

I go to work while Cecchi sweats. We hear creaks and groans but no one calls for the elevator by the time I've opened five. I push the black button, the machine en-gages, and we start to rise.

It's only now that I'm really frightened. What will we find? I pray it's an empty apartment.

When we reach five the elevator stops and the door yawns open. We step out. To the right is Susie's door. To the left is someone else's. We tiptoe, try the door, and find it unlocked.

My detective's heart galumphs. It might make it easier for us but it's a terrible sign. Cecchi and I wordlessly agree. I push open the door; we step inside and close it behind us without a sound.

The place is dark but I remember that the apartment opens right into the living room. Cecchi takes out his penlight, snaps it on, and makes a narrow sweep, showing bits of white furniture and plants. My feet feel as though they're stuck in glue.

Cecchi takes the first step.

Reluctantly, I follow.

The penlight finally reveals a switch and Cecchi flips it. At either end of the couch a light comes on. The room is empty.

There are two doors off the living room; one is partially open, the other closed. Instinctively we head toward the one that's shut and position ourselves on either side. Cecchi reaches for the knob, twists, flings it open. He moves through the doorway in combat stance, gun in both hands, pointed in front of him. I feel around for a light switch and snap it on.

This is a study. A gray desk faces a window and the walls are lined with books. But no one is in here. I check the closet, same procedure, and find that it holds clothes.

It's then that we both hear something, stop still, listen. We hear it again. To me it sounds like a moan; a human one. Again without words we connect and head out of the study, back into the living room, where we wait. The moan seems to emanate from the room with the partially opened door.

Carefully, we make our way to it, step inside. It's dark and we wait. When the cry of distress comes again, I flip the switch I've found and an overhead light illuminates the room.

Susie Mcmann lies on the floor; blood seeps into a white rug. She's clearly still alive. I go to the phone and call for an ambulance while Cecchi attends to her.

I sit in the emergency room of St. Vincent's Hospital on Seventh Avenue between Eleventh and Twelfth streets and sip feeble coffee from a paper cup. It's almost 6:00 A.M. and I've been here for hours.

Getting Susie seen to was a nightmare in itself. We didn't know if she had insurance. Cecchi had to show his badge and generally throw his weight around, which is something he doesn't enjoy doing.

I pointed out to those concerned that since she's an actress and a SAG member, she almost certainly did have insurance. Reluctantly, they agreed to treat her while I went back to her apartment and looked for an insurance card.

I'd been correct and brought the card back, satisfying the *caregivers*. Whatever happened to care*takers?* As far as I'm concerned these people aren't care-anythings. *Care* is a word that's lost its meaning where hospitals are concerned. Perhaps *care* applies only to insurance, as in "they care about insurance."

Cecchi has left me to wait for news of Susie while he gets an investigation going into this latest development. For a start, Susie's apartment will be gone over by Forensics.

I look around me. There's the usual array of people one finds in an emergency waiting room. It's been fairly quiet but then it's a weekday. The rough stuff happens more on weekends. I know this from my own experience and from my doctor friends. Still, there're enough people with problems I don't wish to look at, so I keep my nose in a magazine. You'd think this would be a sign to anyone that I don't want to speak, but there are plenty of people who either don't know how to interpret correctly or don't give a damn.

I'm just lucky enough to attract one.

"It's a conspiracy, you know," a male voice whispers in my ear.

I understand that to pretend not to hear will only delay the inevitable, so I turn and look at him. He's a fright, but living in this city, a familiar fright. Again, I have to ask myself, why do I stay here?

Crazy blue eyes, the color of a baby's blanket, the size of quarters, implore me to pay attention. I have a choice? He is wraithlike, clothes dirty and smelly, worn in layers despite the heat outside. His uncombed hair is thin; wisps whirl from an accidental part like petals on a stem. The nose has clearly been broken more than once, and his lips are dry and cracked.

It's the stench from his mouth when he speaks that makes me recoil more than anything. He doesn't notice.

"You do know that, don't you?" he asks.

"What?"

"About the conspiracy?"

"Which one?" I ask.

This gets a smile. I believe he believes he's found a kindred spirit as I'm admitting to the fact that there are tons of conspiracies out there.

"Good question," he compliments. "However, there's really only one that counts."

I nod.

He leans into me, whispers: "The Buttafuoco one."

"Oh, that one." I'd expected Kennedy or Elvis so this comes as a surprise. An unwanted one, I might add, as I've heard entirely too much about Amy and the hideous Buttafuocos. "I know about that one," I say quickly, hoping this will stop him from going on about it.

It doesn't. "Mary Jo is still in grave danger," he says, referring to Mrs. B.

I nod sagely.

"Amy is the child of Marilyn and Bobby."

Aha! I knew the Kennedys would be in here somewhere. I open my mouth, madly tempted to point out the impossibility of this, if only in years, then immediately pull myself together, nod again.

He pulls back from me, narrows his eyes. "Wait a minute, you saying you know this stuff already?"

"Well. . . ." I make an equivocating gesture with my hand.

"You heard it from Rocking Roberta, huh?"

"Well. . . ."

"That bitch. She got a mouth on her like Martha Raye. She's not supposed to be giving out this information because it's highly classified, as you could imagine."

I wonder (certainly don't ask) why it's all right for him to be giving out top secret stuff like this.

"Joey Buttafuoco is a innocent."

"He's the worst," I slip.

"You don't know the whole thing if you think like that."

What have I done? I've never cared about this case, refused to look at even *one* TV film about it, and never read more than a paragraph or two in the paper. Now I've responded to a loon because I know in my heart of hearts that Joey is slime. I can't believe this.

"Joey is the son of Elvis. How could he be bad?" the man asks.

Omigod.

"The truth about the whole thing will come out one day and then you'll be sorry you said anything against Joey."

"I'm sorry now," I tell him.

"Good. That's good." He nods with approval. "So, as long as you know that Joey's the son of Elvis, and Amy the daughter of Bobby and Marilyn, you might as well know the most important part."

"Ms. Laurano?" a woman's voice calls.

I'm almost sorry I'm not going to hear the most important part because I can't imagine what it could be. On the other hand, I feel saved. I jump up and walk toward the woman, who's holding a chart, a stethoscope around her neck.

"You're Laurano?"

"Yes."

"Come with me."

I follow the white-coated woman through a door and down a tiled hallway. We go into a room where there are beds with patients. The woman pulls back the green curtain surrounding the third bed down and exposes the form of Susie Mcmann, face pallid, eyes closed.

"We're going to admit her," she says as though this should come as a surprise, and perhaps I should be grateful.

I refrain from any smart-ass rejoinders. "How is she?" I ask sensibly.

"She was wounded by a knife. Luckily it's not life-threatening, because her assailant missed any vital organs. It's too soon to say definitively, but I think she'll be okay."

"Good." When she awakes will she know who did this to her?

White Coat opens the chart, pen poised. "What exactly happened?"

This is the nine thousandth time I tell the story. But what's one more time, in the grander scheme of things? I fill her in as we draw nearer to the millennium.

After determining that I've not committed a felony, the doctor tells me to go home because Susie won't wake up for hours.

On my way back through the emergency room, my crazy accosts me.

"What happened in there?" he asks, panicked.

I lean as close to him as my stomach will allow and say

softly: "They've finally removed the bullet from Mary Jo's face."

"My God," he says.

I leave him there to ponder this very important news bulletin.

Chapter

Twenty-five

OUTSIDE THE HOSPITAL the sun is a bright tangerine in a clear sky. Though it's only seven in the morning it's already warm, a not so subtle hint that it might be another hot, sticky New York day. The kind that will raise the urine smell to new heights, perhaps even make the *Guinness Book of Records*.

I walk down Seventh Avenue, which is fairly quiet at this hour, but by no means empty. There are those strange people on the streets who go to work at normal hours; men dressed in suits, women in dresses. I wonder briefly what it might be like to live an ordered life where one knows what's going to happen that day. The thought depresses me.

I cross the avenue and breathe easier when I see that there are no film trucks on Perry. I've lost track of the schedule and have no idea where they're filming today.

As I approach my house, William comes out. He's wearing a black T-shirt and sweat shorts. His gorgeous legs are tan.

"Just coming home?" he asks, arching a blond eyebrow.

"Case," I explain.

"I don't know how Kip puts up with it," he says face-tiously.

"Not graciously, I can assure you."

"Who could blame her? Out all night God knows where and with whom."

"William, you *are* kidding, aren't you?"

"Why would I do that?"

I smile.

He bends from his great height and gives me a peck on my lips. "I'm off to the gym," he says. "One has to keep one's body in good repair as one never knows when one will be called upon to display it."

"Display it?"

"Cover of *Vanity Fair, GQ*. You know, the usual."

"Oh, that. I thought you meant somewhere really important."

"Don't be so sarcastic, Lauren. It could happen. One never knows when *Popular Mechanics* might call."

"Well, that's true."

We wave good-bye to each other and I put my key in the door. Kip will be having breakfast because, I know, she has an eight-thirty today.

I walk through the quiet house to the kitchen. I'm right. She's there . . . but so is someone else. "What is *that?*"

"It's a kitten," she says, all charm.

"That I can see. What's it doing here?" I think I know the answer and I can't believe it.

"It's living here," she answers without guile.

Yup, that's the answer I expected. What I'm looking at is a tiny white ball of fur. Sitting on the table.

"I can't believe you did this unilaterally."

"I had no choice."

"Really? Why is that?" I ask.

"You weren't here and the decision *had* to be made one way or the other."

"And you decided on the other."

"Yes. Isn't she adorable?"

She is, of course. Only an idiot would think otherwise but I'm not about to give in so easily. As I'm set to protest I feel something bite my ankle and I scream. When I look down it's another white ball of fur. "What the hell is *this?*"

"A kitten."

"Will you stop it, Kip? I know damn well it's a kitten and . . ."

"Well, you *asked,* Lauren."

"Don't. Just don't. Tell me you didn't really get two of them."

"I can't."

"Because you *did* get two of them."

"Yes. Lauren, she would've been so lonely. It's always better to have two. Everyone knows that."

My mind sees the dozens of Collins cats; my nose remembers the smell. I feel something happening at my feet again. It's chewing on my laces.

"You have to admit," Kip says, he's adorable, too."

"*He?* I thought you didn't want a boy cat?"

"He won my heart. They were only two-fifty apiece," she says, as though telling me she'd gotten a BMW for a dollar.

"*Only?*"

"That's very cheap for silver-tipped Persians." Her stance now is to be indignant.

"If we have to have cats why can't we have mongrels? What's this pedigreed stuff about?"

"That has nothing to do with it. I mean, it's just that they're so cute. Look at them."

"I am. They have no profiles."

"Of course not."

"Plate faces. How can I ever trust a cat who doesn't have a profile?"

"I don't even know what that means," she says.

In truth, neither do I. And I try to remember that this has something to do with losing Tom. I have a choice here: I can either make a thing of it or acquiesce now.

These kittens are here and she needs them, so what's the point of giving her flak? On the other hand, she did do this without me agreeing and if I roll over on this one, what next? I simply don't know how to play it. Meanwhile, the thing at my feet is making my laces slimy. I bend down and pick it up.

I hold it in the crook of my arm and look at its face. My person's heart tumbles. I don't think I've ever seen anything so cute. It opens its mouth as if to speak but nothing comes out.

"It hasn't got a voice," I say.

"Sometimes he just does that."

"Opens his mouth and says nothing?"

"It's his way."

"Have you ever heard it say anything?"

"Him," Kip corrects. "Yes."

Right then he squeaks. I jump. "What does he want?" I ask, panicked.

"Pet him. Rub his tummy."

I do, and a sound like an out-of-control air conditioner starts up.

"Purring," Kip says.

"I know what purring is. I had cats when I was little."

"I didn't know that."

"There's plenty you don't know about me, sister," I say Bogart fashion.

"One of the reasons I love you. You continually surprise me."

"Don't bother, Kip. We're keeping them."

She grins. "Oh, thank you, massa."

"Stop."

We both know there was never any doubt about that. Kip picks up the other one and comes over to me. I look into its face. This one is more beautiful than the other. He's cute but she's like a movie star or something.

"I assume they're related."

"Brother and sister."

"Have you named them?"

"No. I thought we'd do that together."

She's throwing me a bone. Or in this case, a mouse. "But I suppose you have ideas."

"Actually, I don't. I thought we'd live with them for a while and names would come to us."

I throw her my best curveball. "I don't need to. It's obvious to me what their names should be."

"Really? You hardly know them."

This is true but it doesn't matter. And I know she'll have to agree after having done this without my consent. "I don't have to know them. I have the perfect names."

"Oh, Lauren. This isn't fair."

She knows how I'm thinking. "Since when is life fair?"

"Okay. What do you want to name them?"

"Nick and Nora," I say.

She says nothing. Looks from one kitten to the other, then at me. "As in Charles, I presume."

"Exactly," I answer.

"Perfect." She grins, kisses the head of Nora, then of Nick, and then my lips.

"One thing. I don't want to come third on the kissing line."

"Sorry, darling. It'll never happen again."

"Tell me something, Kip? Do you feel like a *real* lesbian now?"

"Absolutely authentic."

"As long as that's settled. It was frightening there for a while thinking I was a fraud. Nick, Nora, thanks for legitimizing us."

This time she kisses me first.

After breakfast and a shower I call the hospital. Nothing's changed with Susie. I phone Cecchi. Out. I go into my study, turn on my computer and modem, then dial the Invention Factory, where I download mail from David, as well as others.

Suddenly I hear this squeaking and look down at my feet. It's one of *them*. How will I ever know which is which? And then it does its thing of opening its mouth with nothing coming out. It's Nick Charles.

"What do you want?" I ask him.

He looks at me. I pick him up, put him on my desk. He wanders around and then, to my surprise, he lies down next to the computer, crosses his front paws, and goes to sleep. I have to admit, he's very cute, especially seen head-on.

A musical signal alerts me that my mail has been downloaded. I log off I.F., get out of my communications program, launch my reader, and open my packet of new mail. I go to Personal messages first. There are five. I click the index button to see who they're from. David, Eric Loeb, Pearl Greenberger, Bob Blank, and Bill Slattery. They are all regulars except for Bob Blank. I've never heard of him before. I see that he's left me a message in the *Strange* conference. I don't always read everything in this one because it attracts a lot of . . . well, strange people, and why wouldn't it?

I bring my cursor down and click on the Bob Blank message. This is what it says:

Lauren,

　　I know you post and read this conf. so I'm almost sure you'll read this. What I wish to say to you is that a strange experience can be anything. It can be encountering twins or triplets or quintuplets. Death is also strange. Also murder. Strange encompasses so many things. Strange is also sometimes a place not to be. I hope you understand my strange meaning here. I think you will because you're a bright girl, though strange yourself.

　　　　　　　　　　　　Bob Blank

At the bottom of every message the bulletin board's name and phone number are listed. This one is called Bango Bingo and the area code is 914. This is the area code for Ulster County, New York.

I feel frightened, because I don't have to get out my Dick Tracy decoder ring to figure out what's being said here. Clearly, this is from someone who knows about the triplets and is warning me to back off.

What I especially don't like is that this person knew that he/she could reach me by bulletin board; I feel invaded. Bob Blank is obviously a pseudonym. Most BBSs check out their customers and won't let them use aliases or handles or plain old fake names.

I write down the phone number of this bulletin board and quickly close up my mail packet, switch over to my communications program, and dial the number.

Because I've never been on this board before, when it picks up I have to register as "New." Then I have to go through a questionnaire about myself. So I know this is a board that appears to check people out. But my experience tells me that while some boards say they are going to voice-verify you (call you from their phone to yours), they never do.

When I've finished filling out the form I'm told I'll be voice-verified within three days and that now I have a hot fifteen minutes on the board to look around. The main menu comes up. As usual there's a listing that reads "(P)age Sysop." This means you can try to get the systems operator to talk to you in a live-chat format. I click on the (P) and wait. I don't feel hopeful as usually the Sysops aren't around. But suddenly I'm surprised when the screen shifts and I see this:

S.O. hello how may i help you
L.L. i need to check on a user on your board (I type)
S.O. why

L.L. i'm a private eye working a case and
one of your users left me a cryptic but
intimidating message
S.O. what was the name of the person
L.L. bob blank
S.O. hmmmm i don't know offhand who
that is

I don't know why this is, but when people are typing to you in real time (especially Sysops) they always type out *hmmmm*.

L.L. can you check
S.O. why should I
L.L. because this involves a murder case
S.O. rotfwl!

This means: Rolling On The Floor With Laughter in computerese. I type:

L.L. this isn't a joke my life may be in
danger
S.O. hmmmm
L.L. i know this sounds crazy but it's
the truth
S.O. yes it does sound crazy what conf
did this blank person write to you in

I was afraid of this. How can I tell him it was the *Strange* conference and expect him to take me seriously? But I don't have a choice because he as the Sysop is privy to all messages. Oh, well, the worst that can happen is that he'll throw me off the board.
I type:

L.L. it was the strange conf
S.O why didn't you say so right away
hold on

He disappears. I know he's checking. I sit staring at my screen for a month. He returns.

He types:

```
S.O. i don't know who blank is i've
never seen his name before and he's not
listed in the membership roll  he might
be a hacker who got in  sorry i can't
help you but i can trace it if you want
L.L. yes please
S.O. call back in a few hours
L.L. can i call you on the voice phone
S.O. hmmm  ok
L.L. thanks so much
S.O.  no sweat    (914) 256-1761  bye
```

X

EXITING CHAT

I'm returned to the main menu, where I hit G for good-bye and log off. Nick opens his mouth and makes a squawking sound that I guess is his idea of a mew.

"Good idea," I say. Clearly this cat is going to be a great help with my work.

I go back into my mail reader and check out David's message. It's short and to the point:

```
Dear Lauren,
   If you get a chance come over. I'm dying
here!
                                  David
```

He knows not what he sayeth! I intuitively know that he's not literally dying. I'll have to tell him that in the future he can't use expressions like that to a detective.

I save the rest of my mail for later, shut down my machine, carry Nick out of my study, deposit him in the living room, and head outside. I need to go to my office, where all my notes and phone numbers are. And I have to try to get in touch with Boston Blackie again. He might want to see his mother in the hospital.

Chapter

Twenty-six

TIFFANY'S IS ON THE GROUND FLOOR of my office building. Since it spruced itself up a number of years ago from your regular old Greek coffee shop to a regular old Greek coffee shop that serves alcohol, I haven't felt the same about it. I'm not a teetotaler and I'm not a big drinker, but I can't imagine who would want to have cocktails before dinner here. Ambience is not its middle name. But for a coffee and bagel to go, it's just fine.

I drag myself up to my office feeling the effects of lost sleep. This is a perfect example of what I hate about growing older. I fondly remember the days when I could do an all-nighter with ease.

I put the key in the lock but it's unlocked. This again. Someone has obviously been in here and it wasn't my shapely blond secretary named Dora. On the other hand, since my life has become a movie in more ways than one, maybe I *do* have a shapely blond secretary named Dora. How would *I* know?

Nevertheless, I take out my gun and prepare myself for whoever might be inside. I put my brown bag on the floor and slowly turn the knob. It makes no sound because I keep it well oiled for such eventualities. As it swings open I hear this:

"C'mon in, the water's fine."

Boston Blackie himself.

"The very person I want to see," I say. "But what's the idea of busting in?"

"Not me. This is the way I found things."

I give the office a superficial once-over. Nothing seems out of place. I'll check the file cabinet later.

"I got your message, thought I'd come in, see ya. I like the personal touch. Ya know who killed my mother?" he asks.

As I take my seat behind the desk, pop the lid of my coffee, and place my bagel on the brown paper bag, I realize that this isn't going to be easy.

"She's not dead." Direct is always best.

He sits up straight, scoots his ass to the front part of the chair. "I saw her in the morgue."

"You saw her sister."

"Sister?"

I delay the triplet rap. I feel confident now that he didn't know and he's not the perp. Call it instinct. "She's in St. Vincent's Hospital if you want to see her."

A look of alarm crosses his face like a flash of lightning. "She's sick?"

"Not exactly. Somebody tried to kill her." I spend the next ten minutes filling him in. And as I tell him it sounds more insane, more like a movie, than ever. Saying the word *triplets* gets more difficult instead of easier. I don't tell him that his mother was/is a lesbian. That's up to Susie.

"So yer saying that somebody killed her . . . whadda ya call them?"

"The question on everyone's lips," I say. "I guess *sisters* will suffice."

"Right. Somebody killed her sisters and then tried to kill her?"

"That's what I'm saying." Suddenly I realize that, as far as Blackie's concerned, this time the job is really over.

He stands up. "Okay, I'm going over there. To the hospital. And yer gonna find out who killed the other two and tried to waste my mother, right?"

"If that's what you want."

" 'Course it is. What kinda person ya think I am, huh? Hey, they were my aunts. And my mother's my mother."

I could almost kiss him. I would've gone on anyway but now I continue to get paid. No small thing.

"I can't get over it," he says, walking toward the door. "Triplets."

When he leaves I phone to make an appointment with Nicholas Parrish. He has some explaining to do.

"Ah, yes, Ms. Laurano," he says. "How are you?"

"I'm fine. Mr. Parrish, I have to talk with you again."

"Come up."

"Will we be able to talk without Rebecca?"

There's a long silence.

"It's like that?" he finally says.

"Yes."

"I see. All right. Meet me at a place on Broadway called Walker's. We'll do lunch."

I can't believe he's said *do* lunch. The whole world has become like Hollywood. Everything is like everything else. Parrish gives me the address and we plan to meet at noon.

My phone rings the moment I put it down. It's Kip.

"They're sending Tom home," she says.

I know what this means. "I'm so sorry, darling," I say, and wonder if the words sound as hollow to her as they do to me.

"I've canceled the rest of my patients for today. I'm going with Sam to help."

"Do you need me?"

"No. We can manage."

"I'm not talking about managing, Kip."

"Oh. Well, even so. I'll be all right."

I sigh. It's the WASP curse.

"I will. What do you want me to say, that I'm going to fall apart and I desperately need you to be with me?"

"No. This isn't about me. It's only that sometimes I'm afraid you're not clear on what you want or need."

"Lauren, I'm a therapist," she says.

"Exactly." In my experience they're the last to know their requirements.

"I can't joke," she says.

"I'm not. Is there anything I can do?"

"Not right now. Give me a call at their place later, okay?"

"I will. I'm so sorry this is happening. I love you, Kip."

"Me too. You."

We hang up. I feel paralyzed. How long will Tom wait once he's home? A tremor of fear quivers through me and for a moment I wonder if I can comply. I shake away my doubts, tell myself a promise is a promise. And it is.

It's Kip who really worries me. Will she be able to express her grief? How will I reach her? Perhaps she'll need to see Dr. Lubow. I hope, if Kip needs her analyst, she won't have to wait until her back is against the wall, the way she usually does, before taking action. An enormous feeling of helplessness overwhelms me and I reach for my bagel. Yes, I know what I'm doing.

But why isn't a bagel satisfying like a container of Ben & Jerry's Coffee Heath Bar Crunch? Yeah, I know.

By eleven forty-five I'm at Walker's restaurant. It feels run-down. In fact, it is. I've chosen not to sit outside in the heat and horror and, instead, have picked a table in the large room beyond the bar. Overhead fans spin slowly but it's so cool in here I suspect that real air-conditioning does the trick. For the moment I'm a lone diner. Still, it's early. Waitpersons remain idle except for mine who delivers my diet cherry Coke.

"Here you are," she says, smiling.

"Thank you, Linda."

For a moment she looks startled and then remembers her name tag. "I can't get used to it. But it's better than having to say who you are. You know that thing they do in some restaurants?"

"I do. I hate it too. I always say 'I'm Lauren and I'll be your customer for tonight.'"

"Yeah, lots of people do that."

I'm crushed. I thought it was original. Nothing is, it seems.

Linda goes on. "Actually the name tag thing is stupid too. Most people still hiss at you or call you miss, or even better they say 'Excuse me.' I've never understood that one. You're probably one in a thousand to use my name. Maybe that's why I can't get used to it."

"Probably."

"It's Spume." She wrinkles her nose. "My last name. Do you think I should change it?"

"That depends. Are you trying to be an actress?" I've yet to meet a waitperson who wasn't.

"Yeah."

"Linda Spume," I say.

"Terrible, huh?"

"Different."

"Yeah? You think so?"

"Yes. I'd keep it."

"No kidding. Huh. Thanks."

As she walks away I wonder why she cares what *I* think. Am I a producer? A director? What makes Linda Spume think I know what's a good name and what isn't? Still, it makes me feel worthy. I've solved a problem. And that's more than I can say about this case.

What have I really got here? Triplets. Two dead. One almost dead. A person who doesn't exist, Almay. A phantom named Blank who sends me mail. A life like a movie and a movie like a life.

"Hello, Miss Laurano."

It's Parrish. Today he wears a seersucker suit and a blue bow tie. Nice with the white hair.

I stand. "Please sit down."

He does and so do I. "Thank you for seeing me," I say.

He smiles. "You mean I had a choice?"

"Actually, you did."

"A faux choice, wouldn't you say?"

"I couldn't force you to see me."

"But you could have the police pay a call," he says.

"True."

"I'd rather see you."

"Thank you."

"So what have you uncovered?" His brown eyes are flecked as though he has miniature floodlights within.

"Triplets." I let him have it straight.

He smiles, nods, and rests the tip of his finger in the cleft of his chin. "Yes, it was wise of you to ask to meet here."

"I'm aware that Rebecca doesn't know."

Linda approaches and Parrish orders a gin and tonic, turns back to me. "That's right. What would be the point?"

Suddenly I feel angry. This man gave away two children without the consent of the mother. It's an outrage. "How could you do that?" I ask more stridently than I should.

"You're annoyed," he says.

"I'm furious."

"But why?"

"Because you made a decision that should have been Rebecca's."

He presses his lips together and runs a wrinkled hand through his hair. "I suppose that's so."

"It *is* so," I affirm.

"You have to understand the times, Lauren. Things were different then. It was bad enough that she was having my child. How could she have gone home with triplets?

William Mcmann was a treacherous person. As it turned out he didn't believe Susie was his child anyway."

"But you gave away Rebecca's children without consulting her."

"I can't deny that. They were my children, too, however." Gingerly he sips his drink. "I tried to find them much later but it was only Susie I could keep track of."

"So you lied to me about seeing her."

"Yes."

"Why?"

"Forgive me, but I had no idea who was paying your fee. Why should I tell you where Susie was? And Rebecca was present."

I understand.

"It seems you all kept a lot of secrets from each other. You didn't know that Susie knew her sisters, did you?"

The white shelflike eyebrows rise like two dashes. "No. What do you mean *knew?*"

"They've been murdered."

Parrish sucks in his breath and his skin color pales a shade.

"It's been in all the papers."

"I don't . . . we don't read the papers. They always bring bad news."

More and more people, I've discovered, are isolating themselves from the horrors of the world. It may not be such a bad idea.

"Then I suppose you don't watch the news on television."

"Heavens, no. Susie? Is she all right?" He seems genuinely concerned.

"No. She's also been attacked and is in the hospital."

"Good God." Parrish takes a large slug of his drink this time. "Who's doing this and why?"

"That's what I'm trying to find out. Do you think it could be Harold Black, Susie's ex?"

He shrugs. "I wouldn't know. I suppose it could be anybody."

"No. I don't think so. Are you leaving your money to Susie?"

"Yes."

"And should she die before you?"

"Next of kin. What about this grandson you said we have?"

"I don't believe he knew anything about the triplets until I told him. So who's next of kin other than him?"

"Well, I honestly never thought about it. I'm not sure."

Mr. Parrish, all three of your children, the triplets, became actresses. Is this in your background?"

"Acting?"

"Yes."

"In William Mcmann's family there was quite a bit of that."

Who were these people, the Barrymores of Ulster County?

"But that wouldn't explain it," I say, "because the girls weren't related to him."

"True." Parrish looks sheepish as though he's lying. Then he permits himself a stifled laugh.

"What's funny?" I ask.

"Forgive me. I shouldn't be laughing at a time like this but I couldn't help thinking about one of the Mcmann boys. A second cousin once removed of William's, I believe. Left his wife and ran off to Hollywood after a few years of appearing in local amateur theater productions. Pathetic, really."

My detective's heart gives a funny bump and I'm not sure why. "What happened to him?"

"Oh, he came home, tail between his legs. The really strange thing was that this man loved playing women's roles and did so whenever possible."

"You mean he was a transvestite?"

"I don't know. He was married and had children. But that doesn't mean anything, does it?" Parrish asks.

"No."

"In his youth he was damn good at it. I remember he

once came to a Halloween party dressed like a woman and all the men were horrified when they discovered he was a man because they'd found him very attractive. This was before he started acting, so no one knew that this was his bent." He laughs. "Oh, dear, that's what they call it, don't they? Bent?"

"I think that applies to homosexuals," I tell him.

"Ah. Well, anyway, apparently he went on to appear in local shows. I heard his Maggie in *Cat* was superb."

"And now?"

"Now I wouldn't know about. I've lost contact with people there. But I was told he stopped doing it when he filled out, lost his hair. He could've played the older male roles but that didn't interest Bud."

"*Bud?*"

"Yes. Bud Mcmann. Perhaps he's next of kin."

The heart vibrates. "But I thought you weren't related by blood to the Mcmanns?"

He gets that slightly embarrassed look again. "There was some marriage that tied our families together."

"You mean a Mcmann married a Parrish at some point?"

"Yes."

"You know what, Mr. Parrish? I think Bud Mcmann is still doing drag."

Chapter

Twenty-seven

BUD MCMANN = Almay = Bob Blank.

No wonder the bastard looked so familiar when I saw him at the deli that day. I'd seen him earlier dressed like Almay. And, of course, when I called the house he answered and directed me to the trailer. But how did he know to do that? How did he know it was me?

There is only one explanation. An accomplice.

I can't believe how wrong I'd been, because there can only be one: Boston Blackie himself. And I'd sent him to see his mother! The woman that either he or Bud had tried to kill! Money, sex, and revenge . . . everything always comes down to that. Bud has money and sex as motives; Blackie, money and revenge.

As I figure all this out I'm on the subway heading downtown. I get off at Forty-second Street to phone Cecchi, have him pick up Boston Blackie. I'm not worried that Blackie has been able to do anything to his mother, because the police have a twenty-four-hour guard on her. Still.

"You sure?" Cecchi asks.

"I can't swear to it, but it looks that way."

"Okay. I'll get on it. What about this Mcmann mutt?"

"He could be in New York or upstate. I'm going to call his house now," I tell him.

"Lauren, you know you're in danger, don't you?"

"A lot of people are, I think."

"Don't go up there without me," Cecchi warns.

"I'll call you back after I make contact."

We hang up and we both know I haven't agreed not to go upstate. I check the Mcmann number in my book and place the call. It rings fifteen times before I give up. I'd hate it if someone did that to me.

Should I go upstate or not? What if Bud's in town? The thought of driving up there again is not appealing. I decide to wait until I make contact with someone at that number.

Back downtown I try calling the Mcmanns again but there's still no answer. From the corner of Seventh Avenue and Tenth I see the film trucks around the Three Lives area, which reminds me that Barry Berry had asked me to locate Susie for the part her sister was going to play. Of course he'd asked me to have her on the set by 7:00 A.M., so by now he's got to know she's not coming. Still, it's only polite to tell him what's happened.

I head toward the store and the filming. Thank God it's Ed who's on the corner stopping people. At least he knows who I am and I won't have to go through all the rigmarole again.

"Hey, kiddie," Ed says. "Gotcha covered."

What could this possibly mean? I smile. He lets me through because they're not in the middle of a shot when I arrive at the store. I go inside. Susan, Rick, and the Js are eating lunch. Theo is watching.

"Hey, Lobes," Susan says to me. "Thought you were going to get the sister here for the part."

I explain that Susie's been attacked and is, even as we speak, in a hospital bed.

Rick says, "It doesn't matter. We got someone else and we'll have to reshoot the other scene. It's a pain and costs but we have to do it."

"You know, Rick," I say, "it *does* matter. The woman was almost murdered."

He flushes. "I didn't mean it that way, Lauren."

I'm not sure if that's true or not, but I say I'm sorry anyway.

Rick smiles, relieved.

Jenny says, "This whole thing is freaking me out. I wish this shoot were over. It's not worth the money."

"Who knows who's next?" Jill says.

"If it's anyone it'll probably be me," I say.

"What?"

"You?"

"I hate this," Jenny says.

"Don't worry about it, I'm on to something. Who'd you get for the part, Susan?"

"An agent sent over a woman who looks sort of like Shelley McCabe. We can get away with it by not doing close-ups."

If this were a cartoon instead of a life that's a movie or a movie that's a life, I might have a lightbulb over my head. Maybe I do. "What agent?"

Rick and Susan look at each other, shrug.

"Where's this actress now?"

"She's gone. We don't need her again until later. What's up?" Susan asks.

"So she's coming back?"

Rick looks at his watch. "In about an hour, I think."

"Her name?"

Susan says, "Uh, I can't remember. Can you, Rick?"

"No. What's going on, Lauren?"

"Who'd know who the agent was and what the actress's name is?"

"Barry would, I guess. And his A.D., Micky. Barry's not here now."

"And Micky?"

"I think she's in her trailer," Susan says.

"Jill, I hate this," Jenny says.

I leave the store, locate Micky's trailer, and rap on the metal door. She tells me to come in.

"So what can I do you for?" she asks.

Cute. Micky's tall and thin. She wears red sweats to her knees like pedal pushers and a purple tank top. Standing at her sink, she washes lettuce.

"You want some salad?"

"No thanks. I'll be quick. I need a couple of names."

"Organic. This lettuce. The whole salad is. You don't know what you're missing."

This is a health nut and she must be ignored. "Could you tell me the name of the actress who replaced Shelley McCabe?"

"Sure."

I wait.

"Raw kohlrabi, beet greens, knob celery . . ."

"Micky? The name, please."

"Allison Mayer. You know, you should eat some of this. You have a cholesterol look."

I cannot engage. "And the name of the agent who sent her over?"

"You know how I can tell?"

I wait.

"The color of your skin and the white of your eyes. Well, I should say the nonwhite of your eyes. You know what color your . . ."

"The name of the agent, please."

"Doyce Schroeder."

Back in my office, I call the Sysop for Bango Bingo. He answers on the first ring. I tell him who I am and he tells me that Bob Blank is definitely a hacker but there's no way to trace who it is.

I try Mcmann's number next and Anne answers.

"He's in the city today," she says.

"Does he own a computer and modem?"

"Does he? He's practically never off the damn thing."

Zing zing zing go my heartstrings! I think about telling her where Susie is, but until I'm sure of who's in on this whole thing I decide silence is best for now. So I thank her and hang up.

I feel I've confirmed that Bud Mcmann and Bob Blank are one and the same. And then I remember David's message. I have one more suspicion.

When I arrive at the theater, David is pacing the stage like a caged animal. I call to him and he comes down.

"You got my note. I can't believe it," he says. "Twice in a week."

"Why are you dying?" The lecture will come later.

"The whole show is falling apart. Destiny walked out on me and now an actress, with a small but pivotal role, has vanished. I hate the theater."

"The actress," I say. "Was her name Allison Mayer?"

"How the hell did you know?"

Barry Berry has set up the shot by the time I reach Three Lives. There's no way for me to get inside so I have to wait. Nothing will get the director to stop, especially if I tell him I have to talk to one of his actresses. But it's given me time to call Cecchi. He jumps out of a blue-and-white.

"We picked up the kid at the hospital," he tells me. "He's at the precinct. But I won't be able to keep him long, Lauren."

"No need. I don't think he's involved, after all."

"You're kidding."

"Sorry, Cecchi. But I'm not positive. I won't know for sure until this shot is over and the actors come out."

"Want to tell me what the hell is going on?"

"How's Susie Mcmann? Her injuries even less than we thought?"

"Yeah. How'd you know?" he asks.

"I'm a detective," I say.

"And a comedian."

"That too."

"The doctor said the wounds could've been self-inflicted," he tells me.

"Thought so."

"But why?"

"I really loathe this," I say.

"What?"

"Having a woman be a perp. And a lesbian, too."

"They're human," he says innocently.

I smile but don't reply.

"So how do you figure it's Susie?"

"She didn't actually commit the murders," I explain. "She just planned it."

"Then who did?"

"Bud Mcmann."

"Why?"

"Money, sex, and revenge. See, Susie had an affair with Bud's wife years ago. Bud knew about it and somehow he and Susie got together when the other Parrish triplets showed up. And even though Susie'd told the other two their parents were dead, she knew that when Parrish and Rebecca kicked off, the truth would come out. She needed her sisters dead."

"Pretty cold-blooded. Her own sisters."

"That's one of the reasons she couldn't do the dirty work herself. She's got an alibi for the time of their deaths, doesn't she?"

"First thing we checked out. I still don't see how any of them knew that Blackie'd hired you."

"Doyce Schroeder."

"The agent?"

"Yes."

"He's in on it too?" Cecchi asks.

"Not knowingly, but he was."

"If this is going to be some cockamamie coincidence then I'll . . ."

"You'll what?"

"I don't know. I just don't believe in them. I mean, what the hell is this, a movie or something?"

"Yes."

He stares at me with that cop look.

"Face it, Cecchi, life is a movie."

"I thought life was a fountain."

I laugh, getting his allusion to the old shaggy dog joke. "So life isn't a movie," I say, a parody of the joke's punch line. "When I was in Doyce's office I looked at some pictures on the walls. You know, stills of his clients. I didn't recognize any as big names. There were two in which the actresses looked familiar but I couldn't really place them. The background in one appeared to be in the fifties. I didn't think anything of it at the time. Then Nicholas Parrish told me Bud Mcmann had run off to be an actor many years ago and I put two and two together."

"What two and two? You said the pictures were act*resses*."

"Exactly."

"Exactly what?" Cecchi is annoyed.

I start to tell him when I hear Barry Berry yell "Cut and print" from inside the store. I know this means the shot's over and the actors will be coming out.

"Get ready to make an arrest, Cecchi."

"Lauren, you're working my nerves."

We move in closer to the door.

The first one out is Cybill. "Hi, Lauren. Any news on the case?"

I tell her there is and hurry her out of the way. She's totally cooperative. The Js come out next. I wave them to the side and then come the techs, Jimmy Daniels first.

"Hey, babe," he says to me. "Let's not forget to do lunch."

"Right, doll," I say.

And then, between two techs, comes Allison Mayer. This time I have no trouble recognizing her.

"Lieutenant Cecchi," I say. "Meet Bud Mcmann."

At the precinct everything unravels.

It's all as I'd laid it out to Cecchi with an important addition.

Boston Blackie had neglected to tell me one small thing about himself. He is a drag queen. The second picture on Doyce Schroeder's wall that had looked familiar was of him.

All of them having the same agent wasn't coincidence at all. Blackie had heard the story about Bud Mcmann, his third cousin once removed, running away into show business and had looked him up some years ago. It was then that Bud dropped the name of his agent, Doyce. When Blackie wanted to follow in the family tradition, he went to Schroeder.

Blackie hadn't turned his back on Doyce when he became ill and, in fact, had seen him as a father figure, making him a confidant. So when Blackie hired me to find out who killed his mother, he told Doyce, and Doyce told Susie during idle conversation, having no idea Blackie was her son.

Then Susie warned Bud I was on the trail. He was ready for my call and turned himself into Almay, hoping to throw me off. Nicholas and Rebecca would've been next, Bud and Susie sharing eight million dollars.

By the time Barry Berry was looking for a replacement, Bud was in rehearsal with David, the only place he could find work. But then Doyce, having heard from Berry, called Bud because he remembered the slight resemblance to the triplets, and Bud couldn't resist a part in a movie. It would be his first.

If it had actually worked, my guess is that Bud would have killed Susie. Or maybe Susie would've killed Bud.

Somehow I can't imagine them sharing the money. They were, at bottom, rivals.

Blackie sits slumped in Cecchi's office. "I can't believe my mother's a murderer."

I can't believe he's a drag queen but I don't say this. After all, why shouldn't he be? I realize I've fallen into the stereotype trap and I'm shocked at myself. Nobody, absolutely nobody, is free of conventional thinking.

"I'm sorry," I say. "At least you know now."

"Yeah. And the whole world's gonna know, too," he says, looking sheepish.

I understand that he's talking about his proclivity, not his murderous mother. Funny what becomes a priority.

"Nobody has to know if you don't want them to."

"You mean it won't come out that I'm a . . . cross-dresser?"

"Not unless you want it to."

"I don't. It's the last thing I'd want. The guys in my other businesses would . . . well, ya can imagine?"

I've never known what his other businesses are but I suspect he deals with a fairly rough crowd.

"I don't think you're going to need your other businesses," I say. "You're going to be a rich man someday. I'm sure your grandparents are going to change their will in your favor."

"But what happens when they find out about me?"

I laugh. "Trust me, Blackie, Nicholas and Rebecca would be the last to care."

"Ya think so?"

"I know so."

He brightens up like a polished penny.

Cecchi comes into his office. "Blackie, pick up the phone."

"Who is it?"

"Oprah on three; Donahue and Geraldo on four and five."

Somehow I'm not amazed by how fast the word has spread. "You don't have to talk to them, you know. They'll want you to tell the whole story on national TV."

"No shit," he says as he lifts the receiver, hesitates only a moment, then pushes three.

Chapter

Twenty-eight

===

KIP IS WAITING FOR ME, coat on, when I arrive home. I can tell immediately that something is very wrong. I think I know but I shove it from my mind like dust balls under a bed.

We look at each other. Kip says, "It's time."

Two words. Two horrendous words. I don't know what to say so I open my arms. She rises and comes into them. I hold her close, encircle her body, lightly kiss her neck.

We leave the house, hail a cab. On the trip uptown we hold hands, unspeaking. There's nothing to say because in a way it's all been said. There's no more time for nego- tiating, questioning, dealing with the big issues. We made our decision, committed ourselves to this day. Still, the weight and magnitude of what's about to happen seem to push all the air from inside the cab and I feel as though I'm unable to breathe.

The cab pulls up in front of Tom and Sam's apartment house. The elevator rises slowly to the tenth floor. We walk down the gray-carpeted hall to the end. The door is closed but unlocked.

Inside, sitting in the living room, are six of their friends — Bob and Phillip; Marsha and Terry; Rich; and Claude. The couples have both been together a long time and the other two men are old friends of Tom, Sam, and each other. We know all of them but not well.

We greet one another solemnly. We're all cognizant of why we're here, the covenant we'd made some time ago. As I look into the eyes of Marsha and Terry, I wonder if Kip and I reflect the same fear and despair that they do. Glancing at the others, I suspect we do, all of us, look the same.

"Where's Sam?" Kip asks.

"In the bedroom with Tom," says Rich.

This isn't a time for idle chitchat, yet not for deep discussion either.

Terry says, "We've been waiting for you."

Kip goes to the bedroom, presumably to tell Sam that we've arrived and to see her dying brother. I elect to stay with the others, giving Kip a chance to say good-bye alone. And clearly this is what is happening because Sam comes out of the bedroom and joins us. He kisses me.

Sam's eyes are red with lack of sleep and crying. He's lost weight since I last saw him, but it's from illness of the soul.

"I can't believe this day has come," he says.

Nor can I. I squeeze his hand, which is still in mine.

Sam says, "He's amazing. He's so ready." And then he breaks down, sobbing. We crowd around him, each of us touching a part of him, holding, supporting.

None of us cries. There are glistening eyes but everyone is under control. I think we all know that our tears must be constrained for now.

Kip comes out of the bedroom. "He's ready," she says in a flat emotionless voice.

I'm shocked by the jolt of fear I feel and wonder if the others are experiencing this. It's not the illegality of what we're about to do, of this I'm sure. I believe we're doing the right thing, what Tom wants. Still, it's an enormous step; it's playing God.

We all hesitate, stare at Kip as if she's a stranger calling us to join her in an endeavor we've never anticipated. Nothing could be further from the truth. I think back on the meetings the ten of us have had; the endless discussions of morality, dignity, and the right to die. There's a part of me that wants to talk it all through again but I know this is merely a delaying tactic, that there's no time left.

Sam leads us into the room. Tom lies in the center of their double bed. He looks extraordinarily tiny, pillows under his head and surrounding him. Only a sheet covers his frail frame. We gather around the bed.

Tom's face is skeletal, dark patches like burnt grass under his eyes; the eyes themselves are recessed. He manages a smile, like the flap of a bird's wing.

"Hel-lo," he whispers, lips dry, cracked.

We greet him in our own ways.

"I wish I could speak bet-ter," he gets out.

We assure him he's doing fine; he needn't talk at all.

He smiles again. "I app- . . . appre-ciate . . ."

"We know," Sam says. "Save your strength."

"For what?" Tom asks, smiling.

We laugh and the tension breaks, the room appears lighter, Tom bigger.

Tom says, "I want . . . to . . . thank you."

"Tom wants to thank each of you individually," Sam says.

We stare at him, like he's speaking in tongues.

"One at a time," he adds. "Rich?"

And then we comprehend. Rich is first. We form a kind of line, each of us taking a turn to say good-bye to Tom. Yes, that's it. Good-bye.

Suddenly it's my turn. I feel as though I'm unable to move, my feet not listening to my brain. Someone touches my shoulder and I move forward, carefully sit on the edge of the bed because every movement appears to cause him pain. I take his birdlike hand in mine, lean into him, my ear to his lips as I've seen the others do.

Tom whispers: "Lau-ren. You're my favorite sister-in-law. I feel happy that Kip will always have you . . . whatever *always* turns out to be for you two." He gives a raspy, ragged laugh. "Thank you for ever-y-thing." I feel him turn his head and he kisses me on my cheek with dry hot lips. I move away, then kiss those lips.

"I love you," I say.

"Me, too," he answers and he closes his eyes, signaling the end of our farewell.

Marsha and Bob are behind me. I take a place next to Kip, fumble for her hand. We wait.

And then the good-byes are done with.

Sam takes a beautiful Mexican basket from the top of the dresser. "Everyone take two," he instructs.

He passes the basket. When it comes to me I reach inside, feel for the capsules, and remove two. I find that I can't look at them but clutch them in my fist like a child with pieces of candy. Not that looking at them will tell me anything. All the capsules look alike, which is part of the point.

Sam and Rich gingerly lift Tom so that he's sitting up in the bed, then Sam pours a glass of water from a porcelain pitcher. He is the first to give Tom the pills.

It is a moment I will hold in a mind snapshot forever. A beginning and an end. A new journey for Tom, an end for the rest of us, because we are about to lose him.

Sam has obtained the drugs that will allow Tom's life to end. One or more of us is holding them in our capsules, the rest are placebos. It's on the order of a firing squad; no one will know who has given Tom the lethal dose.

Will I always wonder? Will I be haunted with the need to know? The guilt factor is something that I dealt with when all of this was decided. I won't do that to myself or I would have declined a role in this endeavor. I *do* believe we're doing the right thing for Tom. It's his life, his death, and there's no reason for him to suffer any longer than necessary.

Suddenly my turn has come. When I hold out the two green-and-white capsules in the palm of my hand, I see that I'm shaking. Tom reaches up, taps my fingers reassuringly. I lower my hand and he takes the capsules from me. Sam helps him with the water. I watch while, with some difficulty, Tom swallows the first one and then the second. My part is over. He looks at me gratefully as I fight not to cry. We smile at each other and I move away so that Terry can do her part.

Time passes slowly. And then as if no time has passed, Tom has swallowed the last capsule. We've agreed ahead of time that with the exception of Kip and Sam, we will all wait in the living room.

I take my last look at my dear brother-in-law, who is now lying down, eyes closed. Silently, I say good-bye again and leave.

It's five to midnight when Kip and Sam come out of Tom's room and we all know that it's over. As if by design we rise, and one by one we embrace each other, tears flowing freely now. At last I turn to Kip.

She is sobbing and I hold her close, stroke her hair. My tears mingle with hers.

Eventually we say our good-byes and leave Sam to be alone with Tom. In the morning, Sam will call the proper people and Kip will call the rest of her family.

I take my darling home.

Fade to Black.